ISLAND SONG

ISLAND SONG

M. A. Hassan

New York City

CAT'S PAW PRESS

Copyright ©2009 by M. A. Hassan

All rights reserved. Published in the United States by Cat's Paw Press™

This is a work of fiction. The names, characters, places, and incidents are entirely the products of the author's imagination or are used fictitiously. Any resemblance to actual persons living or dead is entirely coincidental.

Cat's Paw ISBN-10: 0-615-31133-4
Cat's Paw ISBN-13: 978-0-615-31133-3

Book design by E. L. Cenac

www.island-song.com

Printed in the United States of America

For Lynn

Behold! The many intertwined, part with
part, though distinct, in working harmony
each others' arm or leg. By fate or
chance or divine purpose who can say,
but what e'er, all is community.

Oh, vision grand…
                    …you mock me still.

> –J. W. von Goethe *Faust Pt 1*
> S. Pelligrew, trans. 1986

*For Carolyn, who helped me find my way back.
I hope you find some pleasure in this.*

Michael Hascan
Bunker 10/17
7·29 – 8/4, 2018

ISLAND SONG

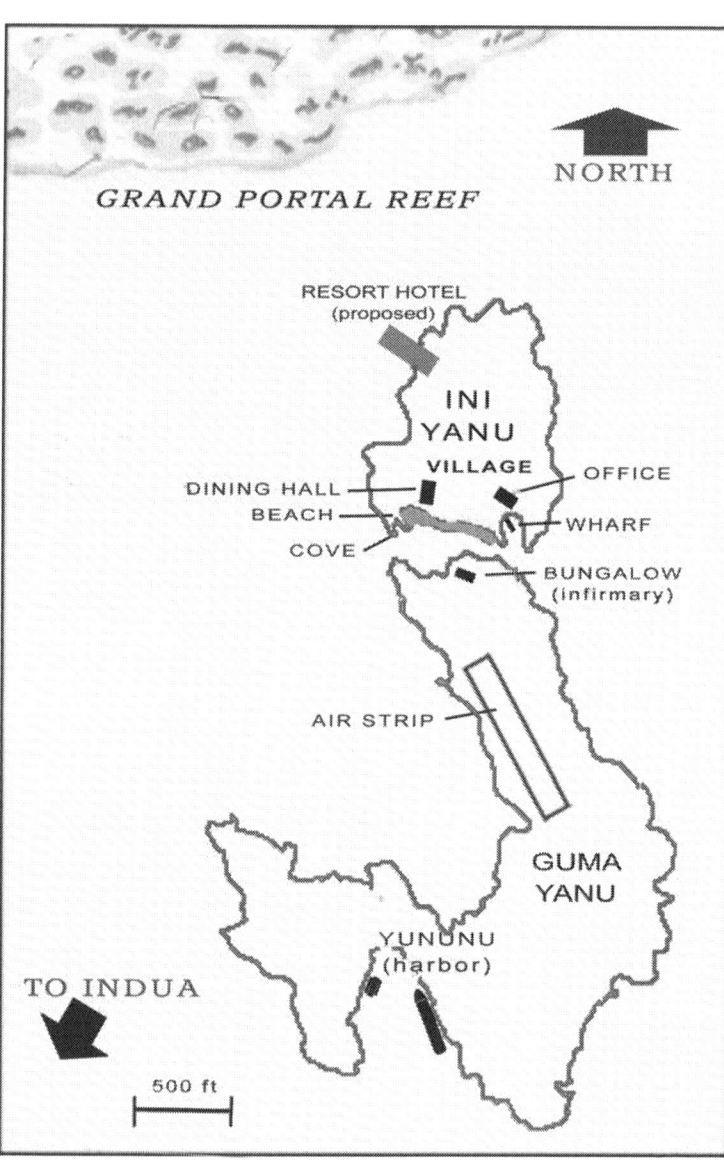

I

The *Annubis*

M
R. LANDIS, HIS RUMPLED whites stained with sweat, leaned over the railing and thrust his clipboard energetically toward the near calamity of dumped freight on the foredeck.

"My god!" he shouted. "Get that thing righted! Quickly! Hurry!" He glanced at the clipboard. "We'll have hominy all over the deck!" The porkers tethered nearby were honking and slavering at the prospect. Two of the men he shouted at were already in motion. One leaped out of the way of the teetering pallet as the other lurched hesitantly forward. The third, huge, a newcomer, non-native, neither Indian nor Anuap, a European or Aussie vagrant by the look of him, hung back and screwed a toothpick between his teeth. "You too!" Landis shouted again, his choked voice approaching an hysterical falsetto. The man looked up at him, then looked at the tip of his toothpick.

Who is that guy? Mr. Landis wondered. He had come on deck not a half-hour before, presented his papers to the bos'un who put him immediately to work with the cargo. It was only normal for crew to come and go. But this had been oddly abrupt: The sudden removal of one man, his sudden replacement by another. *Ah, well, not that unusual after all*, Landis harrumphed to himself. Especially these days with such turmoil in the air.

There was a clattering on the gangplank and he turned to see a young woman striding up it. She was tall and lean. Lank strands of blond-tinged thick brown hair hung about her face and shoulders, stuck to forehead and neck. It made a nice contrast with her complexion, a bit darker and ruddier than his own. An orange pack, stuffed like a sausage casing, expanded on either side of her narrow torso and rose above her head. He had a quick impression of a pretty face: wide cheekbones, nubby chin, button nose, half-hidden behind huge square sunglasses. She made a fetching picture. Mr. Landis hurried down the stairs from the bridge to meet her.

"Hi. I'm Teddi Shepherd," she said as she approached the top of the gangplank, holding her hand out to him. The mate took it in his own and noted the confidence with which the girl's fingers wrapped his.

"Ah, how-dee-do," he said, smiling into dark full-browed eyes. A quick scan of his clipboard discovered Theodosia Lakshmi Patel Shepherd, ticketed by Hop Chin Ltd.

"Ah, how-dee-do. Might I see your ticket, Miss Pa…?"

"*Shepherd*," she quickly corrected him. "There's no hyphen."

"Ah. Yes. Miss Shepherd, then. I'll need your passport too."

She slid a folded document out of the pocket of her shorts and handed it to him. He flicked it open and glanced briefly at the Hop Chin letterhead, quickly turning his eye to the more satisfying specter of the girl pulling a pouch, damp with sweat, from the high neck of her tank top. She caught his gaze and flushed a little as she extracted her passport from the pouch.

"Just a peek," he said, and she held it open for him to look at, allowing him another moment to enjoy the prettiness of her face, now fully revealed. He marked the sheet on his clipboard and handed her the ticket.

"This way miss," he said, glancing over his shoulder just long enough to note that the nearly capsized pallet was now properly settled on the deck, the two native sailors lounging on its white sacks.

SITTING AT HIS PLACE in the captain's mess, the master of the *Annubis* contemplated his tablemates. The captaincy of this wretched tub could be seen as a come down at the end of a long career—the big shippers were not interested in an old man with two heart attacks in his dossier. But, in fact, chugging about the usually calm waters of Anuapúa was just his speed. There were certain pleasures attached to it, the almost daily injection of new faces being, for the most part, one of them. Amidst the tedious routines of the management of this rundown inter-island barge, they provided entertainment of a certain delectable variety, a kind of piquant strangeness that helped make up for the loss of the energy and range of his youth.

These two, for instance—hurried aboard, their arrival announced by two-way at the last minute—were a sort of odd couple. Their brief conversation, while they awaited their third dinner guest—an attractive young woman, as he had been told by Landis with a wink after the mate had seen her to her cabin—had yielded some scraps of information. He already knew they were somehow hooked in with his famous employer Kambula Iratago—a.k.a. Sir Jason Featherstone—the owner of InterFreight Lines, and currently the head of the National Council of Chiefs. Now he learned that they were going to Guma Yanu to pick up the trimaran which had been sailed over from Australia for them. They would pick up their boat at Yununu on the south side of the island—itself little more than a wharf and a fueling depot. They would then sail round to a little island just across a narrow channel to the north. Looked at on a map, Ini Yanu—Little Yanu—was to Guma Yanu like a dot to an upside down question mark, or an eyelet at the top of hook. They had some business there.

"I'd've had Simon 'ere sail her over," said the older man, "but he was otherwise occupied. Right m'boy?" The other nodded. When Captain Percy looked at him inquiringly, he said, in a voice oddly thin for a man of his size, "Big rugby tournament in Toronto. Just got in here yesterday; Tu Vua, that is. Drove here to

Indua with Harley late last night. Pulled me out, he did, of some fun I was having at a club to make me come with'm." His speech was clear, good-natured, somewhat clipped, a bit ironic. He lacked his companion's taste for the oratorical flourish. He was a soft featured, round faced young man, not older than thirty. His look, also, contrasted with his eagle-eyed, beak-mouthed companion. The captain's eye traveled from the loose waved corona of light honey hair to the darker honey tones of skin. *Likely some Abo runs in his veins*, thought Captain Percy pursuing his natural inclination to estimate the racial origins of his varied guests. His own was native Anuap, strained through the gene pool of Europe, Britain mostly, as was the case of many of his countrymen. The other man, freckles gathering around the pink skin of his narrow high-crowned forehead was, he surmised, Scotch Irish with ancestors gutterized in Liverpool before being transported with other hapless petty criminals to New South Wales sometime in the 1800s.

The young man had been introduced by his older cohort as Simon Glimmer. The other, Harley Stable-Birns, frankly gave their host a mild case of the creeps. There was no particular reason for that, except that the captain sensed something churning inside the man, like the tumblers inside an old calculating machine that spun and spun until it finally spun up the number. The other one, the younger one, seemed more straightforward; a model young fellow outwardly—handsome in a way that suggested his varied origins, well put together as befits an athlete, pleasantly present, alert. But, perhaps, there was something too pat about him, too good. But, well, good enough. He let the thought go, only noting to himself the uncanny sense he got from the combination of these two. An odd couple, to be sure.

At the moment, this Harley fellow was opining on the social problems of Anuapúa, the conflicts of a bi-racial society that had its ups and downs; the conflict being high at the moment.

"You can't ask them all to leave, of course, can't make them. But, we know them in Sydney. There's a clot of 'em in Belmain. A troublesome bunch. Making inroads, taking over wherever they can. The one's *you've* succeeded in pushing off the table, like the ones that have gone to the U.S. or wherever. Before we know it, they'll be sliding into every seat of business and government. You mark my words. Leave those Bengalis where they are, is my advice, and they should be grateful." He was referring, as the Captain knew, to the upcoming Anuapúan Constitutional Convention, in which the legal status of ethnic Indians was to be decided once and for all.

Captain Percy chose not to engage the issue. Clearing his throat, he asked, "And what is your line of work, if I'm not being too personal?"

"Not a bit. Happy to share that, aren't we Simon?" The young man looked blankly at his partner.

"Resort development," the man continued. "We're on our way..."

Just then, a boy appeared at the door, the cabin boy who doubled on this small ship as the steward: young Michael Pelligrew, Captain Percy's cousin's son, and a relative on his mother's side of his employer, Kambula Iratago. Beside him stood a young woman. She was, as Landis had said, quite fetching. She wore a soft blouse and a short shimmering flowery skirt that together nicely revealed her womanly lines. American, but something else, he thought. She held his eye for a long moment before the steward said, "Miss Shepherd," and gestured for her to enter the room. The three men rose in their seats.

"Teddi," she said in a warm contralto with an undercurrent of a nervous twitter, like a stream running over submerged roots. The three, for the moment caught in the posture of acolytes before a figure of devotion—which for the moment, all three virtually were—made their own sounds and gestures of welcome. The young steward held her chair as she sat. Introductions went around.

Resuming his demeanor as host, while the young steward poured wine, Captain Percy found himself almost caught in admiration at the ease with which this Harley slid from distaste for what he touted as the parasitism of Bengali-Australian émigrés from Anuapúa, to nearly slavering solicitude for the young woman who just joined them. He quickly saw that despite her thoroughly Anglo name, and thoroughly American-girl manner, she was related to that despised tribe. A thin gold ring would not have been out of place at the edge of one of her delicate almond hued nostrils, or a red *bindi* between her thick expressive eyebrows.

She was fidgety, this one. Her manner lacked anything of the decorum of an Indian woman in the presence of strange men. Captain Percy thought, as he often did, of his late friend Gopal Gupta's wife Samhita, whom he had always admired; and more than admired. She could sit still, hands like the Buddha's in her lap, and give patient attention without limit where it was needed. This one hardly sat still in her chair, slithering on her bottom to make herself comfortable, gabbing amiably about the spread on the table.

"And where are you from, if I may ask?" he asked, and was delighted with his correct estimation when she said,

"L.A. …Oh, I mean Los Angeles," and giggled for no apparent reason.

"And what does Miss Shepherd—sorry, what does Teddi do in L.A.," Stable-Birns inquired with an oily smile, handing to her the platter of roasted parrotfish. "No, let me guess." He tapped his boney forehead with a long finger. "Ah.…Your very presence here suggests an uncommon interest in the varied way stations of humanity…otherwise you'd be camped out at the Club Med near Tu Vua." He gave her a look that intended to be penetrating, which brought more giggles.

"May I…" he said, reaching for her hand. Teddi looked at the hand which hovered over the platter of parrotfish. The nails were deeply scooped, trimmed long. The knuckles of the long fingers thickened between swirls of dark hair. There was something repellently aggressive in that hand, something that, even so, compelled her to set down the platter and lift her left hand toward it. It rolled over to receive hers, and seemed to claim it. He inspected it, breathing and smacking his lips, which moved like the mouthparts of a voracious insect. "As I suspected. All the signs of authority. That pretty girlishness is just camouflage." Small raptorial eyes crinkled.

Her own eyes narrowed and she pulled her hand back as he released it.

"You are a doctor," he said, raising a finger authoritatively. "Or almost a doctor, an intern or resident or something. Right?"

She shook her head, her lips tightening into a stiff smile. "Ah well. Can't be right all the time. But, you could be, say, a diagnostician of *some* sort." He wagged that knowing finger at her. "Astute judgment is written all over you. Well," he said, abruptly withdrawing his attention from her. "We were just about to tell the Captain here about our own business in these islands, were we not, Simon?"

As Simon nodded his agreement, he looked toward Teddi. His look held a question, as if there was some other conversation he wanted to have with her. He smiled, and there was something in the smile, the deepening crescents on either side of his lips, that rang with familiarity bringing up confused faint images. Something more than his immediate appealing presence vied, for a brief moment, with whatever Harley was saying. But, Harley's voice could not be denied.

"As I was about to say," said Harley, sighing as if he had been forced reluctantly into this recitation, "we're here on a little project. After we pick up the *Hespera*—our boat—" he addressed this information to Teddi, "we head over to Ini Yanu."

"Really!" she said, her mouth full of parrotfish. "That's where I'm going."

"Well," said Harley. "Quite amazing. Such a small world."

"Indeed," said the captain. "This one especially. Not that much to choose from out here."

"Oh," said Harley. "I wouldn't say that, Captain. Every small world has its many parts. But, this Little Yanu, is a particularly lovely one. You are going there to play in the sun and surf, my dear?"

Teddi, having in the meantime forked some manioc concoction into her mouth, nodded and said "Moftly."

"Ah, mostly. Now you've made me curious again. A woman of intrigue."

Teddi was about to offer the explanation he seemed to want, but his curiosity was too short-lived. He went on:

"Our business in Yanu, if all goes well, is to give the charming little place a bit of a makeover. Am I right Simon?" he again turned to the younger man for confirmation.

"Righto. Quite a *bit* of a makeover." His eye went to Teddi and hung there, inquisitively for a moment, causing her to look away in confusion. The sense of familiarity that had been hovering around her suddenly struck home, flooding her with the image of a smiling face with wide lips incised at the sides with deep crescents, soft blondish curls bobbing around it, flecked with light from a dance-ball. But, that recognition took second place to a stronger sense of alarm.

"A makeover?" she asked, the nervous quaver strong in her voice.

"You might even call it an *augmentation*," said Harley, laughing, looking around shrewdly at the company.

"Oh? Like a boob job? Not good enough as it is, huh?" she said sharply, with a brittle smile.

Harley looked at her open-mouthed for a moment. Then his mouth snapped closed. His eyes traveled to her face, scanning it, scanning her, as if she were a specimen.

"Even natural beauty can be improved upon, no?" he said.

She looked away from him, catching Simon's contemplative glance toward her. The mutual recognition was now obvious. They held each other's gaze for a moment and then both turned back to Harley who, having to his satisfaction neutralized her rebuke, continued.

"The ancestral owners, the Pelligrews—don't be put off by the Anglo name, many hereabouts have them, am I right, captain?"

Captain Percy nodded. "We all—or most of us, god help us—have the common taint of Anglo ancestry. Ogden Pelligrew is a cousin of mine, on my mother's side."

"So, at any rate," Harley went on, "the Pelligrews have come to the conclusion that the beauty of their sanctuary—and not least its ready access to the Grand Portal Reef—is wasted on the few and wish to offer it to the many. The many, that is, with well-lined pockets. So this is where we come in." He shoveled a forkful of fish into his mouth and chewed reflectively before going on. "If all goes well, Ini Yanu will, in two year's time, boast a glamorous new addition to the tourist trade hereabouts. Am I right, Simon?"

Simon looked up at him, then at Teddi. Captain Percy looked from one to the other. He had been quietly observing the ebb and flow of the interactions at the table, had noted the visual exchanges that had been going on between Simon and Teddi; and now Teddi's stunned reaction. She sat quietly with her eyes to her plate, fingering her fork beside it. What, he wondered, had this Harley character said that so completely shut her down? And then, when she did speak, it was as if she had suddenly returned from a dream, had not really been paying attention to the remarks that followed her rebuke of his mild jest.

"Really?" she said, looking up when Harley had finished his exposition. "A makeover. How about that?" At which point, she seemed to again withdraw into herself.

Harley, having made his case, turned his attention fully to his plate. Simon, pushed food around on his, glancing frequently toward Teddi. Captain Percy called the cabin boy for more wine, and again wondered what it was that turned this seemingly happy go-for-broke girl into a sullen misfit. He felt some relief when, lifting the glass to her lips and taking a healthy slug she said, the quaver back in her contralto,

"Well here's to the success of your project." This acknowledged by grateful nods from Harley. She added, with slightly waspish humor, "and to me for my good luck in coming here now instead of waiting for two years."

Harley's smile fell momentarily, and then he responded,

"See. As I said. You're one for the out of the way. Yes, yes. I guess you are lucky. Although…tell me if I'm wrong Simon…" he said, patting the latter's hand, "if you were a more typical young lady you'd be more likely to find a typically playful young male in the envisioned paradise than in the current one. But, to each her own. Cheers!" He raised his own glass to her.

If Teddi had not been entirely clear up to this point what her feelings were toward Harley, he had just succeeded in clarifying them. However, the same feelings did not contaminate Simon, from whom she received a sympathetically apologetic glance, suggesting that she tolerate the old lout, if only for his sake.

II

Break In

COFFEE AND A DESERT of mango frappé were served on the afterdeck by the young steward. When they had finished, the captain excused himself for duties that called him to the bridge, and Harley for business that he said awaited him in his cabin. Teddi and Simon sat silently for some minutes, the only sounds the harmonized murmur of the engine and the screw churning the water. Simon spoke first.

"You really didn' recognize me?" Teddi turned her head just enough to be able to see him out of the corner of her eye.

"Of course I did." She slid her tongue over her lips.

"You're lying," he chuckled, leaning toward her and giving her a familiarly rebuking tap with the back of his hand on her bare shoulder. "You didn't. You'd've let me know if you had. You played it like I was a complete stranger."

"Okay. It took a while, but I did. They were slightly different conditions last night, right? More like this," she said. The single bare light bulb hanging over the deck cast his face in shadows, creating an atmosphere much more like the dance-ball flecked gloaming in the nightclub than the brash light of the captain's mess. They emphasized his prominent brow and deep-set eyes, giving them an almost dangerous intensity, like an animal at bay peering through the underbrush. They had some of that look now, as he said,

"We were having fun, weren't we?" His voice was softly earnest. "Before all that boisterousness started up? *I* was, at least."

" 'Boisterousness,' huh? More like 'attack' maybe."

"Okay," he laughed. "Attack. Some girls'd be flattered."

"By those clowns? *Some* girls would go for their mace." She slid her eyes towards him.

He smiled. She liked the deep parentheses at either side of his full mouth, his deep eyes.

"I take your point. But, it all worked out, didn' it? Those bruisers, those big Anuap boys from the club hustled them out okay."

"And there went our fun," she said.

"Yes. Sorry. But me mates weren't to blame. I got a high sign from Harley. He was ready to take off. I had to go."

"You just *jump* when he calls. Who is he anyway, apart from your meal ticket?"

"Whoa girl! Speaking of jumping, you *do* jump to conclusions. Well, you *almost* got that right. But, he's only *a part* of me meal ticket. He's not the whole show. At the moment we're more or less in this together."

"*This* being the extreme makeover of paradise?" she said. He smiled again, his eyes darting over her face.

"Correct, so to say. You have problems with that?"

"I have some interest…" she rolled her tongue over her lips. Her eyes leaped away for a moment.

"In what, precisely? Protecting native habitats? I hadn't realized I was in thrall to a keeper of the faith."

She looked back at him, feeling the flush of warmth flowing between them.

"In *thrall!*"

"You're not the only one whose fun was interrupted, y'know,"

The growing buzz of pheromones between them didn't require that specific confirmation. And as to her own general willingness, she had already verified that two nights before in the Ohanu Maile in Waikiki where a nice anonymous boy with everything in good working order seemed to come packaged with the pool bar and a mojito. But, now, something—*dammit!*— was holding her back. "What *faith* is it that you think I'm keeping?" she said, clearing her throat, conscious of the heightened quaver in her voice.

He pulled his head back, so that it was almost lost in shadow. A long moment passed before he replied.

"Oh, you know. Protecting the environment, maintaining native cultures, that sort of thing. I'm wrong?"

"Partly yes, partly no."

"Then what is your deal?"

She hesitated for a moment, unsure what she wanted to reveal.

"In my own business I have to face these sorts of things all the time; environmental impact studies, and so forth," she said, and then thought *I don't trust you.*

"Oh, so you're an…"

"Architect."

"Ah."

He seemed himself to pull away a little at this. His hand slid roughly against his muscular tan-panted thigh. It was a thick soft hand. She had felt it in hers the night before, on her bare shoulder, against the small of her back. She had liked the way it felt. She had liked the way his thighs pressed against hers.

"And so," he said after a moment, "you've come here to …?"

His eyes closed on hers and smiled. She liked the smile again too, and she had to stifle the impulse to blurt out all the current facts of her life. The warm feeling passed. The shadow of mistrust came back. Her fun was being spoiled again, by herself this time. She somehow couldn't just tell him that their project was an insult to her; that she had her own project on Ini Yanu, or had thought she had until she found out about theirs. And what was hers anyway but a kind of a gift—a consolation prize—that her dentist, Horatio Cook, her father's friend, a native of Anuapúa, had engineered for her with some relatives of his who owned this island resort. So what if it turned out to be just a vacation, just surf and fun, instead of a working vacation? What was her problem now? A little thing, her ego under attack? Was it only that that was standing in the way of her fun? She wanted nothing more, as she returned his smile, than to throw that thing off and get back to the pheromones. But, the insult hung in the air, buffeting that multitude of travelers between gonads, driving them off course.

"Kinda snoopy, huh?" she chided him, hoping a playful deflection would shut the door on it and let the travelers continue their jubilant journey.

"No worries," he said raising his hands to wave off her objection. "Just natural curiosity. Anyway, thanks to Harley at least, I'm an open book."

Ah, Harley! she thought. His fingers like furry tarantula legs grasping hers. A bat's wing beat against her heart. She wished Simon hadn't refreshed *that* subject, left it buried under the quickening flight of feeling between them. But, there it was, a stain.

"To set the record straight," she said, trying to scrub it out, "I'm just a normal girl on a normal get away." She ended in a tense, tight-lipped, squinting smile. She would have been happier, just then, if they could achieve the sort of anonymity she shared with the boy in Waikiki.

"Righto," he said, his own smile falling a bit. His eye flicked up at her as he eased back in his chair. "We all need to go walkabout now 'n again."

The moon cut free from the horizon, threw its light across the water. Teddi got up and went to the railing at the stern next to where the ship's ensign fluttered limp in the light breeze. Spray from the shining braid spun out by the ship's propeller fell like warm dew on her arms and shoulders. She sucked in the sea air, trying to change the conversation inside herself, to detach herself from the man sitting in half-shadow behind her, at least long enough to figure out what she wanted. There would have been no such problem with the Simon of the night before at the club in Tu Vua. This was a different Simon, who seemed to have suddenly emerged full blown into her life, complete with a future, with his strange stain-producing spidery cohort.

She felt a presence behind her, and starting, turned suddenly to see Simon take a quick step back and raise his hands.

"Oh!" she said.

"Sorry. Just thought I'd join you."

"Oh! That's fine," she said, but her heart was beating furiously. She slid to the side, indicating that he should take the space next her. He stood close, with his elbows on the railing, leaning far over toward the water, stretching up on his toes.

"Careful you don't fall in," she said loudly. After a moment, he pulled himself up.

"Never fear," he said. "Me and water are…" he held up his hand with his middle and index fingers pressed together.

"Well, anyway," she said with a laugh, having quickly made a decision. "If you do, I'm afraid you'll be on your own. Jet lag seems to have caught up with me." She paused at his objecting grimace. "I must have been going on sheer adrenalin last night. Guess I used it up."

"Ah. There's no way I can inject some more…?" He eased a bit closer. When she pulled away, he said, "Well. Best to leave you to your own devices. Guess I'll just go see what me mate's up to. He always finds some way to keep me entertained, Harley does. G'night."

He turned and walked quickly away. Teddi looked after him, surprised by the speed of his departure, and annoyed at herself. She quickly laid plans for wooing him back—surely he wasn't just going to turn in, not on a night like this. There was a ping-pong table somewhere. There was a special tube top and a small bottle of cologne nestled in her pack. She'd freshen up and hunt him down. Maybe they'd skip the ping-pong. What was his big rush anyway?

She hurried to the companionway leading down to her cabin on the engine deck. A pair of tan-trousered legs, unnoticed by her, appeared for a moment in the corridor below, then quickly retreated at the sound of her footfall on the stairs.

She turned the key in the lock, then turned the knob. The door didn't give. She tried it again, putting her shoulder against it. This time, it gave way easily and she stumbled into the room. Catching herself against the desk just in front of the door she felt something move roughly against her and she quickly twisted around to see a large figure already halfway through it. Light from the corridor showed a glistening bald head, a beefy shoulder and arm, and something gripped in thick fingers. She lunged, throwing her hundred and twenty pounds against the door with enough speed and force to trap the man, who squirmed like a cat in an unwanted embrace. He almost managed to pull himself through, but one arm lagged. She gave another thrust that trapped his wrist. He barked in pain, but held onto what was in his hand. As Teddi grabbed for it, she relaxed her pressure on the door, which flew open, flinging her backward, slamming her into the desk. She recovered quickly, lunged forward again and found herself facing a huge man whose gapping teeth glistened around the dark hole of his mouth. Dipping quickly as she came toward him, he caught her on his shoulder and threw her backward over the desk. Her skull cracked into the closet wall behind it and everything went black.

When she came to, she was curled on the floor between the desk and the berth. Her head hurt, her lower back ached as if it had received a blow. There was a strange stench. She pushed herself up and rested her back against the berth. She was dizzy and it took her a while to recall where she was. The cabin was quiet, dark except for shafts of moonlight coming through the twin portholes that peered at her with dark pupilless eyes. She tried to push herself up, but she was too weak and dizzy. She sank back down against the berth. For a long while she sat quietly with her hands in her lap, humming tunelessly to herself. She thought about Simon hurrying away from her, and again regretted chasing him off. She had a sense of rough hands against her stomach, pressing and lifting, of being airborne, and the insulting crack at the back of her head. She slid her hand over it lightly, feeling a tender bulge. She fell asleep to the sloshing sound of water coming through the portholes with the moonlight.

III

A Package

IN THE MORNING SHE found herself lying in her berth under a thin blanket. The sun was not yet up. Through a porthole she saw the faint shifting line of the horizon. She lifted the blanket away. She was still dressed in the blouse and skirt she had worn to dinner the night before. Only her shoes were missing. She felt the bed beside her. She was alone. There was a light knock on the door.

"Miss Shepherd, are you all right?"

She recognized the voice of the ship's officer who had greeted her when she came aboard and shown her to her cabin.

"Yes, fine," she said, wondering why he would have thought otherwise.

"Miss Shepherd?" came the voice, louder, more anxiously.

"Yes. I'm fine," she said, more loudly. To demonstrate that she pushed herself up by her elbows, sliding her head against the steel bulkhead, feeling the pain of the bruise. *Oh, not so fine* she thought.

"Can I get you anything, Miss Shepherd?"

"Coffee would be good."

"Coffee it is."

He went away. Sitting with her back to the bulkhead, feeling the extent of the raised area at the back of her skull, it occurred to her vaguely that something had happened. She surveyed the cabin. Her pack stood on a chair below the portholes, its flap undone as she had left it after she had changed for dinner the night before. A piece of folded green paper lay on the desk on top of a couple of manila envelopes. The sight of it sent a shock through her, and a vivid image of a hand flailing between the door and the jamb, gripping a flat green object. Shock and image dissipated as quickly as they came, like a thought before sleep.

She pushed herself to the edge of the bed and sat there for a moment, fending off dizziness, eying the little pile on the desk. Then she reached across for the folded green sheet that lay on top. She studied it. It was a common kind of wrapping paper. Dull white on one side, shiny light blue-green on the other. She held that side up. It was badly torn along one edge. Within a rectangle of folds she found written in ink in careful handwriting underlined with a flourish, "For Steve." She looked at it quizzically for a moment, then it came to her as an obvious fact. The tall graying man with the surgical mask askew on his neck, held out the green package in long fingers. "You don't mind, I hope. For ma cuz." Ah, yes. *Steve*. That would be Stevenson Pelligrew, her prospective host and employer in Ini Yanu, into whose hands she was asked to deliver the package by Horatio Cook, her dentist, her father Joe Shepherd's longtime friend. Of course. How could she mind? It had travelled with her from L.A. sequestered among books and drawing pads in her orange backpack. So, how come here, detached from its contents? Only a vague thought. She hadn't a clue. Evidence only that something had happened. What? She couldn't say. She was dizzy. The back of her head hurt.

She set the wrapper on the bed beside her and reached for the envelopes. That made her dizzier still. She swooped them into her lap and eased herself down to the floor. There was a knock at the door.

"Coffee," said another familiar voice. It was the steward.

"Come in," she replied. The young man entered, holding a tray with coffee and a bowl of fruit. He was very pretty. Teddi smiled up at him and pointed to the desk.

"Evating a'right miss?" he said, repeating the words of the ship's officer in his soft island accent.

"Of course," she said, shrugging a little. It came to her that he was responsible for packaging both herself and her pack. "Just great. Thank you."

He smiled shyly, set his burden down and left.

She looked at the envelopes in her lap. With fingers that were not quite in control, she picked at the clasp of the larger one, lifted the flap, and pulled from between two protective pieces of cardboard a clear plastic bag that held a folded architectural drawing. The style was archaic, especially the lettering. It brought to mind old drawings of Victorian architecture she had studied at UCLA, in Wallenheim's art history class, in the days before her decision to become an architect had taken absolute hold. She remembered her paper—something about conflict between the architects of the British Parliament, Barry and Pugin, the Protestant and the Catholic. Marveling at the strange leaps of her memory, she noticed that the drawing she held seemed, in fact, to be some sort of public building, even reminiscent of the Parliament. She slid it carefully from the protective plastic, and held it gently between her hands. All awareness of her bruises evaporated as she looked at it, feeling the old sense of mystery and admiration that those earlier antique drawings had given her. It was folded in quarters. She was tempted to unfold it, but the first move made her realize how brittle it was. It also showed clear signs of decay. It would have to be steamed to have any chance of being unfolded without being completely destroyed. Even then, there was a risk of turning it to useless mush. Great care and a practiced hand would be needed. *Hers*, for instance. She gently slipped the plastic covering back over it and turned it over. Parts of words in large elegant lettering appeared against a faded blue background. "MBLY" she read, and below that "UA". There was a date in script and Roman numerals: June 10, 1886. It was indeed very old. "A gift for my cuz," Horatio Cook had said. An interesting gift. But, what was it doing here, its wrapper torn open? Why...? *A sudden light as the door flung open, the stench of a hairy sweating body, catching her, their grunts married in half-light, half-darkness, flinging her, skull cracking against closet....*The momentary clarity faded, leaving only the ache at the back of her skull, and a general sense of distress and agitation, of disorientation of thoughts that came and went and couldn't be grasped. Heart beating, fingers shaking, she slid the drawing with its envelope to the floor beside her, and felt the bulk of the other one—thick and spongy, pregnant.

There was another knock at the door, followed by the voice of the ship's officer:

"Fifteen minutes to disembarkation, miss."

Fifteen minutes! Quickly, with frantic fingers, she opened the envelope, tilted it and shook it impatiently so that its contents came out in a bounding rush and the heap scattered in a ragged flow from her lap to the floor. Envelopes, small opened envelopes, some sliced carefully, some torn roughly through their flaps. She flipped one over and saw a scrawled address: *Miss Ruth...* it looked like; *Somewhere-Somewhere, Anuapua* she could barely make out. And the return address, a smaller scrawl, harder to read. She blinked at it. Her interpretive skills were definitely not in high gear. She flipped over a couple more. All to *Ruth* whoever. The return addresses gave the single name *Shepherd*. What coincidence was that? A few more bore the same result, exciting interest and alarm. *Who* Shepherd? Oh, but such a common name. She turned over the mother envelope. The same hand as the big envelope that held the drawing, Horatio Cook's. This time "For Shepherd." Oh, okay, okay. Another Shepherd. The world is full of Shepherds. And vague questions fluttered around her, questions her mind would have usually pinned to the wall and torn apart, but which now bent and curled in a breeze of uncertainty, hiding their faint writing, getting lost in the thrum of the idling engine, completely swept away by the returning voice of the mate:

"And, oh, miss, I forgot to say. The captain would like to speak with you in his cabin before you go off.

"Okay, I'll be ready," she said, catching her breath, fingers clumsily gathering the little envelopes together, jamming them back in the larger envelope and closing it. Looking at her pack, it came to her that it likely had been completely rearranged, and she wondered just where in its dense disturbed strata she could now find a clean tank top. The sweat drenched one from yesterday still hung from a knob on the closet door beside the desk. Worse than that, there was that unexplained stench still clinging to her. She grabbed a towel from the small dresser below the portholes, and made a dash for the shower across the corridor.

THE CAPTAIN ASKED IF she wished to file a report. *About what?* she wanted to know. A look of surprise came over his face, his full brush mustache pressed over his lower lip. He explained in a soft voice that it had to do with the incident in her cabin during the night. Her first response was to feel defensive, and she told him she knew of no incident. His response was still more surprise, his grizzled eyebrows lifting, his head cocking slightly to the side.

A flash of memory came, a hand squeezed by a door, something falling from it. The package from Horatio for Stevenson. The torn wrapper. The drawing. The envelopes.

"Oh," she said softly.

"Yes?" the captain inquired, his look full of concern.

But she said nothing more. Then he told her that the mate and steward had found her lying on the floor of her cabin, and she had another flash of memory: a large man, sweating, fangs bared, pale hairy arms thrust at her. She told the captain all this and apologized for not remembering anything more clearly. He said that it was for him to apologize, and he would do everything in his power to find the scoundrel.

Despite saying this, he doubted that he would find anyone. Mr. Landis, who was busy at another desk typing as Teddi spoke, already had a suspect. The man who had mysteriously signed on at

Indua. But, he had disembarked just as mysteriously when the *Annubis* had put into a small port during the night, sometime before the steward had noticed the door of Teddi's cabin ajar and discovered her lying on the floor, asleep or unconscious, amidst the disarray of strewn clothing and other possessions. He had gotten Mr. Landis, and together they lifted Teddi into the bed and stretched the blanket over her. In addition to his oddly abrupt arrival and departure, what bits of description Teddi now had to offer sufficiently confirmed that that man was the likely culprit. But, all that remained of him was the order Mr. Landis had received to take him on as a replacement for a suddenly departed crewmember; the order which came from the InterFreight head office in Tu Vua. It had been signed by someone the captain recognized as one of his employer Kambula Iratago's lieutenants. It all struck him as very strange, but he would not inquire about it. He had no doubt that his young steward, Michael Pelligrew, would convey all that had happened to his elder brother Stevenson. Making a mental note to hang onto the hiring order just in case, he apologized again to Teddi, wished her a quick recovery from whatever distress she was in—that it was significant was obvious to him if not to her—and wished her a happy stay in Anuapúa, repeating the traditional greeting that some other Anuapuan elder had offered her—the old man from the plane? from the bus? she didn't remember; something about mango and frangipani, which she only half heard.

Mr. Landis pulled the report from his typewriter, looked it over officiously, approved of his work, and handed it to Teddi, asking her to review it and confirm what was written with her signature. Teddi held it absently in her hand for a moment, then asked for a pen. She steadied herself at the desk with one hand. She was feeling a little faint. The words swam before her, making no sense whatever. She signed where he asked her to.

Mr. Landis then ushered her out of the office and to the head of the gangplank.

"That's your bus," he said, pointing to one a short way from the wharf across a dusty street. It was a smaller version of the bus that she had taken the day before from Tu Vua to Indua; chalky pastel, rusted in places, windowless. A half-dozen people were already on it. It stood parked beside what seemed to be a utility building, a hundred or so feet from the wharf. "It will take you over to the other side where you'll be met by a launch from the village."

A voice behind her said, "Shame you can't join us."

She turned to find Harley bearing down on her, a panama hat swinging between his fingers.

"Look," he said, pointing away from the bus, to the other side of the wharf where a large blue-hulled trimaran was tied up. "Simon's already aboard, getting ready to cast off." As if on cue, Simon looked up and waved at her. She waved back. "It would be much fun, and mean only a slight delay. If all goes well, we should be in Ini Yanu ourselves by early afternoon, I should guess. There's a lovely lunch awaiting us on board. Not too late."

"I think Miss Shepherd's hosts are expecting her," put in Mr. Landis, holding his hand out to Teddi, to help her onto the gangplank.

Teddi nodded and took his hand.

"Thanks anyway, Harley," she said weakly, and started down. "See you there, I guess."

As she made her way down, she glanced over to where Simon had been. But, he had now turned away, occupied with issuing orders to a crewman on the *Hespera*.

IV

Ini Yanu

OGDEN PELLIGREW WATCHED CASPER, his third eldest, standing on the wharf, tying the small boat off to a cleat. His few passengers were gathering their belongings and lining up to hand them up to him. There were, according to the list on Ogden's desk, a couple from somewhere in the US, a pair of women from the UK, and one more, whose name had been added in pencil. Her name was Theodosia Shepherd, and she was still sitting in the stern beside the outboard, looking around uncertainly.

She was already a problem. She was not expected to arrive this way. She was supposed to come in by plane, at the airstrip across the channel on Guma Yanu, with some others who had arrived earlier. She was supposed to have spent the previous night at the Tukulu, the Gupta's motel near Indua. But, for reasons unknown, she had made a sudden change in plans, and had instead taken one of Iratago's tramp freighters. She never stopped at the Tukulu, throwing everyone into confusion, like a disturbed nest of *mabudju* ants. It was only because Lorraine at Hop Chin had conveyed the message to Samhita Gupta that they had learned of this at all; that she hadn't simply dropped off the radar. One consequence was that Stevenson, his eldest, who was supposed to greet this young woman in Indua—where he was on business of his own, personal business that distressed Ogden to think about—was not here to meet her. This meant that he himself would have to make excuses. Furthermore, there had been a problem. Her cabin had been broken into, she had been roughed up. This news had been reported by a phone call from his youngest son Michael, who served as steward on the *Annubis*. How badly she had been hurt he didn't know. She would have to be watched. Fortunately, medical attention was available in the form of that Tedescu fellow.

He lifted the small binoculars he kept on the sill and peered through them. The focus was already set, and he had a clear view of her face, which she just now raised, seeming to look directly at him. It was perhaps a pretty face, but now it was a face in distress. It seemed confused and pleading. Looking at it, he felt a mixture of concern and annoyance.

She would have been a special case regardless. Due to the conniving of his son Stevenson and his nephew, the dentist in California, and abetted by his wife Mona, she was to spend part of her vacation designing the dive shop that Stevenson had been on him for years to build. It was, he had to admit, a reasonable idea, especially given the rapid increase in traffic they had seen over the last several seasons. And, even if the vastly more elaborate scheme of this Stable-Birns fellow should work out—a scheme decidedly *not* abetted by Mona—that would be several years in the offing. The small, simple dive shop would be a useful stopgap. But, this girl herself…?

He put down the binoculars and turned to study himself in the mirror, to gird himself for the performance he was about to stage for the second time that day. It had always been his prerogative and his pleasure to do this. But, lately, it had come to feel more like an obligation, one that he was required to undertake, rather than pass on to Steve, which at this stage of his life might otherwise have been reasonable. But, it afforded him an opportunity, which he could certainly not entrust to his son, to promote native priorities; a necessary opportunity especially now that it was all being challenged. He could only rely on himself to make these travelers understand how important, it is to make sure that the basic institutions of his country remain in the hands of its original inhabitants, never to be fully shared by interlopers, however long they had been living there. Or, even, however close their relationships might be. His with Gopal Gupta, his long dead friend, rose in his mind as always when these thoughts came to him, as they did much too often these days. It brought to mind other losses, even closer. There was much at stake. It seemed, he mused, that that was what life had been coming to—a series of losses.

As he smoothed his thick mustache, he quickly surveyed the picture that hung beside the mirror over a handsome mahogany table on which were arranged a colorful array of Anuapúan tourist magazines and a sweet smelling bowl of frangipani. The picture was large, nicely framed in wood with silver details, covered with glass. Five young army officers smiled from it, arms wrapped around each other. An inscription was scrawled in loose looping letters on a diagonal across the bottom: "To Kambula Shangano Ogden Pelligrew, the best man to have with you in love, war and good food." After the inscription, the names: Iratago, Amatosi, Rotanu, Bokanjo. His attention hung for a long troubled moment on the face that belonged to the last name, the one next to him in the picture. The embrace between them was perhaps the strongest. His loss was most painful. A severe loss. He had left for the States during the troubles of '69, as had others in their situation; left with his wife, Samhita Gupta's sister, and their young son. That son was now the very Horatio who was in league with Stevenson about the dive shop. And not only that. He pushed the thought away.

Turning from the picture, he squared his shoulders, and walked out onto the low wooden porch. Putting more spring in his step than he honestly felt, he stepped down and three strides across the thick grass brought him to the new arrivals.

"Welcome to our circle of friendship," he said, after they had followed his lead and settled themselves in a circle on the grass. He was, he told them, Kambula Shangano Ogden Pelligrew. He explained how the parts of his name conveyed both the history of his country and his own lineage. That "kambula" identified him as a chieftain. "There are as many chieftains here as there are Princes in Saudi Arabia," he added with a chuckle. Shangano was his traditional name, Ogden his Christian name, and Pelligrew his legal surname. The latter two were, he noted, inheritances from British rule.

He welcomed the new arrivals on behalf of his entire family, and particularly his wife Mona, to whose family the island belonged. He added that land inheritance through the mother was the strongest rule in Anuapúa, stronger than any inheritance the British had left behind them. "Including their genes," he added with another chuckle. He then said a few words about the duties of hosts and guests to each other, the traditions that bound people of different tribes together.

"So, it is on behalf of my family, my wife's family, on behalf of those who inhabited these islands untold years and centuries ago that I welcome you to Ini Yanu, our beautiful Little Yanu."

He told the story of the Great Mother Turtle who began the world. He told the story of the island song, the song of the ocean rolling along the sea cave walls that are themselves the remains of the giant sea turtles whose joyous copulation, he said, gave birth to these islands.

"If you want to hear the island song you must listen very carefully. And when you hear this—*bungshalo!*—you will find what you seek. "

He spread his warm smile around the circle, letting the mystery generate its own meanings. But, he added that legend also had it that Ini Yanu had been in Mona's family almost since the time the Great Mother Turtle had created these islands; since the time she had coupled with the first man who had come from across the oceans and with him made the first Anuap woman to be his bride, and thus kept the line of possession of the islands pure for all time. Of course, he admitted, his face creased in mock seriousness, that might be a bit of an exaggeration. But it was true, he insisted, that it had been passed down through the women since long before the white men came.

"And we hope," here a somber tone clouded his voice, "that this chain, this circle of family and land will continue and continue."

Teddi, who sat opposite him, whose attention had wandered to the tableau of frond roofed huts and leggy palms and bursts of red bougainvillea beyond him, was caught by this change of pitch, and noted the darkness that flickered across his face, as if a bat had passed between him and the sun. But, his voice quickly regained its buoyancy, his smile its charm.

A young boy had quietly arrived from the adjacent maintenance yard carrying a machete and a pail full of large green coconuts. One by one he hacked off the tops with a single backhanded stroke of the machete. The little girl who accompanied him carried them solemnly to each guest, demonstrating for each individually how the hacked-off top should be used to scoop out some of the soft glistening meat.

"Your presence here is our blessing," Ogden Pelligrew concluded. "May fragrant flowers mark your trail. My grandchildren will now show you to your accommodations, your *endugas*." His broad hand swept the air behind him indicating the huts scattered on the open green or peeking from clots of foliage. With that, he got up, made a courtly bow, and walked off toward the building from which he had come. The little girl, whose name was Gola, walked shyly over to Teddi and slipped her hand into hers.

"C'mon," she said. "I'll show you where."

They had just started off across the green in the direction of the pigpen when Ogden turned and walked toward them.

"Just a minute, Gola," he said. Then, "Miss Shepherd I have a special greeting for you. I hear you are going to do a wonderful thing for us."

Seeing that Teddi was about to demure, he raised a gently reproving finger.

"No, no. I'm sure you are. But, I must apologize to you that Stevenson is not here to greet you, as I'm sure you had expected. He had gone to Indua to…well…on personal business. But, he should be here soon. It was not his wish to neglect you."

He took her hand and held it for a moment, searching her face with concern. "You are, I hope, feeling well?" he said.

"Sure," said Teddi, not feeling at all well. "Of course."

"Very good," said Ogden, no more believing what she said then she did herself. "We look forward to seeing much more of you."

He turned and walked away and Gola pulled Teddi off in the direction of the pigpen. Twenty yards from it, she turned up a conch shell lined path leading to a small hut.

"This is your *enduga*," she said with giddy excitement, pushing open the door and signaling Teddi to enter.

There was one small window in the mud and wattle wall. The thatched roof was dense. A single bed stood against one wall, on it a small stack of towels. Against another wall was a rough wooden table on which her pack lay. Next to it stood a chair of the same rough construction. She turned to thank Gola, but the little girl was already skipping away down the path. As she made the turn beyond it, she looked back at Teddi with a broad smile and waved, then ran quickly away.

ANOTHER WOODEN BUNGALOW housed the dining room. One side faced the beach, the other backed into the jungle. As Teddi was about to enter a stout woman in a green muumuu bustled past, holding before her a large bowl in which something white sloshed thickly. "Welcome, welcome," she said as she passed, dipping her head with its thick shrub of grizzled hair.

Lunch, a cold soup of some sort—the sloshing contents of the bowl—with salad and sliced mango, was served family style. Teddi avoided the soup and grazed ambivalently at the other things. The others seemed to plunge into their food as they did into a general enthusiasm ignited by the odd looking man at the end of the table about whose pink face, mounted with coke-bottle glasses, curling russet hair fell like spaniel ears.

"You've stolen my heart again, Mona," he called over the chorus of happy chatter to the woman in the green muumuu who dipped in a brief curtsy as she carted off the bowl.

"Sometimes I think I come here just for her cooking," he said, turning his crinkling magnified eyes on Teddi. "And what brings you here?"

She wasn't ready for this assault on the retort into which her spirit seemed to have crawled, and said, irrelevantly, "Oh. I'm from California," before she shrank away.

His smiling expectant gaze lingered for some moments before he turned to the others. From what he said she learned that he was Bagram Tedescu, a psychiatrist from Sydney, formerly of Kluj Napoca, a city in Romania. He had been forced into hiding and then finally out of that country by the tyrant, Ceaucescu. His psychiatric practice involved, among other things, leading a group of bipolars. As part of their commitment to the therapy, he made them tell jokes about bipolars. Anuapúa, he said, and particularly Ini Yanu Village, was almost a second home.

THE END OF LUNCH came as a relief. She returned to her enduga immediately after. She hoped that a nap would clear her head and restore her. But, the baking closeness of the hut and the squeals of shoats and sucklings from the nearby pigpen made her decide on the beach instead. She pulled open her pack and lifted the package for Stevenson onto the dresser, its torn and rumpled wrapper held in place with a rubber band. The thought of the mysterious letters it held made her pause for a moment before she turned to rummage in her pack. She came to the net bag holding her swimsuits and pulled out the most modest of the three she had brought with her. She slipped it on, put her tank top and shorts back on over it, grabbed a towel from the bed, and headed for the beach.

She followed a trail that went past the dining room and through a short stretch of jungle. On the way, she came upon a little clearing in which leafy green tops of plants of some sort marched in orderly rows. An old man sat on his haunches, digging in the earth. He had a little basket beside him full of fist-sized white chunks, which he stuck in the holes he was making. He looked up and greeted her with a wan smile and a soft lifting of one hand. Teddi smiled and waved back at him. He was sweet, probably senile, maybe the last of his generation, filling out his time with work that was still basic and important. *Joe would have loved this*, she thought. She saw her father on his knees in the garden, a small plateau of vegetables that Chender had created, with its view out to the valley. He had found some solace there in the years after her death. Teddi had also. It was the one place where they could meet without sniping at each other, where that was absolutely ruled out. She felt the pull, back into their old argument, back into the miseries of his death. She pushed these thoughts away and, waving again at the old man, continued down the path.

Some of the others from lunch had gotten to the beach before her. They sat in a clump off to the left, not far from where the beach was stopped by a ridge of rocks. Behind it grew a grove of trees of various sorts, a magnificent giant ficus rising regally from it. One woman waved, calling for her to join them. Teddi waved back, shouted "Maybe later," and headed off in the opposite direction, down a narrow strip of sand that also came to an end at a rocky point a hundred or so yards away.

The strait between the two islands lolled like a great tongue sending rushes of water in staccato rhythms against the beach. She slid easily and softly through the sand, comforted by its fine warm grain against her feet. Approaching the point, the beach deepened invitingly, the long unswerving strand threw a shoulder into the jungle. She had a momentary impulse to spread out her beach towel there in the partial shade of the trees. But looking back to where the others sat, a need for more solitude pulled her forward and she continued on to the point. Getting around it required climbing over a muscular arm of sharp-edged rocks that reached some distance into the water. She climbed them carefully, unsteadily, her attention entirely fixed on planting her feet and keeping her balance.

It was not until she was fully on the other side, standing in shallow water, that she saw the place: a small cove, beautiful by any ordinary measure, that curved back deeply like the apse of a gothic cathedral. At the top of the curve, a trail, thickly groined with branches, peered onto the beach; more a crawlway or a cave, than a path. Filtered, shadowy light moved among the branches. A strong odor suddenly came to her, a rancid, putrefied odor, a peanut-oil-like mixture of engine grease and stale sweat. But it was the brambled opening that held her attention. Something seemed present in it, seemed to move, seemed almost to speak to her. She heard a voice roaring in her ears. The smaller branches, filtered light falling on them from above, took on the look of thick fingers. Then the putrid odor took over, filling her nostrils. Gasping, she scanned the cove, looking for its source. Not far from where she stood was a low curved mass which she thought was a large rock. But then she saw the patterns in the sun baked surface and followed the curve to the large eyeless skull of a giant turtle which nestled on thick white finger bones. With each breath, the putrefying odor intensified. She turned away and saw, tangled in the overgrown path, clutching fingers and a face with bared fangs. Holding the towel tight against her like a shield, she scrambled back over the rocks and threw herself down on all fours in the sand, gasping to get control of her breath.

As the foul odor and frightening image dissipated, she felt a sharp burning in her left foot and sat up to inspect the damage. In her panicked dash over the rocks, one had sliced into her. She peeled back the tender, sand-encrusted gash. It was minor, superficial; more an additional insult than a wound. She carefully wiped it with her thumb. She would rest for a moment and then bathe it, and all of herself, in the purifying salt water.

Absorbed by this, she didn't see the blue-hulled trimaran slide between the headlands, or the man on the deck waving furiously and calling out to her. Perhaps if she had, it would have distracted her enough to keep the foul scent and frightening image from reasserting themselves. But, she didn't, and they did. She was suddenly overcome with retching, and seized with wooziness as if from a high fever, which in fact she had. The blow she received on the back of her head when the intruder flung her against the wall did more than addle her a little. Her brains plowed into her skull, capillaries broke, blood leaked, and she had, without her or anyone knowing it yet, a serious concussion. As Simon yelled his greeting from the deck of the *Hespera* she felt herself whiting out. She rolled over onto the towel, and lay there, staring at the man who came running down the beach toward her. Suddenly he was standing over her, looking down with large insect like eyes that reflected back to her in duplicate her tiny form lying demented in the sand. His wide mouth moved like a loop of liver-colored taffy. Words seeming to float toward her as if they rode in bubbles through thick water. *You... doan... loo... so... goo.* Long, brown arms reached toward her. The mouth moved again, and words again paddled slowly toward her: *You...reeeel... doan... loo...so...goo*

MINGA LAID BACK ON the throttle of the Xanadu Reefer and, cutting the wheel hard left, let it slide into the wake of the Hespera and sidle up to its own berth, leaving the big trimaran to go through its own more complicated docking procedures. Her little sister Gola stood on the dock in a slightly tattered frilly dress, bouncing a ball. As Minga jumped from the boat, the little girl ran off. She chased after, catching her by a flying pigtail.

"Let go, sis, you're hurting me."

"Not until I give you a hug am I gonna let go."

Gola giggled, twisted around, and threw her arms around her big sister.

"What you doin' here, baby?"

"Came to see you come in."

"And how'd you know I was comin' in? Who told you my secret?"

"Nobody. I was just down on the beach, following a new lady, when I saw you."

"No kidding. Well, you're just lucky I guess."

"Guess so. You gonna stay for a while?"

"Oh, no longer than usual. Stevie said he needed me here, so here I am. Lunch over?"

The little girl nodded.

"Well. Guess I'll just rustle up something for myself. There'll be leftovers."

"Guess so," said Gola, sliding her hand into her sister's as she headed up the stairs with her.

Long dreds shuddering against bare light-brown shoulders, Minga took the distance between the grassy vestibule and dining hall in long strides, the little girl running ahead, half-dragging her excitedly along, forcing her finally into a laughing trot to keep up. They arrived at the ramp leading up to the dining room just as the door banged open and Ogden appeared. At the first sight of her, his face arranged itself into a smile that could not entirely conceal a frown.

"Ah," he said with an equally ambivalent chuckle. "My daughter visits us."

Minga, brought up short by this, dropped the little girl's hand.

"Hi, Pop," she said, and walked in measured steps up the ramp to receive her father's embrace. Before another word could pass between them there was a sound of rapid steps coming up the path from the beach and an urgent voice:

"Pop…! Oh Minga. Glad you're here." It was her next younger sibling, Casper, his lean-muscled chest panting hard. "Problem down on the beach. Steve's down there with someone. You better come."

V

Awakening

LIKE A STOCK SCENE from a horror movie, rhythmic lumbering crunching and heavy breathing seemed to come from everywhere. When she turned to face her pursuer, she saw a bright ocean with pretty yachts drifting on it, white hulled, white sailed. As she ran toward the water, it lifted like a great tongue exposing beneath it a seabed of thick grass where Mr. Landis, holding the hand of a little girl, waited to show her to her cabin. As she stepped forward, a wide rift opened at the border between sand and grass. She tumbled head over heels down through the rift. Then she floated like a leaf in a light breeze, drifting across a sparkling blue sky.

She opened her eyes to bright daylight coming through the window. Blinking to adjust to it, she saw beyond it a sparse array of palm trees set against a cloudless sky; beyond the trees, water.

She felt comfortable, as if she had had a very good sleep, a very long good sleep from which she was in no hurry to get up. A muffled voice, a female voice, said something. There were slow footsteps and another voice said, "Oh, awake is she?" This voice was deeper, masculine, with a built-in smile. She liked the sound of it. Sliding her eyes in its direction, she saw a tall figure beside her, looking down. The smile in the voice was duplicated in the face, which was a little long, a little fleshy, a little pink, with curls of graying reddish-golden hair that parted loosely over a high forehead. A mustache drooped over the lips, almost concealing them; eyes smiled behind thick glasses. As hers lingered on him, his smile broadened. He spoke again.

"Well, Minga, it looks like Miss Shepherd has decided to rejoin us after all."

Teddi looked past him to see the person he addressed standing at his shoulder. Lean and athletic, her complexion in the range of a walnut shell, dark next to the man but lighter than her own; her head a medusa tangle of swirling brown snakes. Her broad face held a wide-mouthed, toothy smile; brown eyes squeezed into feline slits beneath a broad shining forehead. Teddi had never seen her before. But, she now recognized the man. She had last seen him at lunch…oh, when was that? He was the jokester, the psychiatrist that made everyone introduce themselves.

Her eye traveled over the bed, over the flattish mound of her body under a thin blanket. She saw the slender tube taped to her wrist. She looked up at the man and said thickly,

"Was that in doubt?" Her voice seemed distant to her.

"That you'd rejoin us?" He shook his head, his smile softening.

"What's wrong with me?" She looked at the tube. He took her hand in his. It was large and soft. The hand of a doctor. With his smiling voice he said,

"Oh, not much. You have a pretty nasty bruise at the back of your skull. Looks like you took a pretty solid blow. But, you're tough."

She tried to smile back at him.

"Don't feel tough."

He laughed lightly. "Tough doesn't mean you can't be hurt a bit."

She lifted her arm, turning it so that the tube faced him.

"What's…?"

"Fluid, electrolytes, a little bit of sedative to keep all systems calm. Always a small chance of seizures when someone's taken a blow like that."

"Oh. Concussion."

"So it seems. Everything adds up to that. Afraid we don't have a CAT scan handy," he laughed.

"What happened?" she said.

"You passed out on the beach. Stevenson was just coming down to find you. Seems he caught you mid-fall."

"Stevenson? Oh…"

"You remember Stevenson?"

"I don't think so. Don't think I met him."

"You're right," said the woman. "He was in Indua when you arrived. He flew back as soon as he heard you were here."

"Who're *you*?" said Teddi abruptly, startling the woman

"Minga. Minga Pelligrew. Stevie's sister."

"Oh," said Teddi, looking at her vaguely, then looking away, as if the information held no particular interest. Something was trying to sort itself out inside her. She looked from the woman to the man, to the room—boxy and simple—to the palm trees outside the window and the water beyond. She felt herself retract like a snail pulling back into its shell as the cove came back to her, along with the ominous vision in the undergrowth, the stench of the decaying turtle, and her terrified flight over the rocks.

"I mean," she said, furrowing her brow, straining to keep her mind on one track. "I mean, what *happened* to me? *Why* do I have a concussion? Something *happened.*" Her eyes narrowed on the man's face, which was no longer smiling, his brow now furrowed with concern. She pulled her hand away from his. "Do you know?" she said.

"Well, we're not sure, exactly. Except it seems you were attacked by an intruder in your cabin. Michael called to let us know."

"Michael?"

"Yes," said the woman. "Our little brother. He's the steward on the *Annubis*. He said he and another guy found you…"

A sharp memory came to her.

"They put me in bed."

"That's right. That's what Mikey said. They found you in a heap on the cabin floor. Seems your pack had been torn into. Your stuff was all over the place. Whoever did it also saw to it you got a nasty crack on the skull."

"Voila! Concussion."

"Voila concussion," said Bagram. "And some amnesia along with it, apparently. But, it seems your memory's waking up, along with the rest of you. Maybe you can fill in the rest."

Teddi thought. She now remembered awakening in the bunk in the ship's cabin, her pack placidly on a chair, the torn package on the desk. And then later in the morning, making the report in the captain's cabin; she had a vague recollection of apologies; reassurances that if anything were amiss the company would restore it; regret that there wasn't a gendarme on the scene. It was an asteroid of memory, fragments somehow stuck together in no particular order, large gaps making clear meaning impossible. Her brain rummaged among the debris, trying to formulate a question that might lead to an explanation. But, it found nothing.

"Sorry. Only bits and pieces. Except…except…"

"Yes? Except?"

There was the package, its slick pale green surface with the hand-scrawled note by Horatio Cook for Stevenson, its contents lying in manila envelopes on top of it. She told him about it. He nodded, but seemed unimpressed, which made her think he was withholding something from her. She pressed on:

"One of the envelopes had a drawing, an old architectural…"

"So you saw that? Yes. We…he'd been expecting it. Steve had. You conveniently left it all sitting on the dresser in your enduga. Minga grabbed it when she went in there to get your stuff for you." He nodded to the pack standing in a corner of the room.

"How long? How long has it been anyway since…"

"You went under?"

"Yes."

"Oh, I'm not sure. What do you say, Minga?"

Minga looked at the thick chronometer on her lean wrist, thought for a moment.

"Forty-eight hours or so. That's about how long I've been here."

In the time it took to make this calculation, Teddi's eyelids had dropped and she was asleep.

SHE AWAKENED AGAIN to the screech of a macaw winging high overhead. She felt sharp and energetic. A young man in cutoffs and flip-flops was asleep in a chair in a corner of the room, head sunk on chest, lean legs stretched out before him. Outside, the gray first light played on the sloshing water of the channel. She could see across it, not more than a hundred yards away, the trimaran tied up at the village wharf. Bobbing at the wharf on the near side of the channel was a sleek powerboat. Bold lettering on its prow proclaimed it to be the *Xanadu Reefer*.

Without thought or hesitation, she pressed herself up into a sitting position. Her scalp itched. She dug her fingers through her thick hair, which felt like it was covered in a coat of slime, and scratched hard. She smelled bad. She was parched. The I-V still hung from her left wrist and slid down over her breast like a dingy yellow worm. She was tempted to peel off the tape and pull the thing out, but thought better of it.

"Excuse me," Teddi said to the boy in the chair, not wanting to shock him. After three such attempts, she didn't care.

"Hey!" she called out sharply, and he opened his eyes in alarm.

"Oh, miss, you're awake," he said. "Wait. I'll be right back."

He dashed out and Teddi could hear him running through the adjacent room calling, "Minga! Minga! She's awake!"

A TABLE HAD BEEN SET on the veranda just outside the room in which Teddi had spent the past two days drifting unconsciously. Five places were set with plates. The boy Teddi had awakened—Alyosius, one of the younger of the Pelligrew children—brought out a pot of coffee, a pot of cream, a pot of coconut cream, a plate of sliced mango and a plate of fried plantain, a plate of toast. Teddi, Minga and Bagram sat at the table, awaiting the arrival of two others. The first, Stevenson, her official host and presumptive dive shop client, arrived shortly and joined them at the table. He expressed his relief that, after the scare of having found her collapsed on the beach, she now seemed to be okay.

The sun's rays broken over the jungle and sparkled in the channel. It beat intensely through the veranda's frond roof. Little was said as they helped themselves to the spare breakfast and awaited whomever it was the fifth chair was set for. At one point, young Alyosius made as if to sit down in it, but Minga spit at him and waved him away.

"Aw Minga," he complained. "Just until…"

"Never mind 'until.' You just go find something else for yourself to do. There'll be time later." The boy walked disconsolately into the building just as footsteps were heard on the gravel, and a man came around the corner of the bungalow and stomped up the stairs onto the veranda. He was of medium height and build, of about the same walnut shell coloring as Stevenson and Minga. He had loosely curling dark hair and wore dark sunglasses.

"Ah, here he is," said Stevenson, turning toward him with a welcoming gesture as he strode across the deck toward them. Sliding into the vacant chair between Stevenson and Teddi, he apologized for his late arrival, saying that he had been delayed by business in Tu Vua. He accepted the cup of coffee that Minga offered him, poured cream into it, took a sip. Then, hands clenched before him, he sat for a long minute, twisting and fidgeting in his chair, as if he were about to do something momentous that he was not quite prepared for. That was, in fact, the case.

After a long silence, Stevenson said, "Teddi, this is Shepherd." He waited for a moment. When the man merely nodded, his attention still seeming to be directed to his hands, he added, "Shepherd Pinkerton," as if to goad a response from the man.

A smile spread over Shepherd's lips, making a deeply grooved dimple in his cheek, and he finally, it seemed reluctantly, looked up and turned his sunglass-covered eyes toward Teddi.

"You're Teddi Shepherd," he declared, as if informing her of the fact. His voice was husky, slightly gravelly; it was a deeper voice than his size and bulk suggested; an oddly familiar voice.

A ray of sunlight breaking through the overhead fronds glinted off the black lenses of his sunglasses. It annoyed her that he kept them on, and made her wary. When she said, "Hello," there was a faint impatient questioning in her voice, as if challenging his presence. She looked quizzically around at the others, whose attention seemed to have gone elsewhere. What the man said next, stunned her.

"You're my *what*?" she barked at him.

At that, he pulled off his sunglasses. Small hazel eyes set close beside a triangular, low-bridged nose, looked intently into hers.

"I'm your brother," he said.

The brow, which bulged over the eyes, the straight dark eyebrows pulled together in anxious uncertainty, vied with the smile offered by the wide thickly mustached mouth. Deep vertical dimples on either side were framed by the tense jutting angle of his jaw. Like his voice, his look struck her with uncanny familiarity. Almost inaudibly, he repeated yet again the alarming words:

"I'm your brother."

"That is, of course," he went on, the smile for the moment winning out, "I'm your *half*-brother."

She stared at him, her head askew, eyebrows raised, lips compressed. Seeing that his effort at a friendly overture bought him nothing, he looked sharply away, first to Stevenson, then to Minga. The latter had pulled out her Polaroid, as was her habit whenever a moment struck her as being particularly noteworthy. Her boating customers loved her for it. He would have preferred she skipped it at the moment. Bagram, sensing an impasse, sought to smooth things out and get them moving again.

"Not surprised you're a bit distressed at this news," he said sympathetically. "Not everyday that someone discovers they have a long lost sibling. Especially while recovering from a concussion. Why don't we just take it easy?" His smile was all encouragement.

She looked back blankly, as if his words didn't compute. In fact they didn't. At the moment nothing did. She drew into herself, half-swooning at the flood of information. She felt as if she had been lifted out of her own world and dropped into another, into another self, that the armature that supported her own life had suddenly been stripped away, leaving her floating amoeba-like in an inky void. A quick glance at Shepherd suggested he wasn't in much better shape, despite his amiable efforts. The newfound siblings each seemed to be wandering adrift. As Teddi tried to gather herself, she heard Minga say "Watch the birdie."

She and Shepherd simultaneously turned their heads toward her, and she triumphantly snapped a picture. As irritating as that was, it at least served the purpose of giving them something specific to do. A minute later, she was pushing it at them across the table.

"Here, look you two," she said.

Shepherd took the picture out of her hand and held it so they could both look. Teddi felt immediately comforted by the ordinary gesture. They studied it together. The resemblance between them was clear. Their coloration was different—hers rosier, a little darker than his; different brows and eyes, different noses, but the same strong jaw and wide knobby chin. *Swish-swish* went the camera again. When the second picture arrived in their hands, showing them looking at the first, the resemblance was still more striking, especially around the mouth, despite his being partly hidden by the full brush of moustache. And between Shepherd and Joe, their common father, the likeness was more striking still. Shepherd's low-bridged nose, triangular, broadening out at the bottom, was different. Joe's had been high-bridged and narrow, almost femininely delicate. But, the narrow set of the eyes, their luminous hazel, the strong, prominent brow were all Joe's. Teddi was more like her mother, Chender, in that way: wide, deep set, dark brown eyes. They lingered together on the photograph, then turned toward each other with a shy effort at good humor.

"Woo-eee mama, is this fun," said Minga, taking yet another.

"Minga, for chrissake, cut it out!" snapped Shepherd, the underlying tension he and Teddi both felt suddenly rising up in him, souring the brief amiable moment. Teddi looked from one to the other. Then sitting back in her chair, playing with a strand of hair that fell over the light robe she wore, she cleared her throat and said,

"So, how come you're my brother?"

"Joe Shepherd's my dad, he's *your* dad. I'm your half-brother."

"Right. I already figured that out. But..."

Shepherd looked away, still clearly annoyed by Minga's

documentary efforts. As Teddi had already sensed, this business of recovering a sibling was evidently no easier for him than it was for her. He turned to Stevenson who gave him an encouraging look; and who, finding no taker, took up the baton while Shepherd sank into himself.

"He was here in the early sixties, your dad," Stevenson said. "A Peace Corps worker. Shepherd's mom, Ruth Pinkerton, was a local community worker. They met, worked together…" He stopped talking and lifted his hands to suggest all that followed.

The attention fell on Teddi, on her response. For her, it was both too much and not enough. For all these years, it seemed, there had been this lie in her life, like a snake hiding under a rock. Why Joe had kept this from her made no immediate sense. But, that was not what she was mainly reacting to. Rather, the final effort at manipulation that was so typical of her struggle with her father throughout her adolescence and then her adult life. It was a struggle that was never reconciled, only made finally irresolvable by his death. She was left to love the ghost of a father with whom she was joined by anger more than anything. It was an anger that grew out of his efforts to preside over her choices, efforts she had battled all her life. Feelings swirled and raced in her. Another immediate deception occurred to her: she now clearly saw that Horatio Cook, her dentist, the man who was mainly responsible for her coming here, was not just an old college friend of Joe's, but was somehow connected to his hidden life in Anuapúa. Horatio Cook himself, whom she trusted as a sort of confidant as well as being her dentist, was part of the deception, the manipulation, under which she had been living.

She felt herself go rigid, whirling inside with anger. She couldn't think. She was reduced to childish fury; a little girl, cajoled by her elders, running in a flood of outraged tears to the safety of her backyard swing set. She pushed back in the chair and folded into herself. Like the little girl, she wanted to flee and saw the impossibility of it. That little girl, perched in the safety of her swing, had plotted for years, and had made her escape when she could. She had no intention of going back now. She gathered herself and stood up. She felt a little wobbly and had to steady herself against the table. Then she turned away and walked to the railing at the end of the veranda. From there she could look out to the channel as it met the ocean, and the headland that bordered the cove where she had had the alarming experience just before her collapse. Nothing about it registered now as she looked across the water, no fear or disgust. That had been completely absorbed by the old irritant, the frustration that still burned in her. She had not yet absorbed the fact that she was free. She still struggled for it, whenever the question came up. Now here it was again. She turned and looked at the others, addressing them from the short distance, leaning back against the railing, gripping it to steady herself.

"Look," she said huskily. "I'm sure you're all really nice people. But, this just wasn't my plan. My poor old dad had some weird ideas. But—I don't know if you'll get this—I just don't want to be, you know, the final step in some sort of master *mea culpa* of his. I really don't know what the hell he was trying to do. Nothing against you Shepherd, but I'm just not in the mood to be anybody's long-lost sister, never mind part of the price being a crack on the skull and whatever." She paused for a while, her arms stretched out on either side, clutching the railing, head bowed. "The best thing you could do would be to help me get myself together and get out of here. This just doesn't feel right. Okay?"

None of the others moved. They looked at her furtively, sheepishly. Even the ebullient Minga, seeming to have fallen back at her onslaught. Finally, Bagram got up and, in his shambling gait, walked over and leaned against the railing beside where she stood, now turned away, her back to the others.

"You know," he said quietly, working to meet her levelly, "I'm not really surprised at your reaction. I mean, the whole thing is completely unimaginable. And, here you find yourself kind of waylaid. It seemed to make such sense. Two orphans—that's what you both are now—find each other. It sounds so right in the abstract. Great theatre, right? Who wouldn't want to support such a coming together. You two could go on Oprah." He looked to see if he had managed to raise a smile. No such luck. He continued. "'Course everybody has their own baggage, not always computable. Who could know that you had a pile of other issues, and that you wouldn't be so pleased about being hijacked?"

She looked sharply at him, then quickly away.

"Right. Surprise, surprise. Well, anyone really thinking about it might have thought that. But…well, you've made it clear to us dunderheads that whatever was going on between you and your dad is still alive and well. Big, surprise. So much for my psychiatric credentials, eh?"

Horatio should have known! she thought to herself, feeling especially his betrayal.

"My whole point in coming here was to get away from that. Now it seems Horatio's decided it's okay to rub my nose in it. He should have understood. He knew what was going on between us. I just don't get it. He could have told me what this was about. Why the big fucking mystery? I'm sorry, I really just want to get the hell out of here. That guy doesn't look too happy about this either. He's got plenty of issues of his own." She gestured toward Shepherd.

Bagram bounced his hands softly against the railing a few times.

"There's something else," he said. "You're probably not going to like this either. But, I wish you'd give us a hearing. It will at least explain some things."

After a long pause, she shrugged, pushed herself upright and followed him back to the table.

VI

The Plan

ALYOSIUS APPEARED WITH a pitcher of fruit juice and went around the table filling their glasses. They drank and sat silently for a while. Then Bagram said to Teddi,

"I need to set the scene for you." He looked around at the others who nodded their approval.

"Anuapúa," he began, "is about to have a Constitutional Convention to settle once and for all the status of the two major communities—the indigenous Anuaps and the ethnic Indians, Bengalis mostly. This status has been carefully left undecided since the British gave up their authority here in 1966, thirty-four years ago. The result of that indecision has been periodic outbreaks originating on one side or the other, and the general suppression of Indian interests except where they agree with Anuap interests. Small concessions have been given to the Indians. But, they're half the population and they have, by specific statute, only two-thirds of the constitutional power of the Anuaps. The good old double standard. The Indians are second-class citizens. If things are allowed to just follow their natural course, this upcoming so-called Constitutional Convention will engrave that status in stone. But, some Anuaps…"

"Many, actually," put in Stevenson.

"…these guys for instance," said Bagram, gesturing to the others around the table, "have good reasons for opposing this. Good political and economic reasons, for one thing. The Indians do a lot of the heavy lifting in the Anuapúan economy. And they hold down much of the bureaucracy. They run a lot of the tourist industry. They own no land, are not allowed to, also by statute, but they've historically managed the agriculture industry. Even now, they plant, harvest and ship all the considerable cane produced on these islands. And so forth. If they're made permanent second-class citizens, a good number, maybe most, probably a lot of the best qualified, will leave. Many have already: for Australia, New Zealand, for the US."

"Its not just economics," put in Shepherd. "There are also personal reasons. Intermarriage is a problem for everyone, but especially for Anuaps. That's what sent Horatio Cook's family to the U.S. You probably know that his dad was Anuap and his mom Indian. It's a problem for these two." He pointed to Stevenson and Minga.

"That's right," said Minga, "Stevie's wife is Joyeeta Gupta. My sweet boyfriend is her brother Sanjay. Someday, when all this shit gets fixed, we're going to get married."

"It makes for lots of problems," said Stevenson.

"So, a major opposition has developed," Bagram continued. "Mostly among young people, these guys' generation and younger, mostly. Some elders, Rotanu and Amatosi, for instance. You'll meet them."

At the mention of the last name a shadowy recollection crossed Teddi's mind, then faded as Bagram went on: "But most, that is most Anuap elders, are for status quo."

"Like Pops," said Minga.

"Yes," said Stevenson. "Our father's old school. We try to change him, but no dice so far." Teddi remembered the somber expression that flitted across Ogden's face at the welcoming ceremony as he spoke of keeping his community together.

"To say they're *for* the status quo is way too mild," said Shepherd. "They're absolutely hell bent on keeping it going. Some would rather eat us for breakfast than change."

"Ogden too?" asked Teddi, turning to Minga and Stevenson.

"You bet," said Minga, who had slouched down in her chair and pulled the beak of her battered Dodgers cap over her eyes.

"He's not as bad as some of the others. But…yeah, probably, if push came to shove," said Stevenson, reaching over to pat Minga's hand. She jerked it away with a grimace.

"So, a big battle is looming around the Convention," said Bagram. "They have the power. And they're supported by some of the Indian establishment; the ones who've benefitted from the system, the yea-sayers and kow-towers. They have the army, they control the media, even the part of it that serves the Indian community. And they have the Bukharat."

"Stick around here long enough and you'll run into them," said Minga, lifting her cap and looking at Teddi. "Surprised you haven't already. They *love* to perform for tourists. They really do. Really screw things up."

"That's right," said Stevenson. "These days they limit their activities to a kind of vigorous guerrilla theatre aimed mostly at tourists."

"Which really makes no sense," said Shepherd.

"Well, whatever. But, anyway, you never know when they're going to pop up with their grotesque costumes and cute little spray bottles of sugar syrup. And we just don't know how they're going to react when things really get going."

"Get going?" said Teddi.

"Yeah," said Shepherd. "When our followers hit the streets and start whooping it up outside the National Assembly."

"The hell we don't know," said Minga. "You can be damn sure they'll be beating the crap out of any AMNUP they can get their hands on."

"And with the consent of dear old Iratago—currently and probably forever President of the Council of Chiefs—and his *official* hoodlums," added Shepherd.

"A buddy of Pops," Minga sneered.

"*Official* hoodlums…?" asked Teddi.

"I mean the army," said Shepherd. "As chief-of-chiefs, he runs it. The Bukharat are unofficial. They may act like a bunch of hyperactive goofball performers now, but they have a history."

"Blood-and-guts thugs," said Stevenson. "They're the local equivalent of that guy in Haiti's—what do you call them?—Tonton Macoute. They went to town with clubs and machetes after the Brits left in '66."

"That's right," said Bagram. "That's why all Europeans, at least the ones who weren't already tied into the government, had to get out then, why the Peace Corps shut down."

"Yeah. Some *peace*," said Minga.

"Then who are *your* 'followers'?" said Teddi, addressing the three Anuaps. Bagram answered for them.

"You, Miss Shepherd, are in the company of roughly half of the steering committee of the Agarbathy Mango National Unity Party."

"Otherwise known as AMNUP," said Shepherd.

"Agarbathy," began Stevenson, "is for the Indian contingent. It means…"

"I know what it means," said Teddi. "It's what my grandma, my mom's mom, called joss sticks, incense."

"Ah. Well, right you are. And the mango is the national tree of Anuapúa, so…"

"Got it. And you all are the steering committee?"

"Half of it," Stevenson said. "The other half are, well, let's see. Rajiv and Sanjay and Joyeeta are in Indua. Amatosi should have just returned from some government business in the States."

There was that name again. The fleeting memory returned: two images, cut of the same cloth, vied for attention. The first, the old man on the bus from Tu Vua, a sweetly romantic old uncle, full of talk of vivid sunsets and moon-swept oceans, who had suggested the change of plans that brought her aboard the *Annubis*. No name attached itself to him. It wasn't him, but the other they were referring to.

"That *I* can confirm," said Teddi. Below an embossed gold seal on a plain white business card, three lines stated: Kambula Amatosi, Minister of Commerce, Anuapua. *That's just the official nonsense,* he had said, holding out his broad hand to her. *My civilian name is Jack Sprague. Please call me Jack.* As they stepped from the air-conditioned cabin into the sultry heat of the tarmac, his last ceremonious words to her—*may your days be tangy as green mango and your nights filled with the sweetness of frangipani*—were unmistakably twisted through with irony. The recollection of this now made her wonder what he had already known and anticipated.

"He was my seatmate on the plane here from Honolulu. He told me to call him Jack."

"Right," said Minga, looking around to the others in a way that put Teddi on heightened alert. "That's Uncle Jack. Mom's brother."

"And," Stevenson went on. "Rotanu is...Where the hell *is* Rotanu?"

"He's been tied up with family business the last few days," said Shepherd. "He'll show up eventually." And, looking to Teddi, added, "My uncle, my mom's brother."

"Ah. Well, that's it, pretty much," Stevenson went on. "The steering committee. Young, old, Anuap, Indian. There're some other ethnics involved also."

"Like me, for instance," said Bagram. "Although I guess not technically. I'm more like honored guest. Right?" he said, looking jovially around the group. They all fell silent, leaving Teddi to again ponder what had not yet been said. She waited expectantly for a while, and then said,

"And...?"

Bagram, who had become occupied with watching his thumbs spin on his stomach, cocked his head toward her as if he were just reminded of her presence. "And?" he said. "Oh, yes. Well, the thing is we need your help."

"Which," said Teddi, her tone baffled and impatient, "is the other reason why I'm here? You need my help?"

"Yes," Bagram continued. "You see, the thing is we really have no power. I think we made that clear, no?"

"I guess."

"Well, we don't," said Stevenson, "Our only hope, where we think we have a chance, is by turning the eye of the world on this little crumb of dirt."

"That's never really happened before, you see, except as a playground." said Bagram. "It's not like what happened in my country, when we finally managed to string that bastard Ceauşescu up while the whole eastern block was more or less going topsy turvey. Or in what used to be Yugoslavia. All of that mattered big time to a lot of other people. There it was, smack in the middle of European history. But, what is this? A very minor side show. No one's really interested. Nothing that happens here is even news anywhere else. Except maybe in the little Anuapúan Indian émigré community in Sydney or someplace."

"So, okay. I get it. You have to make it matter somehow. And…" she looked from one to the other, "…you need *my* help?"

"This is going to sound like a joke," muttered Minga, from under the peak of her cap. She lifted her head and leveled her gaze on Teddi. "We need you to help us find something."

"Me? Find what?"

"That package for me you brought from Horatio?" said Stevenson. "What was in that package, in one of those envelopes, is a drawing of the National Assembly building. That's where the Constitutional Convention will take place in about two weeks. It's not an ordinary drawing. For one thing, it's very old, a relic, dating from the time of the building's construction, late 1880s. It's been in Horatio's family since that time. There were rumors of its existence, as there have been about other things relating to it. I'll get to that. Also, there are these markings, sort of a doodle and some scribbles. They're part of what you'd call its legend. They're supposed to be a code of some sort. It makes the thing kind of like a treasure map. That's there all right, right on that old drawing. And we've been able to verify that it at least *could* be a code. We're still working that out. That is, he is," he said, indicating Bagram.

Teddi turned toward him.

"You read codes? I thought you were a psychiatrist."

"Also certified cryptographer. First training in Romanian army, Second Kluj-Napoca Brigade. Thanks to Ceauseşcu for that. One thing about dictators. They recognize talent when they see it. I knew Reagan and Gorby were going to meet before they did." He clearly got a kick out of his joke and laughed loudly for a while. The others sat silent. He continued. "I escaped before they make much use of my talents. So, yes. True. I decode other things beside souls. I am convinced there is something to the doodle. I'll show you later, if you like. Please…" he said, turning to Stevenson, who continued.

"So, it's the idea that this doodle is a code that makes the drawing you brought important. Otherwise, it's just a nice old drawing. If it is a code, it means the other part of the legend might also be true, the really important part. And this is it: the original British colonial administration, who were responsible for and oversaw the building of the Assembly, didn't feel entirely safe here. They were afraid that the indigenous folk, our Anuap ancestors, might get stressed out and forget their new cloak of civilized Christianity and— as incredible as it sounds—decide that they, the Brits, were edible. You've heard, of course, about the cannibalism practiced on these islands. Yes, yes. I know. It sounds like a racial slur put out by the colonials to justify their messing around here. White man's burden kind of rot. But, you will not find many Anuaps who say that. Most of us think of it with a kind of pride. Anyway, according to this legend, fearing an out of control uprising, they built into the Assembly an escape hatch, so to speak. A tunnel or whatever, that would take them out of reach of the cauldrons."

"Actually the barbecues," put in Bagram. To Teddi's astonished response, he added, "As incredible as it sounds, there *are* archival photos of nursing Anuap mothers, placidly gnawing on the arm of someone else's child hot off the spit."

"As if that proved anything," said Teddi. "You believe that, you probably believe in the moon landing."

"Of course," he responded, chuckling appreciatively, "simulation being one of the delightful discoveries of the early photo-documentrist. But you won't find many here denying it. As Steve said, it seems to be a point of pride."

"Yep," said Minga, impishly. "We Anuaps just *love* the sweetness of human flesh."

"Dad used to say the skeleton you let on is in your closet is as good as the one that's actually there," said Teddi.

"Smart Dad," said Shepherd, flashing Teddi a quick smile.

"It seems strange to me," she said. "Why would a British administration so certain of its place as to throw up a building like that have any such fear? I don't remember The Brits being bashful about putting down native revolts."

"Not so strange," said Bagram. "Other justifiably paranoid and efficient potentates—Norman dukes, Alhambran emirs, bit players like Transylvanian counts, my dear countryman Vlad the Impaler, for instance—had tunneled beyond their walls in fear of a bloodthirsty rebellion, if not necessarily cannibalism. And the palaces of Venetian mercantile princes concealed escape routes to the sea from the lands where they practiced their thievery. Guilt, you know, is a great stimulus to all sorts of weird action."

During the brief pause that followed, an idea of where all this was leading began to form in Teddi's mind. Before it could take shape, Stevenson continued.

"No one's examination of the official construction drawings of the Assembly—we have a copy of them; you'll need them if…" he stopped mid-sentence, then began again. "Neither the drawings or anyone's investigation of the building or the surroundings has turned up anything."

"That's right," said Shepherd. "It used to be a kind of schoolboy's game to try to find it. Especially for those of us that had the run of the place, sons of kambulas mainly. We were all over the place, inside, outside; not a crevice or cranny of building or sea that didn't suffer from our probing little eyes."

"Great for Fox and Hounds," added Stevenson.

"And so now this old drawing turns up. So…?" said Teddi.

"Yes. Well, it's the most amazing piece of luck. The fact that after his mom died, Horatio found it in her stuff…"

"Why would she have it?" asked Teddi caught up now in the puzzle, which further distracted her from the idea that was dawning on her.

"Good question," said Stevenson. "Part of the legend was the existence of the drawing itself, and its disappearance. It most likely came to her from Horatio's dad when he died, whose ancestry, on the Anglo side, went back to the time of the building of the Assembly."

"Ah," said Teddi. "So *his* ancestor nabbed it?"

"Well, maybe," said Stevenson, smiling brightly at her. "Or maybe he created it."

"I've done a little genealogical research," said Bagram.

"You would," said Minga, offering him a crooked smile.

Bagram reached over to give the bill of her cap a playful yank, then went on: "You'll find this interesting. According to records dug up by one of Amatosi's people, there was a certain Brightman Cook, Esq. who was apparently an adjuvant in the governor's office around the time the building was constructed. The record shows that this Brightman married a chieftain's daughter, and together they produced Horatio's first mixed-race ancestor, one Magulano Claudius Cook. Seems he stuck around just long enough to plant his seed…"

"Just like dad," said Teddi, looking over at Shepherd.

"Well, maybe a bit longer. Long enough for the naming ceremony, anyway. And then…well, it's unclear. He either expired or sailed off. But, any way, that's how the drawing became part of the family trove. Claudius passed it on to the next Brightman who passed it on to Jacob who passed it on to the next Claudius, Horatio's dad, who left it in Horatio's mom's possession when he died. Now, as noted, there's a kind of a doodle on the drawing, a sort of leaf shaped thing…"

"I think I saw it," said Teddi. A musty scent came to her, the feeling of delicate brittleness between her fingers, what seemed to be an idle line, or even a scratch above the fold, with odd random markings. She had paid little attention.

"Ah. Good. Well, it seems it was done by him. There are some faint notations near it. Amatosi got me some documents in old Brightman's hand. I'm well enough schooled in this to recognize handwriting from the same hand when I see it. So, it's at least a good bet that the doodle was done by him."

"Which means he came by it fair and square," put in Stevenson.

"Right," said Bagram. "And the doodle itself..." he paused to look at Teddi and give weight to what followed, "...is a code. At least I'm fairly certain it is. But, we'll get into that later. If I'm right about it, it will help you..."

At this, the part of Teddi's mind that had been lulled by Bagram's story woke up and, like a shark circling in deep water rose toward the surface, bringing a renewed sense of alarm with it.

"Help me? Help me do what?" she said.

"Well," said Bagram, clearing his throat. "Find...the...uh... you know..." This uncharacteristic hesitancy from Bagram heightened her alarm.

"No," she said, her throat constricted, the ever-lurking quaver almost taking over her voice, "I don't know. Find what? What am I supposed to find?" And then, before he could say anything, the shark struck.

"Oh, of course. How dumb. The tunnel? The escape route, whatever it is? *That's* why I'm here?"

Bagram looked around at the others. Their eyes were fixed on her. He went on:

"Well, to put it plainly, yes," he said, with forced joviality. "Give me a good old bi-polar or a coded message to decipher and I'm in my element. Forensic architecture, sorry to say, is just not my bag. But, so Horatio tells us, apparently it is yours. So, we thought, well, since you're going to be here anyway..."

He stopped, observing the stunned look she gave him. There

was a long pause. The others turned their attention fully on her. She herself was occupied with a quickly coalescing swirl of suppositions.

"I hope you won't be insulted," she said finally, controlling her voice with difficulty, trying to inject her own tone of gaiety, "but I just had the crazy idea that you intend to try to sneak into the Assembly and…" as she spoke she saw in her mind's eye the people around her bursting into the council of state. "…and I don't know what," she concluded with an explosive guffaw that nearly drowned out her words, "…take them all hostage?"

She looked around at blank staring faces.

"Sorry," she said, struggling to contain her laughter. "Sorry. I get weird ideas sometimes. Really, I do. Didn't mean to insult…" They sat, unspeaking, stony-faced. They may have been insulted by her manner, but not by the allegation.

"Oh my god," she said. "You are…you do…"

Stevenson looked up at her bleakly, then looked away, toward the channel.

"God!" said Minga, pushing herself back down in her seat. "I knew this was a bad idea."

Shepherd, in the low slightly corroded voice with which she was so familiar, her father's voice, looking down at his hands folded on the table, said, "You have no obligation…"

Teddi withdrew into herself, sat back in her chair, folded her own hands together. "I'm sorry," she said calmly. "I guess I really didn't get it. It seemed funny to me that someone would really think about doing something like that. I'm sorry. I guess I'm just having a hard time tuning in."

No one spoke. In the silence it all became clear to her. The expectations these people had of her—fomented by her dentist, her dead father's friend—were largely responsible for her coming here. They had given her a key role in a kind of comic-opera plot, joined to the melodrama cooked up by her dying father of connecting her with the half-brother whose existence he had concealed from her during his life. As Bagram had already as much as admitted, in cahoots with Horatio Cook, at his instigation, they had basically hijacked her to suit their needs.

"Well," she said, breaking the silence. "I wish you luck. I do. But, sorry. This just isn't my problem. You're all very nice, but, this is not really what I had in mind. Now," she said, her jaw clamped shut, the tendons on her neck standing out, "I will need some help getting a plane out. Right now I need to be by myself for a while. Just need some space. So, if you'll excuse me, I'm going to go for a little walk. It'd be great if maybe sometime later today one of you can help me catch a flight to Tu Vua." She got up and headed for the stairs leading down from the veranda. Stevenson rose with her, moving to block her path.

"Teddi, please, hear us out."

"Sorry. I've heard. I told Bagram I'd do that and I did. I just don't feel much like being hijacked today, if you don't mind. I think I'm done here. I practically got turned into a basket case. For all I know, it's because your little scheme went awry. Enough's enough. I have a bruised head I don't need. I have a brother I don't need. Sorry, Shepherd, but it's true. I'd just like to get a plane back to Tu Vua. I'll figure it out from there, okay. Thanks a lot."

She skirted Stevenson and, seized with emotion, left the veranda and walked barefoot across the gravel toward the dense ficus and fern forest that went from the channel around behind the bungalow. Finding a path into it she walked along for a while. Her breathing slowed. The path was soft underfoot. She came to a rock pool fed by a waterfall. She climbed up the rocks leading up to its source, unsteadily at first, then with assurance, feeling her strength and physical confidence returning for the first time since the attack on the Annubis. She found a flat rock beside the fall and rested there for a while. She saw that she was not really angry with these people. Not even with Horatio Cook who, though apparently acting out of some confused loyalty, had always been her friend. The grotesquely distorted body of her father rose in her mind, mysterious edema from the surgery that was meant to save his life swelling him almost beyond recognition. Heavily sedated, he had wandered off in some strange and distant labyrinth from which he never returned. She would never know what he really intended.

After a while she took off her thin robe, wound it in its belt, threw it clear of the pool, and dove in. The water was cool and healing. Her body knew what to do and she gratefully gave in to it.

VII

Brother and Sister

THE SWIM FIXED her resolve. Returning to the bungalow, she saw Minga heading to where the *Xanadu Reefer* was docked. As she came around the side of the building, she found Shepherd still sitting on the veranda where she had left him. The sound of her footsteps on the gravel brought him to his feet.

"Hello," he said, nodding stiffly in her direction.

"Hello," she said, returning his nod. She walked across the deck and positioned herself against the wall opposite him.

"I don't blame you," he said, after a long pause. "I'd probably feel the same way. That is if I weren't, tied up in all this."

Another silence. She stood, arms crossed, leaning against the wall, waiting.

"But," he continued at last, "I am. We're in a bad situation here. We're desperate for a solution, and it…that is, *you*…seemed like such a natural. *Bungshalo!*" he exclaimed, suddenly interlacing his fingers. She looked at him quizzically. "Ah. Old Anuap idea. Kismet, fate, providence, destiny, whatever. But, with its own special flavor. Two things show up that serve common needs. It's a sign. Or, the other way around, one thing shows up that serves two needs. Pursue it at all costs. In this case, you're that thing. My sister. Our forensicist."

He raised one cheek in a little squint of a smile.

"Worse luck for you. It's no wonder you're upset. And, you're not the first party *bungshalo* has gotten us into trouble with. There's the case of our ancestors' wildly enthusiastic welcome of the Brits. They were both edible *and* they brought us the true religion." He chuckled, intensifying his cockeyed smile. He waited for her response. When she offered none, his laughter fizzled and he turned inward again. She watched the somber face for a moment, his inner workings suggested by an expression she knew well: a dark cloud within, seeded with danger—lurking and watchful, reluctant and purposeful. She could see that she had been right. He was as put off at the discovery of their relationship as she was, no happier at being wound into this web of fate that included her and their father.

"You're not altogether thrilled that I'm here either, are you?" she said. He did not respond immediately. When he finally spoke, it was on another tack.

"I've often wondered what it would have been like to have actually known him."

The look he gave her seemed full of expectation, as if he were counting on her to fill in that blank in his life.

"You never had any contact with him?"

"Some letters, early on. It's not the same, do you think?" he replied.

She shrugged. Her own conflicts rose up to face her: the little girl who nestled into her daddy's touch; the woman who felt herself hounded by the gray shadow of judgment. For a time they were both silent. Then Shepherd pulled out his wallet, extracted something from it, and handed it to her. It was a picture of a young man and young woman, cheeks pressed together, each with a comically somber expression. A worn photo-booth picture. The young woman, darker complected, frowzle-haired, was not beautiful, but her eyes had a sparkling depth, evident even from the faded, creased image. The man was not handsome, but still charming, cute she couldn't help thinking, the impishness around his lips mocking his serious pose, his face also surrounded with unruly waves of dark hair. It was her father a few years before she was born; her father more or less as she remembered him from childhood.

"Oh, god!" she gasped as tears sprang into her eyes. She looked at the picture for long seconds, then handed it back, looking away. Minga's boat was approaching the wharf on the other side of the channel. The tall mast of the *Hespera* rocked above it.

"Do you miss him?" said Shepherd, his voice thick.

"Yep," said Teddi, crushing away the tears with her palms. "That him," she pointed toward the picture Shepherd held between his fingers. "I miss what never quite happened. Never really got to say goodbye."

They were quiet for a while. Then he said,

"I got a letter. It was in the package for Steve you were carrying. There were things in it he thought I should know... about him, my mom, why..."

"You never knew before? He never...I mean in other letters...?"

"Those stopped pretty early on."

"He stopped writing?"

"No. I stopped writing. I was too old. He was still writing to a little boy. He was too far away. I got an occasional note, birthday cards, presents. Anyway, here's the thing about what he sent me. There were some things he just wanted to get square before he checked out. He seemed to know he wasn't going to make it."

"Yes. He was very sick. The surgery was his last chance." Her eyes wouldn't stop tearing.

"It was why he left here that he wanted me to know about. I'd asked. Not him. I couldn't. But I had asked Papa."

"You mean your mom's brother."

"Yes, my uncle Rotanu. He's the only father I've ever really known. But, he didn't want to talk about it either. I mean, he never said more than that it had to do with the times. You know, all the nastiness after the Brits left. As if that said everything. But, I could tell there was more; there was something behind his words.

He just didn't want to get into it. So, it was about *that* stuff that Dad wanted me to know. I don't really know why, exactly. Maybe just to make sure he cleared the air."

"You got the letters too, right? The ones between them, Dad and your mom?"

"Yes. They came from Horatio with his letter to me. You knew about them?"

"I just saw a few. I opened the envelope they all came in. They sort of poured out, and I saw the addresses and the return addresses. I barely had chance to glance at them before I had to get off the ship. I was really too messed up to do anything about it. But, it sure made me curious. Didn't know what to make of it. Now I know, I guess."

"They loved each other, I think. It was just rotten luck."

"Is that what everyone else thinks?

"I can't say. Sometimes, from Rotanu, I get the sense that he somehow blamed Dad. That's what I meant by something lying behind his words. But, that's not what the letters said. It may be though, that's why he had to write to me, that he thought I somehow thought that. Here." He pulled some folded pieces of stationary from his shirt pocket and handed them over to Teddi.

"Those were very dark times for everyone," he went on. "The moment all the royal pomp of the Brit's leaving was over, the old wounds came charging into the street. Whatever voices of reason there were didn't stand a chance, the ones that Dad and others like him tried to foster. Papa Rotanu was one of them. I think maybe he never really accepted that Dad had no choice but to go. But, that's what he said there," he pointed to the paper in Teddi's hand. "He tried to put to rest any idea I still might have gotten that he just abandoned me and my mom. Very dark times."

There was an appeal in his eyes as he looked at her, seeming to take in both the mission he was caught up in, and what they shared.

"Can you believe this? At my age? I'm supposed to be a tough guy."

Teddi thought back to the scene in the bar several nights before, of him sitting watchfully at a back table while his brothers, who were all undoubtedly tough guys, rousted the jerks who had interrupted her dancing with Simon with their drunken lunatic behavior. Her quick impression was of a man in charge of himself and everything around him. A tough guy, to be sure. She shrugged and smiled at him.

"Being an orphan's a new one on me, too," she said, sympathetically. Then she asked softly: "And now? How are the times now? What makes you think anything's really different?"

"Well, we have reason to hope. Things are definitely different. The world's a smaller place. Light shines in places it never did before. Even on a little insignificant speck like us. Yes. Things are more favorable. That's why, when Horatio dug up that old drawing from his mother's trunk, we saw an opportunity to put together some fancy guerilla theatre. And then, that amazing coincidence of you having just the right skills to make it all happen. *Bungshalo!* The breath of Providence. You find this foolish. I'm not surprised." The last was said with a hint of self-contempt. The shared feeling of a moment before suddenly drained away. Teddi registered the change in temperature.

"Insane is what comes to mind," she said, somewhat coldly, throwing up her own armor.

"Yah, we're definitely desperate," he grunted. Then his voice took on a pleading tone, not addressed to her, especially, but to whatever controlled their destiny: "We need something spectacular, however crazy it sounds."

"Taking your country's lawmakers hostage is really crazy, alright." Again, burlesque images came to her of figures hurrying down a torch-lit subterranean passage, scuttling along dark hallways and charging into the Chamber of Chieftains, guns at the ready. "How can you possibly think anything good could come of that?"

"They have *their* guerilla theater. We'll have ours."

"Ha! What makes you think they'll see it that way?"

"It doesn't matter. We need to be heard. We need to turn the eyes of the world on us, on them" said Shepherd, impassioned, whatever calm assessment there was in him having disappeared.

"But what about your demonstrations? You said there'd be thousands outside."

"Yes? Getting pounded on by the Bukharat. And so what? They'll be inside, locked up nice and safe in their chamber of privilege. The Karoja—the Grand Tribal Council—will run things their way. The Indian and other ethnic legislators—all suck-ups, in it for themselves—will posture and concede. Make speeches about realistic compromise, enduring relations, blah-blah. And some small, cosmetic, concessions *will* be made. Any hope for any kind of real equity will be signed away forever. If we can pull this off, they'll at least have to listen, at least have to confront the shame of the world. It will be like Tiananmen Square."

"Yeah? *That* was sure a great success," said Teddi, the image flaring up of the boy being crushed by the tank while a hopeful world looked on helplessly.

"*This* will be different. We'll do it right. We'll make them listen. They'll be unable to do anything until we've had a hearing. Then…"

"Then…?"

He shrugged.

"You don't know what comes next. Great plan," she said impatiently, now feeling out of sympathy with him, with them. "And, anyway, how will you hold the place once you're inside? Isn't there an army or whatever…?"

Shepherd looked at her somberly.

"We have a counterforce," he said. "They'll secure the Great Hall. The Karoja and all the others will be sealed in. We'll be sealed in. They'll have to recognize the strength of our need by the very desperation of our act. And, they'll have to listen. At the end, what happens will happen. But if there's any possibility, we have to give it a try. As Rajiv says, it's the straw that we have to grasp at. Otherwise, they'll point to the protesters outside as evidence of democracy in action even as the Bukharat are beating the crap out of them while the army keeps an eye on things, pat us on the head like demented children, and do what they want. If you can find a way in for us, then this is our chance. We need you to do this for us."

"Hey, wait a minute. I thought I made myself clear. I'm not a participant in this. I just want the next flight out. Okay?"

His look became stern, pugnacious, ferocious behind the dark lenses.

"Oh, so now *I'm* a hostage?" she said with a derisive laugh.

Pulling off the sunglasses again and slipping them into his pocket, in a final effort to win her sympathy, he said softly,

"Look. I guess I'm no happier with you than you are with me. But, of course you're not a hostage. If you could just please…"

"I don't get it," she interrupted him. "You're Anuap. You're not Indian. What's *your* stake in all of this anyway?"

He reached to take the folded paper from her hands. He looked through it and finding what he was looking for handed it back to her.

"Read this," he said, his voice and hand shaking with urgency.

She read:

"…my continued presence was a special danger. The work I was doing for ethnic parity went way outside my mandate. The State Department knew that, the *Karoja* knew that. Even then Iratago was being groomed. He had a special dislike for me. It would have been disastrous for your family, and for the Guptas, had I stayed on, even if I were permitted to. It was why Claudius and Prajita Cook had to get out with Horatio. I know from Horatio where your sympathies lie. It is as much as I could have hoped for. Be careful my son. And, please, greet your sister kindly. This will be a very difficult meeting for her as I have no doubt it will be for you."

Tears welled in Teddi's eyes as she read. It explained nothing really, except to confirm Joe's objectives and Shepherd's commitment to them. But it did have the intended effect of breaking down her resistance. Surprised at the sound of her voice, she said quietly,

"I'll go to Indua."

"What?"

"I'll at least look at the building and the site. See if I can make any kind of sense of it. Can I get inside?"

"Yes. You can," said Shepherd excitedly. "Oh, that's wonderful. There's a regular public tour. In fact, the legend of the escape route is a feature of it. The tour guide does some kind of amusing business. Minga says tourists love it. That would be good. Minga's going to head back to Indua in a little while. If you're up to it, you could ride in with her. You'll meet Rajiv. He can take you there. Oh, that would be very good. You two could talk."

And who is this Rajiv that I need to talk with him? she wondered. Then, feeling a little less enthusiasm for the project, despite the sympathy Joe's letter had stirred in her, she said, "Okay. But no promises."

"Sure, no promises," said Shepherd, still grinning and wrapping her in a very fraternal embrace which, to her surprise, she found herself returning.

VIII

Indua

THE *XANADU REEFER* CAREENED at full throttle around the headland of Guma and south toward Indua. Teddi clutched the windshield to keep her feet as the sleek hull pounded against a strong onshore current. Close beside her, Minga strained at the helm, cap turned backwards, dreds bouncing against the tensed muscles of her lean shoulders. Keeping the wheel cranked to the left with one hand, she pointed behind her with the other.

"The reef's out there," she shouted into Teddi's ear. "Some of the most gorgeous coral and fish in the world."

Teddi turned to look. An awning-covered motorboat from the village filled with reef hounds, some with masks planted on their foreheads, was making it slow way in the direction Minga pointed.

"You'll see it when you get back here," Minga shouted again. Teddi turned to give her a doubtful look. She had left nothing behind. On the deck beside her stood her stuffed orange pack. Her daypack sat on a bench nearby. She had made no promises. She would look at the Assembly, tell them what she thought. As far as she knew, her next stop was Tu Vua; after that, maybe Honolulu. But Minga gave her a broad smile and shouted, "Oh, don't worry. You're coming back."

Teddi shrugged and gave herself over to the pure pleasures of speed, the rush of wind, the sting of the tropical sun now halfway to the western horizon. She was disappointed when, getting into open water, Minga cut the engine to half-throttle.

She settled onto the bench beside her daypack, wrapped its comforting bulk with one arm and let her other hand drop into the water. She wanted to continue thinking about nothing. She looked at Minga, tough and pretty, now slumped casually in her chair, one bare foot on the instrument panel, one finger on the wheel. She could feel a sense of sisterhood pulling them together, and her resistance to any commitment pulling the other way. After a while, Minga turned to her and said, temptingly,

"Want to drive for a while?"

Holding her ground, Teddi replied, "That's all right. I'm fine." But, the sense of connection was there.

The water was calm. The boat moved gently against the soft swells of the inter-island current. After a while, an island loomed on the right, low to the water, a harbor just visible behind a finger of land. As they got within a few hundred yards of it, she could see a small wharf and some endugas arranged nearby.

"That's my cousin Billy's place—a.k.a. Umogoro. You'd like him. Your type."

What type is that? she wondered. It wasn't an idle question, and the thought that there, hidden in the quiet of the little village, lurked something or someone that was her match took on the character of a quest. This quickly dissolved as the island fell behind and her attention returned to the watery panorama. From time to time, sheds of seaweed rode on its surface, which Minga maneuvered carefully around. A couple of dark forms rose from below one of them.

"Look," said Minga, pointing as two giant turtles broke the surface, lazily plowing against the swells of the boat's wake. Teddi heard Ogden's voice recounting the legend of the great Mother Turtle. The *real* original people, she thought, looking at them.

Sometime later, when the profile of the main island began mounding along the horizon ahead of them, a couple of grey-bodied dolphins suddenly showed up on either side of the propeller's spume and started performing giddy leaping side flops.

"I'd give anything for that kind of freedom," Minga said.

"I'd give anything for *yours*," said Teddi. She meant the Minga she saw immediately before her. But, almost as soon as she said it, she knew that was wrong, and the sense of sisterhood with all its implied common troubles rose up in her again. True, here she was, charging around a boundless sea in her boat, part of the favored race, a princess in a land of privilege. But, at least part of that freedom was a serious burden. And, because of it, Minga, like her, was a renegade daughter; like her carrying through her life a heavy sack of expectations, which stirred and rumbled at predictably inconvenient moments.

The hump of the big island now filled most of the view in front of them. Before long, other vessels began to appear within hailing distance. A huge luxury yacht, with a black helicopter mounted like a giant black fly on a platform above its afterdeck, headed around a promontory. On top of the palisade that formed it, half-shrouded by a grove of trees, stood the National Assembly, its tower and roofline strongly echoing the British Parliament, confirming what the drawing had already given her to expect. Smaller boats bobbed behind a low breakwater which protected the marina they headed toward. Nearby, stood the Royal Augusta Hotel, whose Victorian fussiness, like a heavily powdered and primped old duchess, Teddi had admired her first time through Indua several days earlier.

Standing up again, a hand resting lightly on the windshield, she was thrown against it and had to clutch it tightly to be kept from being flung over the gunnel as the boat suddenly decelerated and changed direction. She turned a shocked grimace toward Minga and then saw the reason for this abrupt adjustment. Almost unseen, its blue-green hull nearly the color of the water, its superstructure the color of the sky, a large ship was sliding into the space between them and the view of the hotel. The swells peeling off its bow caused them to rock severely, as Minga slowed them down even more. It was called *Southern Explorer*, and it was an ugly monstrosity of a ship. A complicated grid like structure, like the work of a manic child with an erector set, covered its foredeck; out of that grew a derrick that rose thirty or more feet further into the air. All of it was painted sky blue. Out at sea, it would have been all but lost amid sky and water. It might have here also, if its course hadn't taken it in front of the bone white hotel.

"Oil exploration," said Minga. "They put in here from time to time for r-and-r and reprovisioning."

They were no more than a hundred feet away. As its shadow, thrown by the late sun, loomed toward them, almost engulfing them, Minga brought the *Xanadu Reefer* around to port to ride the swells of the big ship's wake more easily. As they drew amidships, Teddi saw two men leaning over the railing. The sight of one of them suddenly struck her and made her go rigid. She saw beefy shoulders and arms. A deathly scent came to her. She grabbed Minga by the shoulder and pointed.

"That's the guy that was in my cabin. The guy that attacked me," she said. She was not sure that the words had even come out, that she hadn't just thought them until Minga said:

"Are you sure?"

At that moment the two men turned and started walking away from them, toward the prow of the ship, and quickly disappeared into the gridwork on deck. Minga gunned the *Xanadu* and they raced around the ship. They made two circuits of it. By the second trip around, a group of men had appeared on the forecastle, laughing and hooting at them. Minga gave them the finger, gunned it some more, and took off at an oblique angle toward the opening in the breakwater.

SANJAY GUPTA, MINGA'S BELOVED, not a large man but a man with a large smile, stood waiting for them as they tied up at the Xanadu Reefer's slip at the marina. His hair fluttered like a pair of perfectly formed glistening black wings as he maneuvered to help them each up onto the wharf, where Minga attached herself to him like a koala bear to a tree trunk, planting her mouth against his. When she released him, he introduced himself to Teddi.

"We go wiki-wiki now to the best motel in all of Anuapúa, possibly all the south seas," he said, as they walked to the micro van that was the motel's jitney. Its name spanned the side in big white letters disintegrating at the edges, suggesting sea foam: "Tukulu."

"The Turtle," Sanjay translated.

Driving away from the town center, they passed a church, a mosque, a Hindu temple, all interspersed with an assortment of restaurants and motels. Sanjay, full of the spirit of his role as host, exuberantly commented on each as they came upon it.

They had gone about a mile through what had become, on either side, mostly heavily planted fields. Rounding a curve he almost slammed into what at first seemed like a crowd of revelers. A dozen or so costumed people of uncertain gender swarmed around something in the oncoming lane and spilled into their own lane. Whatever these revelers surrounded was at first obscured by a banner held by four of them. They moved apart, revealing a small convoy of minivans. One of the figures, costumed in a parody of a 19th century British admiral, wearing a white, mutton-chopped mask and a sash-draped coat cluttered with ostentatious badges, dragged a limp puppet—a dark, scrawny, diapered body—and threw it into the arms of another figure, wearing traditional Anuapúan dress, kilted, with nose bone in place. This was followed by another of the scrawny puppets and then another, which were dragged out of a shipping crate stenciled with the word "India," until the Anuapúan figure was all but hidden by them. The other revelers sang and chanted, the gaps between them showing the grim-faced occupants of the first minivan.

"Oh crap," said Sanjay, slamming on the brakes. All the joviality squeezed out of his face, he clenched the wheel and leaned his forehead against it. Minga reacted by reaching between him and the wheel and blasting the horn. She leaned out of her window and screamed, "Fucking idiots!"

Sanjay quickly turned to her.

"No, Minga!"

But, she was out of the car, screaming and making for the

performers. Two of them turned her way.

"Hey, look who comes ta join us," a male voice called out of the melee, followed by a chorus of rowdy taunts. As she neared them, they met her wildly expressed displeasure with streams of fluid from the squeeze bottles they were armed with, hitting her in the face and torso. She threw up her hands and was about to launch into them, but was saved from a thorough drenching, and maybe worse, by horns that blasted from a military convoy approaching from behind the minivans. It slowed, swung around them, dispersing the people in their lane. The lead jeep, horn blaring, came to screeching halt in front of Sanjay, who pulled to the side to let the convoy to pass. Minga climbed back in the car. As the convoy snaked through, Teddi could see the soldiers in the lead jeep hail the revelers, and from the trucks behind it, all the young soldiers—dark haired, thickly mustached young men— threw their fists into the air, cheering.

Sanjay drove on before the dispersed revelers could block their way again. As he moved slowly past them, spray bottles let loose at the jitney. One reveler slapped a flier onto a streaming side window.

"It's just cane syrup," said Minga, pulling out her shirt and mopping her face with it. "Welcome to the real Anuapúa. There you have our politics in a nutshell."

Teddi looked at the flier stuck to the window beside her. Slimed with syrup and fluttering, it was hard to read, but she got the gist. It was a crude drawing, done quickly with a marking pen. The distinctive Y shape of the main island had two heads superimposed on it. One, larger by half than the other, was a grotesquely cartoon Indian, a rag wrapped head, glandular eyes, splayed buck teeth; the smaller a heavily mustached Anuap. The Indian was gleeful, the Anuap reeked sorrow. Bubbles filled with text surrounded the sketch. A quick sampling of them told the story: "Parity=Anuap inferiority"; "Equality for Indians: Marginalization for Anuaps"; "Children of Bengal: Everything to

Gain; Children of the Garden: gone forever." Another contained this mysterious phrase: "Save .6 and .3"

The blatant nativist racial paranoia—that was it, pure and simple—made her angry, arousing her in a way that all of Stevenson's and Shepherd's pronouncements and pleas did not, not even Minga's. She also saw the other side of it that she didn't quite get before; the wall of resistance her friends were trying to push through. *By finding a secret passage!* The idea now seemed more touching than ridiculous.

They turned off the main road and headed through a sugar cane field for a while, finally breaking through a mango grove to a bluff overlooking the ocean. The setting was spectacular. The Tukulu itself was like any number of motels from the San Fernando Valley—or even the Gulf coast. Her mother's family owned a small motel in Pass Christien, pastel and blocky like this. She wished for a minaret or a tower to set against that brilliant ocean.

SANJAY PULLED APART a curtain to usher Teddi into the apartment from the adjacent motel lobby. Mrs. Gupta's voice cheerily joined the tinkling of the bells that hung from it.

"Hello," she trilled, lifting a large wooden spoon out of a bubbling pot of *dal*, setting it down carefully, and turning to smile at her guest.

Teddi returned the greeting and took a quick look around the room. Nick-knacks large and small, emblems and tokens out of the huge formulary of Indian folklore and religion covered every surface. A small alabaster Krishna stood close to a jade Shiva on a polished mahogany credenza. A coffee table held a beautiful brass trinity consisting of Vishnu and his consort Pravati with baby Ganesha on their lap. All of it, wrapped with familiar cooking odors, aroused in her memories of Grandma Patel's kitchen in San Jose. She felt immediately at home.

The kitchen and adjacent great room looked out to the swimming pool and patio beyond it. In the far corner of the patio, near a cabana, a man was busy at a barbecue.

Samhita Gupta, a small woman with a scimitar of silver hair peeking from beneath her orange headscarf, her sari swishing around her, bustled across the room and took both of Teddi's hands in her own. She smiled up at her through feline metal glasses and said, "Please call me Samhita."

Still holding her hands, looking past her, she called to Sanjay, who stood with his head poking through the curtain, "We're just fine. You can go run off with your girlfriend now." Then raising her voice a bit, she called out, "Hello Minga my love."

"Hello Ma my love," came the response from beyond the curtain. "See you later."

"Minga must shower first, Ma. She's covered with cane shmootz."

"What? Oh no. Not another…"

"Yes, yes. The natives are restless again. Teddi got very nice local welcome. She'll tell you. Enjoy."

Flinging her hands out as if to dispel a bad odor, Samhita ushered Teddi to a small lacquered table and soon produced tea service for two. She poured and they sat in silence for a while. Teddi idly watched the smoke rising from the barbecue and the man who was busy at it.

"I'm really very glad that you finally came to us," said Samhita .

There was a mild rebuke in that "finally," to which Teddi could not resist showing the sort of contrition she might have with one of her aunts she'd run afoul of.

Samhita waved the gesture off. "No, please. I don't mean to scold. It's just that we were all so worried, especially Stevenson who was waiting here for you. But, it's not your fault. I'm just so glad to see that you're in one piece."

Teddi answered frankly, "I had no idea there were so many people waiting for me,"

"I'm afraid *we* were at fault for depending on you. We had no right," said Samhita. "We loose track sometimes of what is proper. You see, we have so much at stake."

Teddi nodded sympathetically.

Her face grown somber, Samhita went on: "I must tell you, when Stevenson Pelligrew first showed up in our world, towed by my Joyeeta, I thought, 'O, now my life is really going to go upside down.' I'd seen what this could do to families. Parents have their children and grandchildren living in San Jose or Milwaukee. Only so rarely do they see them, if at all. Or their sisters. After my own sister Prajita and her husband, Bokanjo, left with Horatio for California, that was it. I never saw her again. And now she's dead and I never will. I was so frightened I would loose Joyeeta. But, this hasn't happened, because of a miracle: both she and Stevenson are committed not only to each other but are also to their families. It is, I know, very hard for them to be apart so much. But, they're clear about what they're doing and understand the problems." She closed her eyes for a moment and compressed her lips, then went on. "Not so easy for Priya. My granddaughter is half Anuap and half Bengali. She suffers so much confusion. It is especially painful for a young girl."

She lifted her hands in the air and let them drop in her lap.

"One wonders, sometimes, if it just wouldn't be better to leave this place like my sister Prajita did, rest her soul."

IX

Rajiv and Pria

AS IF ON CUE, TWO FIGURES entered the room, jingling the curtain. The first was Stevenson Pelligrew's daughter Pria, a tall lean girl of eleven. Her long bare arms were folded together in front of a loose blouse which hung over knee length shorts. Both blouse and shorts had a much worn look. As she was introduced to Teddi, she unfolded one arm, offered thin fingers, looked quickly at her with dark eyes, then away as she quickly took back her hand. The woman behind her, shorter by several inches, was Joyeeta Gupta, Stevenson Pelligrew's wife and Pria's mother. Round and full-figured in comparison to her lean tautly built daughter, she smiled warmly as she introduced herself to Teddi, taking her hand between both of her own. After introductions, Priya dutifully helped her grandmother bring food to the table. The four of them sat down to eat.

"One never knows when Rajiv is going to show up," said Joyeeta to Teddi as if apologetically, nodding to the place that had been left for him at the end of the table opposite Mrs. Gupta. The apology seemed unnecessary, and Teddy thought she detected a bit of sisterly carping in it. But mention of the name yet again, whetted her curiosity.

When Joyeeta passed the platter of chicken tikka to her, she gratefully took it and passed her back a bowl of dal. The one thing

Teddi definitely was interested in at the moment was food, and she was relieved that they all fell to eating without ceremony. Before long the curtain tinkled again and Rajiv himself entered.

"Don't everyone all jump up at once," he said. His voice had a good-humored softness to it, but with a bit of an edge, like a chamois that had been rubbed into a sheen in places. Teddi turned at the sound of curtain. She found a man of somewhat more than medium height, a bit taller than his younger brother, of somewhat heavier build, but still compact. If Sanjay struck one with his playfulness, Rajiv immediately conveyed, apart from his good humor, a sense of competence, attentiveness to what needed to be done. His brows pulled together, his lips twisted a little in a wry smile. As Teddi turned to look at him, he bobbed his head to her.

"Ms. Shepherd. At long last. Welcome."

"Hello," said Teddi, quietly, a bit surprised by the man's appearance and manner. The few almost occult references to him, she realized, had set her up for someone who would command awe. That's not what she got from the sound of his voice and his look. She immediately liked both.

Pria hadn't bothered to turn to greet him, but continued to gnaw on the piece of chicken she held between reddened fingers. He came up behind her, put a thick hand on her head and, scuffing it, said, "Hey, skinnybones. Don't you give the time of day to your favorite uncle?"

"Stop it," she squawked, her words half lost in the chicken clenched between her teeth. He bent down to kiss her head. "Anyway, you're not my favorite uncle. Sanjay is." She stopped her gnawing and rolled her eyes teasingly up at him, waiting for his response.

"Well," he said. "That's a relief." He settled himself into the chair at the end of the table and started reaching for food. The women passed bowls to him. He took a piece of nan from a platter nearby and tore at it hungrily.

"All that barbecuing has made me ravenous. New guests should be here soon. I left Madhu in charge." He nodded to the window behind the table. Teddi looked out to see a thin column of smoke rising into the evening light, and a man standing near it, waving a long-handled barbecue fork around. "With any luck he won't burn it all. Tikka, tikka. Hand me that chicken," his thick-palmed hand reached out across the table. Joyeeta lifted the platter into it.

"So," he said to Teddi, taking a drumstick from the platter and waving it at her. "I gather from Sanjay that you came across a little of Bukharat theater. Nothing too much, I hope."

"It definitely made things a little exciting. But they didn't seem interested in us. Except, when Minga got into the act."

The others laughed.

"Sanjay sure knows how to pick them," Rajiv said. It was clear from his expression that he entirely approved of Sanjay's choice.

"They're so stupid," said Joyeeta. "I wonder who they think pays for keeping this place going if it isn't the tourists they're harassing."

"Oh," said Rajiv. "I doubt they see it that way. They think they're only doing a bit of strategic advertising."

He turned back to his food. He was just in the midst of ladling some dal into a bowl when Priya, who had stopped eating and was watchfully twiddling her thumbs, suddenly said,

"Hey Uncle Rajivi. Want to see my costume?"

Joyeeta began to object to this intrusion into his dinner, but he waved her off.

"Of course I do. I have a strong interest in this. I'm counting on you as our entrant into the *Durga Purja*."

Mention of a Durga Purja caught Teddi's attention. It had been years since she herself had been an entrant to just such a pageant, sponsored by an Indian cultural group in the San Francisco South Bay, where most of her mother's family lived. She recalled an argument about it between her parents. She had to reach back to the mid-eighties for it, a very different time in her life. She had lost touch with all of that. Especially since her mother Chender's death six years before.

Priya slid away from the table.

"Be right back." She disappeared through the tinkling curtain, her bare feet slapping the floor.

A silence ensued while Rajiv continued consuming hurried mouthfuls of whatever came into his hands.

"I can't understand why you're so hungry," grumbled Joyeeta playfully. Then leaning confidingly across the table to Teddi, she said, "My brother has poor short term memory. He doesn't recall that he had lunch only a few hours ago. Pity his stomach."

"Don't bother your brother, Joya. He's still a growing boy," said her mother, setting an opened beer down next to him and beginning to clear the table.

"Here, let me help," said Teddi rising.

"No-no," said Joyeeta, "you're still an honored guest. Now that you've finally arrived." She gave her a sidelong look, raising her eyebrows. The mild chiding only added to Teddi's sense of family. Her Gulf Coast cousins would have done no less.

"At least for the next few minutes," said Rajiv. He lifted the bottle and drank deeply from it before he went on. "But, yes. Whatever it was that delayed your arrival...*whatever* it was," he said, waving off any attempt at explanation that might have been forthcoming. "...whatever it was, we're very glad you're now safely here. Whatever may come of this."

He took another slug of his beer and wiped his lips with the back of his hand.

"You would, I suppose, not mind hearing something of how we got into the situation we're in, that makes us crazy enough to hatch ideas like the one we've hatched, the one in which we've cast you in a starring role?" His eyes twinkled as he took another, perfunctory sip and set the bottle down with slow precision. Ah, she thought, maybe you're responsible for the mad plan, and nodded for him to go ahead.

"It's really very simple. Just an ordinary tale of hunger and indentured servitude. In the late 1800's two events happily coincided. First of all, a famine in Bengal, brought about by usual cyclical climactic events, aggravated by the idiot policies of the provincial governor, an uncannily devilish Brit. I spare you the details. Then, the Brits in Anuapúa, in their constant quest for moneymaking schemes, discovered that sugar cane grows like a son of a gun here. Sadly, they also found that the locals were too erratic and unmanageable for the assembly line like procedures needed to cultivate and harvest the stuff. The indigenous Anuaps, however much the Brits were in charge of the big picture, still pretty much controlled their own lives, lived in their own little abundant paradise. Their population was small enough, their property well enough distributed to provide all the necessities of life. They enjoyed all the privileges of an aristocracy. So, says Sir British Kingpin to himself: There's productive soil here," he raised the palm of one hand. "There's a bonanza crop there," he raised the other. "And there," he said, wagging his finger as if at different points on a map, "I mean all over the world…hungry markets. Now, who's going to farm the damn stuff?" He had warmed to his subject. He looked over to her with a caustic smile.

"You follow me?"

She nodded. So far everything he said more or less coincided with what she had gotten by osmosis about the Indian diaspora from her mother's family, even if she hadn't paid very much attention to it.

He continued: "The answer: hey, we've got some starving Indians up here who are just desperate and passive enough to plant and hoe and cut from morning to night. Bingo! We'll make the world fit together! And so…"

"And so…?" said Teddi, playing her part as interlocutor.

"And so, they rounded up my great-grandpa and great-grandma, and a few thousand of their friends and said 'Hard times here. How 'bout a party in the beautiful South Pacific. Plenty of food, plenty of land, plenty of money.' And so they came, and came and came until the fields filled up with them, and the offices that ran the fields filled up with them—because they could, a lot of them, read and cipher. And, bingo. Seventy-five years later there are as many of us as there are of them…I mean the so-called indigenous Anuaps. But," he said, biting off his words, "we don't have the same deal. And therein lies the rub."

Rajiv's voice had risen in volume and sarcasm during this recitation. He paused to tear a piece of nan and chew it down with another slug of beer.

"So, you see," he finished. "We're a little overdue for an uprising." He wiped his hands brusquely on a linen napkin, pushed himself back from the table. "And that, dear Miss Shepherd," he said, throwing down the napkin in punctuation, "is where you…"

At which point he was interrupted by a tinkling of the curtain. They all turned their heads. Priya stood there, transformed into a vision of legend. Her face and bare arms were smudged, her eyes had heavy dark circles, furrows marked her brow, her hair was disheveled. Both the yellow sari and the short midriff blouse she wore under it looked unkempt. Despite all, she was beautiful; her tender young reedlike body drawn up to full height, her head bent to one side, her eyes down cast, her hands before her, fingers clutching each other fretfully.

"Wonderful," said Rajiv. "You are Sita in the garden of Ravana, mourning for your Rama. Brilliant."

"It was all her doing," said Joyeeta proudly. "She did all her own research."

"Can I sing my song?" she said.

"If I can accompany you," said Rajiv. He got up and went to the nearby the sideboard on top of which sat a tabla. He sat down on a couch with it. Pria gracefully slid into position and waited while Rajiv began producing a familiar rhythm. Apparently some preparation had gone into this. Priya waited through a drummed introduction. Then, with gestures that pantomimed the content of her song, began to sing in a sweet high pitched voice. The words were English. The sentiment entirely Indian. The song she sang was drawn from *The Ramayana*. It concerned the capture of Rama's queen Sita by the demon king Ravanna, his efforts to seduce her, her attempted suicide, and ultimate rescue by the monkey god Hanuman.

The demon king Ravana has once again
tried to take me for his own.
    O, Rama, where are you?

Surrounded by his monster women
he tries to break me down.
    O, Rama, what can I do?

Ravana does not care that I
am unwashed and ill clad.
    O, Rama, come, I beg you.

He would take me in a sty,
He has no idea of what is bad.
    O, Rama where are you?

I must hang myself to keep
his dreadful hand from me.
    O, Rama, what else to do?

I do not dare let myself sleep,
so I'll hang from this dear tree.

Priya's dance came to an end in a pose suggesting that there was a rope around her neck. They were all applauding while Rajiv played a final flourish on the tabla, when a man walked through the curtain. He was a slight Indian, wearing a simple white kurta over baggy bush shorts—a driver and factotum for the motel. Without acknowledging the others, he nodded to Rajiv.

"Ah," said Rajiv, clearly expecting him. He got up and went with the man. As the two pushed through the tinkling curtain, Teddi heard breathless fragments from the man: "…wanted to jump out…chase Bukharat blighters…very hard to restrain." She got the picture: a replay of the scene she had witnessed. But, who were these tourists who dared to take on those impertinent performers? Riotous laughter and shouting burst through the quiet night as Rajiv herded them toward the dinner that awaited them at the cabana

Priya, clearly fascinated by these proceedings seen through the livingroom window, rejoined the women at the table. Mrs. Gupta served desert.

"I'm sorry Rajiv had to go on that way. A little too much history," she said as she passed out little ornate brass spoons.

"Can I go?" said Priya after a few minutes, for which she received an impatient reproachful look from her mother. Mrs. Gupta seconded this by tapping her finger on the table.

"History sucks," said Priya. She received no response.

"My brother is excitable," said Joyeeta, lifting her head, not seeming to address anyone in particular. Teddi couldn't tell whether the comment was addressed to her or Mrs. Gupta. But, she had gotten the picture. Excitable, and something more.

"I hate this costume," said Priya. In unison, grandmother and mother turned their heads sharply and said "Pria!" Pria bent her head to her mango and ice cream, then flung herself back in her chair and flopped her hands in her lap.

A strained silence followed. During it, the argument between her parents again came back to Teddi, particularly her mother's ferocity. Chender Shepherd, by that time head of cardiology at Marin General, shouted at Joe, the county's chief public defender, "No daughter of mine is going to play someone who has to jump into the fire to prove her loyalty. Not a chance." Joe had tried to appease her: "This is just for your parents. Can't you give a little to make them happy." As a compromise, they settled on Hanuman, to Teddi's delight. Oddly, the young Bengali director of the pageant, a theater student at the community college in the East Bay where the Durga Purja would be held, had at first a hard time wrapping her head around the notion of a girl playing a monkey. Teddi herself loved the idea of playing the monkey god, who could conceal himself flea-sized in a tree or blow himself up to the size of a mountain. The passivity of Sita did not at all appeal to her, even with her serious resistance to Ravana's disgusting advances. The more she thought about the details of the story, the worse it got. Pulling herself back to the present, she looked over to Priya, slumped in her chair, her sari blousing almost into the ice-cream which she had stirred into a soupy mess. Aware of Teddi's eyes on her she looked up:

"I hate this costume," she whispered stagily, leaning toward Teddi, seeking an ally for her subversive position.

"Priya!" said Joyeeta.

"I do," she said, turning to her mother. "Sita's such a wimp."

"Priya!" said Mrs. Gupta.

"She's right, ma," said Joyeeta, giving her daughter a wry approving smile.

"Even so," said Mrs. Gupta. "A little respect for our history, don't you think, Teddi?"

Teddi, wished she could offer agreement, but unable to, instead said to Priya,

"Hey. Wanna show me your room?"

An instant smile spread over the girl's face. Then, struggling to suppress her delight, she said "Sure," as if it were a burden she would graciously endure.

PRIYA LED TEDDI OUT through the office and around the building to the apartment which she shared with her parents; often only with her mother, since Stevenson spent much of his time in Ini Yanu. The night had cooled somewhat. The new arrivals were now arrayed around a couple of picnic tables beside the pool. Shrieks of laughter came from the patio, along with the odor of grilling meat. Rajiv stood with them, beer in hand, playing the host. They were all Europeans, blondes for the most part, as far as Teddi could see. Among the half-dozen or so, Teddi could make out two women. Rajiv waved as he saw them walk by and the others followed suit, shouting a greeting across the pool.

The apartment was smaller than Mrs. Gupta's, less cluttered with Hindu artifacts. Pria opened the door to her bedroom and ushered Teddi in. Here the clutter was of a different sort. A jovial rotund multi-colored ceramic Ganesha stood on a shelf in a corner, over her bed. The bed was unmade, the clothing she had exchanged for the pageant costume lay strewn across it. Stripping off the sari, she treated it with equal lack of ceremony, and quickly slid herself back into her street clothes.

Teddi surveyed the room. She was surprised at the dominant decorations. A full length poster of Britney Spears was taped to the door. On the wall to the left were large posters of the Williams sisters in full tennis gear.

"Like the posters?" Pria said, pulling her shirt over her head.

"Wow, yeah. They're really cool," said Teddi, having some difficulty getting the life she imagined this girl led to jive with them. It took her only a moment to understand Britney.

"What's with them?" she said, pointing to the Williams sisters. Then she saw the tennis racket leaning against a cluttered desk.

"They're kind of my heroes. I know I'll never be as good, but I like to think about them." The girl looked away for a moment, then said offhandedly, "I'm on the national junior team."

"So, you're good?"

"I'm okay. How about you? You play?"

"Nope. Swim. Captain women's polo Valley Hi, 1993."

"Oh. Too bad. Want to see my scrap book?"

"Sure."

For the next hour they poured over a six inch thick binder which was, section by section, filled with memorabilia of Pria's three heroines. When they came to the place in the Britney section announcing a golden disc for "Baby One More Time," Pria said, "I can play that. You want to hear?"

A guitar standing in a corner served at the moment as a hanger for underwear. Pria got it and, sitting at the edge of the bed, sandwiching the pageant costume between her bottom and the mattress, she tuned it. She played nicely, and sang in a sweet, slightly breathy voice.

When she was done, Pria dropped the guitar back onto the bed. As if out of the blue, as if it was the guarded information the entire proceedings had been leading up to, she said to Teddi, "You know my grandpa hates me? He thinks I'm a big mistake."

As Teddi watched the girl, now paging through her scrap book,

Samhita Gupta's words about her granddaughter's difficulties came back to her.

"Hey," she said. "Forget that. Don't even think it. Your grandpa may have some problems, but not loving you isn't one of them."

"Yeah?" said Priya. "So how come he never lets me come to his place? How come he never wants to see me?"

Teddi had no answer for this.

Priya thumbed through some more pages. Then she closed the book, added it to the accumulation on the bed, and said,

"C'mon. I'll take you to your room."

TEDDI'S PACK HAD ALREADY been installed on a luggage rack. There were flowers in a vase, a bowl of fruit stood beside it. The desk lamp was on and sitting on the desk was what she recognized to be a folded set of architectural drawings. An envelope lay on top of it. Beside them, there was a note from Rajiv, in which he explained that he had intended to give the letter to her earlier but had been distracted by the demands of the newly arrived guests.

The letter, addressed to her from Horatio Cook, said many things. It began apologetically. The first paragraph repeated what she had already surmised: that Horatio's friendship with Joe hadn't begun in L.A. but had its roots in Anuapúa, and that over the years he had been her dentist he had conspired to keep this fact from her. It explained that Joe had been instrumental in arranging for his family—himself, his Anuap father and Bengali mother—to come to the U.S. in the nasty aftermath of the British withdrawal, even though he had been unable to get his own all-but-wife Ruth Pinkerton out with his unborn son. It spoke of the young Joe Shepherd that he had known, torn by grief and guilt, who paved the way for him to go to school and ultimately do his dental studies; who had continued his activism as a law student, providing support for civil rights and anti-war activists who needed to be legally rescued, on and off the UCLA campus. It was a praise song from a man whose depth of gratitude toward her father was greater than she had ever imagined. The portrait that it gave was of the father she knew, different only in added detail: righteous, stalwart in his defense of the defenseless. He had been wounded by being forced out of the Movement after Dr. King's murder. But, he was full of forgiveness and understanding, calling it a *reasonable mistrust* on the part of the brothers. It never interfered in his own advocacy of what he thought was important. One of his first official acts as a lawyer in Marin County was prosecuting an anti-discrimination suit filed by two women of color against a local landlord. One of those two women, Chender Patel, MD, became Teddi's mother.

Joe Shepherd expected his attitudes and actions to be reflected by his daughter. He had tried to show her his world, the world the way he wanted her to see it. More than once, when she was little, he had taken her on his own tour of Marin: the barrios near the canals where illegal Central American immigrants waited outside of 7-11s for someone in a pickup truck to come along and give them a day's work; the public-housing ghetto of Marin City down along the U.S. 101 corridor on the way to the Golden Gate Bridge. One day, the summer she was eleven, he took her to what he called "his shop": the Marin Civic Center, Frank Lloyd Wright's otherworldly fantasia, with its sky blue dome and gold towers, nestled in hills near the bay as if it had just dropped down through the afternoon fog from some far galaxy. He took her to court, to hear the stories of the disenfranchised, to impress on her the need to come to their defense. She fidgeted, and slid away, exploring instead mysterious inner balconies that hung over a skylight lit court, lavish with tropical plantings. She was fascinated. She found the library, a large circular room where concealed lights flooded a domed ceiling with ethereal radiance. She was entranced by the room, as she was by the entire building. After that, she begged Joe to take her with him. While he was in court, she prowled the grounds and the building, and poured over books of Wright's work in the library. By the time the summer was over, she was saturated with his work. It was all she could talk about. That must have been when it started, she thought, the tension between them; when she first disappointed him and he realized she always would. He had intended to give her an education in social responsibility. Following her own nose, she was drawn to the fascination of things. That was the rub. The only time he seemed to think there was any hope for her was when, as part of a college project, she used the forensic skills she was learning to help reconstruct a runaway slave church in Maryland. That made him proud, and for a time provided some common ground between them.

Horatio's recounting of his and Teddi's own relationship, his special role in her life, at first just reinforced her sense of betrayal. When she moved down to L.A. from Marin, he became the link between father and daughter, who hardly ever spoke, especially in the years after Chender's death. What Horatio's letter finally came down to was a confession and plea for forgiveness; or, at, least understanding. While Joe, seeing his death in front of him, was responsible for initiating the move to connect her with her brother Shepherd, it was he, Horatio, who was entirely responsible for getting her involved in the AMNUP plot.

When she had finished reading, her eyes pooled with tears, she set the letter back on top of the dresser, beside the folded drawing. The faint, excessively impassioned voice of Brittney Spears reverberated through the wall. She felt tenderness for the young girl who listened to it so ardently, filling her hollow spaces with it as she filled her scrap book.

After a while, Teddi pulled herself up and, reaching for the set of drawings, flipped it open. It was what she imagined: a fresh copy of some sheets of the architectural drawings of the National Assembly. Spreading it out on the dresser, pressing out the creases, she sat before it as if it were a votive object, and spent the next hour studying its several pages.

X

A Tour

For breakfast, the two Gupta women made a dish of flattened rice and vegetables, accompanied by luchi, the delectable little fried dough puffs that Teddi recalled as a regular morning offering at Grandma Patel's table. When Pria came in, ringing sleep out of her eyes with a knuckle, and without a word pulled Teddi's arm around her, it was all she could do to hold onto her resolve. Nevertheless, when Rajiv announced that it was time to leave for their tour of the Assembly, she felt her determination return to fulfill the commitment she made to Shepherd and then go her own way. She would check out the building, give them her take on the possibility of an escape route, and that would be that. So her goodbyes had the ring of finality. As Rajiv lifted Teddi's pack into the trunk of his car, Priya clung to her. She was finally was pulled away by her teary-eyed grandmother.

As they turned onto the main road to town, Rajiv said,

"Looks like Ma's decided you're supposed to belong to her. Not to mention my niece."

She turned her head to look at him. Both hands wrapped the steering wheel, his eyes fixed on the road ahead. His profile—thick nosed, full jawed—had a toughness and composure to it that she admired. It spoke of determination, but also a generous attitude toward the world. He seemed a man who would try what there was to try, come what may; but a man who would not let bitterness rule his life, despite the heat of his feelings about the treatment of his people.

"And you?" she said.

"Have I decided you belong to me?" he said, flashing a quick playful smile toward her.

She slapped his shoulder lightly with the back of her hand.

"You know what I mean," she said, aware that she didn't quite know *what* she meant, but that she liked the smile that he had turned on her, and the unmoving solidity of his shoulder. She went on, "How do *you* feel about my being here?"

He looked at her again.

"Ah…" he said, raising an eyebrow, as if to ask what level of feeling she wanted him to respond with, sharpening her own uncertainty. She looked away to the phalanx of trees lining the road.

After a while he said, "Well, in terms of what Ma seems to be thinking….Look, you seem to fit right in. The way you were with Priya was fantastic. The poor kid lives in a sort of hangdog world. Can you imagine? With all her gifts?"

"She told me Ogden hated her," she said, relieved for the moment, by the way he defined her question, of having to question herself further.

He slammed his hands against the steering wheel.

"It makes you want to weep, no?"

"Does he?"

"How would I know? Who can fathom the mind of…" he paused awkwardly.

"What? An Anuap?"

"No. I know. Stupid. Old mistrust dies hard. Look. Steve's my best friend, in addition to being my brother-in-law. But his dad? There is one confused man. No, no. He loves Priya. You should see him at the tennis matches, when he manages to show up. I think he even loves Joyeeta. He and Mona Pelligrew and Ma are friends from way back. Did you know that my dad, Gopal, was one of his best friends, until one of his other best friends, Bokanjo, married my mom's sister Prajita."

"Horatio Cook's mother."

"Right. That tells you a lot about what's going on here, doesn't it? So, Priya's right. She isn't exactly welcome on Ini Yanu; none of Steve's Indian family is. I'm sort of an exception. I've been there from time to time because…"

He flashed a crooked smile toward her and shrugged.

"Yes?"

"Well, because I'm me, another version of the weird confusions we live with. Stevenson and I sweated through the A-Levels together: 'In Xanadu did Kubla Khan a pleasure dome decree,' and all that stuff. About as useful and harmless as *The Ramayana*. Ogden just takes me for one of Steve's school chums and ignores the rest. It's almost like I'm not Joyeeta's and Sanjay's brother; like I've got no stake in anything. In the real world we're all what in Anuapúan is called *govalanu*, extended family. I tell you, the man's in real trouble. This whole *place* is."

And again, Teddi recalled the troubled look on the elder's handsome face during the greeting ceremony when he touched on these issues.

"I don't get any of this," said Teddi, pulling down her sunglasses, turning her attention back to their surroundings. Rajiv had taken a different route than the one Sanjay had followed the night before. They had by now arrived in the outskirts of the city, where isolated clusters of buildings gave way to neighborhoods with an occasional weathered white stucco multi-story building. The single road suddenly met three others in a tangled intersection of cross-traffic, which seemed to function without logic. Cars entered it from each stream and aggressively competed for the right of way. At the same time they managed to negotiate passage, without the ireful honking and shrill belligerance of rush hour intersections in L.A.

Blocks of buildings were now solidly two or three storied, remnants of imperial grandeur, rows of elegant piles of stone with touches of polished mahogany and etched glass, relieved by an occasional low bungalow set back from the road. They came to a broad avenue along the waterfront. Teddi could see up ahead of them the marina and the frowzy grandeur of the Royal Augusta. Before they got to it Rajiv made a turn that took them through a commercial district of more recent construction. The street was fronted on both sides by austere two story stucco buildings of a dreary post-war vintage. Round steel posts, paint-peeling and streaked with rust, supported second story balconies that overhung cracked and crumbling sidewalks. Everything looked modern, utilitarian, and worn down; thrown up at one moment and, after that, completely left to the effects of time. This section seemed to be an instance of spartan commercial efficiency the British left behind with no instructions for ongoing development and upkeep; another symptom of the actual conditions of the country concealed behind the allure of the tourist world.

"Where the real business of life goes on?" she asked.

Rajiv nodded.

"You'll see some more when we get to the market. We'll park there. It's a short walk to the Assembly. Look here," he said, returning to his subject, "there's a statute that goes back to the British time. The Brits instituted it to take care of the problem they created by importing my ancestors. Simple and brutal. It's called the Anuap Land Inheritance Protection Statute, sometimes referred to as 'Statute fourteen point six', or just 'fourteen point six,' or even just 'point six.' What it says is this: No one whose lineage is partly Indian on either parent's side, may hold ownership of land in Anuapúa, whether by sale or bequest. Then there is another statute: Any citizen whose lineage is to any degree Indian on either side, if empowered to vote by virtue of having been elected as a legislator to the National Assembly, shall have a vote whose value is equal to two-thirds of those legislators without Indian lineage. That is Statute 15.3, known formally as The Legislative Exception Act. So, you see…" he raised a hand from the steering wheel, to signal the end of his exposition.

"Got it," said Teddi. "Land stays in Anuap hands forever."

Rajiv went on: "Ogden doesn't hate Priya. He loves Priya. He hates the *idea* of Priya. Everywhere else he's fine. On the courts during a tournament, he's like any other proud anxious grandpa. But, in his own place, the wholeness of Steve's family—I mean if Joyeeta and Priya regarded Ini Yanu as their home also—would be for him like an infection, a sign of decay, signaling the collapse of the land ownership system, and the final destruction of Anuap priorities, Anuap culture. And, in terms of what he and others like him think is important right now, of what they fear, who's to say he's wrong. That makes it a big hill to climb."

He paused as they pulled into a parking place across the street from the market, a cavernous city block of corrugated sheet metal set on poles, outside of which a line of vendors—Anuap and Indian alike—languidly plied their trade in the sodden heat.

"As far a Priya goes," he continued, "he's the one who buys her tennis rackets. True, it helps to salve his guilt or whatever. But, it's also because he's so proud of her and she's his kid. You see how bad this is? Totally schizophrenic. That's why it's so frightening— it's so totally irrational. That's why we've got to…" He stopped, his voice rising, the calm he had begun with fulminating to passion. He waited for calm to return before he went on. He turned toward her and looked at her levelly.

"So, what do I think of you? I think I wish you weren't such a flea and that you'd arrived where you were supposed to when you were supposed to so we could have talked all this out and you wouldn't have gotten that nice skull of yours bashed. And, I think that I also would like you to stay and help us muddle through this, as crazy as you might think it is. So…there…that's what I think." He bounced his hands again on the steering wheel. Then, resting a hand on hers he said, "Come on. Let's check out this building."

THEY ARRIVED ALONG WITH a small clot of tourists just in time for a tour. Broad shallow granite steps ascended to the entry. Kilted Anuap soldiers manned a massive pair of twenty-foot high, thickly carved mahogany doors. The tour guide, a sweet faced young Anuap, also kilted, but to whose standard full brush mustache was added a wispy goatee, gathered the tourists before the open doors and gave a short introduction. The small group then moved into the foyer, identified as *The Grand Vestibule* on the drawing Teddi had studied the night before. The drawing was an accurate schematic, but it did not come close to suggesting the magnificence of the place. It was a no-holds-barred job. Built in a time when the world's appetites for coconut and sugar cane and parrotfish and sea cucumber were very high, and the British colonial system was working at its fullest, most rapt efficiency, no concessions had been made to cost. It was not vast; rather intimate, in scale with the entire building that was perhaps a quarter the size of its imperial prototype, the British House of Parliament. But everywhere the materials, the attention to detail were the highest quality.

Teddi took note, especially, of the floor itself; the details of the Great Seal that stood at its center, and of the tiles that ran around the walls from the front doors to the entrance of the Assembly Chamber itself. The young guide made much of these details, calling attention first to the "Great Seal of the Commonwealth Nation of Anuapúa." These words formed a border around a central medallion. It had to be redone, he told them, when the Brits gave Anuapúa its independence thirty-four years before. They had to replace the former brass engraving that had read "Her Majesty's Imperial Colony" with the words "The Commonwealth Nation." The central medallion itself, a meter-and-a-half in diameter, consisted of a field textured to suggest ocean waves, filled mostly by the figure of a turtle seen from the top.

"The Great Mother Turtle," said the guide. "Symbol of our national origin." And he went on to repeat the tale that Ogden Pelligrew had told when Teddi arrived in Ini Yanu. What had appeared in the architect's drawing as indistinct irregularities in the turtle's shell, was actually a map of the major islands.

The guide then pointed out the row of foot square rusty orange tiles that paraded around the walls under a palisade of impressive foot high stone copings, bordering the dusky sea-gray marble of the floor. Each tile, he pointed out, was inlaid with a green marble leaf, and each leaf was daisy-chained to the next, tip to stem, from tile to tile. A thick leafstalk with veins coming off of it was deeply incised in each leaf. All this was as she has seen in the drawing detail. And, as in the drawing, at each corner of the room, these rows of tiles stopped at a larger tile which repeated the Great Mother Turtle motif of the Great Seal, but with only a single island represented on the shell, each with its name inscribed below it: Indua, Vu Nua, Alao, Panoha—the four major islands of the archipelago. Across the foyer opposite the lofty main entrance, a quartet of equally impressive fifteen foot high pointed-topped double doors led to the Chamber of Chieftains.

"At the beginning of each session of the Karoja," their guide explained as they regrouped in front of them, "these doors are ceremonially opened and the chieftains of each of the four main islands march into the chamber accompanied by their lieutenants and other honored members of their tribes, all in tribal dress."

He called attention to the names of the chief islands engraved in granite on the floor before each entrance; then to the tiles at either side of the group of doorways, where the mango leaf tiles stopped. Each of these terminal tiles featured an Anglican cross supported by two figures, each identifiable by their dress: one European, one Anuap. "Symbolizing," said their guide, with what Teddi thought was a shadow of a smirk on his lips, "the true meeting of two minds."

Pausing before one of these, as the rest of the tour grouped themselves around the guide in front of the doors, Rajiv said quietly, with a sardonic chuckle, "Like all sound marriages: what keeps in, keeps out."

"Part of the intention, right?" replied Teddi, correctly taking him to mean the lack of any reference whatever to anything Indian in the foyer.

"Let's see if anyone is home," said the guide, playfully. He knocked lightly and each of the four doors was opened at the same time by a tall, kilted Anuap soldier. They walked through, onto a marble porch on which stood four marble columns of different colors supporting a balcony. Several steps running the full length of the curving porch led down to the floor of the hall. At the far end, a dais rose against a background of twenty-foot high pointed arches surrounded by intricate carved stone decorations. It was a good replica of the throne end of the Chamber of Lords in the Parliament. *True to his teachers*, thought Teddi. She remembered again her architecture school studies of that colossal testament to the British colonial system and its architects, particularly Pugin, so celebrated for his profuse Gothic ornamentation. On the dais stood a tall man with trim steely grey hair in an elegant gray *kurta*. He was directing the activities of some young Anuaps.

"The older man is the Sergeant at Arms of the Karoja," the guide explained in hushed tones. "It is a position of honor granted by the Karoja to the ethnic Indian community in recognition of their important service to our nation and their role in it. He is responsible for maintaining the services of the hall. The young men he is overseeing are the children of certain chieftains. Their service is a way of honoring their fathers. The Sergeant at Arm's duties are, in fact, more ceremonial than practical. The practical duties of the Karoja, the hall itself, are carried out by the Services Department of the army."

"So, the marriage has someone on the side," whispered Teddi to Rajiv, who responded, "Part of the pre-nup," and they laughed together bringing quick looks from their party and those on the dais.

Their guide next led them across the chamber, past rows of polished wood desks, each with a damask upholstered chair and green-glass shaded lamp. At the far side of the hall a door stood open to darkness. Pausing before it, the guide, his face darkening, his finger pointing toward it, whispered stagily, "And now, we'll to the catacombs."

He stood beside the door, his hands folded over his kilt, his head ceremoniously bowed, as they passed before him into it. They went a short distance down a dim lit hallway, and then down two flights of narrow stone steps. The atmosphere became dank and forbidding as they descended. At the bottom they came into a room of uncertain size, but large and open enough to give an echoey quality to the guide's voice, which they followed into the room until they were all but enveloped in darkness.

"There is a story," he began when he had them all grouped around him. "A legend," he said, his voice edgy, insinuating, "of a secret escape route the nervous-nelly white administration had built just in case the natives got restless." Nervous titters came from the onlookers. Suddenly, a sharp light from a small flashlight held below made his soft Anuap features, his strong brow and deep set eyes, ghoulish and ominous. After a few seconds of this common campfire trick, he turned the light off and waited a beat while startled exclamations, giggles and guffaws settled down. Rajiv stood close behind Teddi. She felt a charge slide down her spine as her shoulder grazed his chest and took a small step away, forcing her attention back on the docent's voice.

"Of course, no such thing has ever been found. But, who knows, someday it may be" he said, and lights flared on in the room with the exhilarating shock of sudden transformation, met by a few short gasps.

They were in a low-ceilinged room, perhaps twenty feet wide by a hundred feet long; a partial sub-basement dug down into the ocean side of the escarpment on which the building stood. Massive wooden posts—actually lengths of squared off tree trunks—came down to piles of heavy stone that were the building's footings. The posts carried equally massive beams, which then carried heavy closely spaced joists on which lay stone slabs.

"Teak from Burma," said their guide, slapping a post. "Same as is used in ships. The oil and silica in this wood will preserve it for a thousand years." He pointed to the footings and floor slabs below and above them. "All this, solid granite from the Dharamapuri district of Tamil Nadu state in southern India, brought by clipper ship from Cuddalore."

Teddi listened with half an ear. All this simply confirmed what she had already identified as soon as the dim light came on; all materials that were part of her own workaday vocabulary. Her attention was on the space itself and what she could learn about the possibilities of the legendary passage. At least *that* much, the legend as such, was not a joke.

Despite the immediate impression of the building's supports being well-maintained, there were some telltale signs. At the perimeter wall there was an area which, despite the heavy layer of glossy gray paint that covered everything, appeared to be stained by fungus of some sort, possibly algae, suggesting a closer approach of sea water in that area. The heavy paving stones of the floor glistened with the same thick paint. It also seemed in good condition, except, she noticed, one area where the thick grout that divided the stones seemed a bit broken up, suggesting a possible breakdown in the underpinnings there. Nothing remarkable in itself. As she scanned the floor, she observed several in that condition. Cavitations in subsoil occurring through natural action provided a ready explanation, although a man-made void was also a possibility. She surveyed the exterior walls themselves, and imagined beyond them the surrounding mantle of earth and rock. At the far end of the room was a doorway.

"What's back there?" she asked the guide.

"Just more of this, miss. If you want to see…" he said, smiling brightly.

"That's all right," she smiled back.

"Well then," he said, and turning them all around he herded them back up the stairs.

XI

The Mother

AS THEY WALKED BACK to the car, visions of escape came to her. Torch bearing specters ran along a dark, rough-hewn corridor to an opening in the forest that crowded the escarpment to the west of the Assembly, made a dash through it down to a concealed cove and their hidden boat. Other phantoms descended a ladder down a shaft into a sea cave where a coracle lay hidden behind a stone facing. She dwelled on that apparition until it was displaced, this time by spirits ascending in a flood of golden light from the great stone pile like a vision from Revelations. She cackled at the manic turns of her imagination.

"You find something funny," said Rajiv, walking beside her, impatient to probe her for whatever she had discovered.

"Oh, you know, my mind just wanders into nonsense. No, nothing really funny except, maybe, the whole thing." She looked at him sideways and saw his expectant expression muddle to a slightly cross, wounded look.

"Sorry," she said, really not wanting to offend him. Then, addressing herself as much as him, "But, you know, the whole thing's so improbable." And despite that, and her intention to resist it, she could feel sympathy growing within her. The desperate anonymous shadows of her imaginings were ghosts of the real people around her, all the members of the AMNUP steering committee—Rajiv, her brother Shepherd, Minga, their friends.

"I saw nothing, nothing in the drawings, not during the tour, that shed any light on this; no specific clue, or even the possibility of one."

"Nothing at all?" said Rajiv plaintively, making her wish she had something to offer him. A hug came to mind. She put that aside and said, "Oh, a hundred things, but nothing that really stood out. Unless you're prepared to start tearing up the floor and walls…"

Rajiv shrugged at the impossible idea.

"Maybe," she went on, "a look from the water would tell us something, although I doubt it. The site plan with the drawings you gave me pretty much show the lay of the land, how it comes to the sea. There are caves all over the place, sneaky little coves."

"It's touchy. They've got their eye on me anyway. Even doing this tourist act has been a bit dicey. Even with your miss-turista-of-2000 getup."

"Are you mocking my attire, sir?" For the occasion Teddi had tricked herself out in a brilliant yellow tube top, red plaid shorts and espadrille sandals. Total tourist.

"May Shiva strike me with his trident. No. You look very fetching." Their eyes held for a moment. He went on.

"Look. I don't know if this came up with Bagram and the others, but that thing that happened to you on the *Annubis*? No accident. Someone who wants to do us harm is behind it. I'm convinced of this. I don't know who or why yet, apart from their being somehow connected to the Bukharat, part of the nativist cabal. But, somebody learned something—about you, about our plans, about what you brought to us from Horatio. If they know that, they know enough to keep an eye on you, on whatever we do together. The Assembly is just an ordinary stop on the tourist track. But wandering around the coast in my old skiff; I don't know. I guess, if you really need it."

"How's this any different? What could it matter, if they already know what we're up to?" said Teddi, cutting him off impatiently. Then another thought occurred to her. "I just remembered. I wanted to tell you about the guy on the ship."

"What guy? What ship?"

"Some big oil exploration ship we passed coming in. The something-or-other *Explorer*. He was up on the deck, at the railing. He turned and walked away...*fast*...when he saw me, like he was afraid I'd recognize him. And I did. I'm pretty sure anyway he was the guy who broke into my cabin."

"Really," said Rajiv. "Really. There you go. It may make sense. *Bungshalo!* We always just assume the oil guys will do anything to get their way. But, how would that happen? Who knows? Much too murky. What would what we're up to have to do with *their* ambitions. Even more reason, though, to be cautious."

"But, not too cautious," said Teddi."

He looked at her thoughtfully. "No, not too cautious," he said. Then, as an after thought: "It would be very good to know who's up to what."

Her mind had leaped ahead of him, to other imagined specters—those of Harley and Simon, on the *Annubis* with her the night of the attack. All shimmered together in a murky submerged haze, suggestive lines of connection running between them and breaking up. It all quickly evaporated, and she said, repeating what was only obvious "Yes. That *would* be good."

THEY TOOK HIS SKIFF out from the marina. The old wood-hulled runabout looked neglected. Parked in an over-large berth between two greyhound sleek sailing yachts, the grandiosely named *Rama* was a quaint parody of them. As he helped her down into its cluttered hull, Rajiv apologized for its appearance.

"Who has time," he said. "We just use this poor old thing for hauling stuff around. I mostly keep it at a wharf down below the motel."

It took him a few tries to get the outboard cranked up. With Teddi sitting in the stern amid coils of rope and other debris, a sunhat on her head, they putted out past the breakwater and then swung west, following along parallel to it, but veering a little out to sea. When they were a few hundred yards out, Rajiv cut the engine and threw out a sea anchor. As they wallowed in the tide, he pulled a couple of fishing poles from a case that lay in the bottom of the boat, dug for bait in an ice chest, baited both hooks and handed one pole to Teddi.

"Used to go out on the bay with my dad a lot," she said, taking note of his surprise that she knew what to do with the pole. "He called me the queen of the bottom fish." She took a bight in the line, lifted the pole, and flicked the baited hook easily out over the water. "Didn't know what you were getting yourself into, huh?" she said, haughtily raising her eyebrows and sliding her eyes in his direction. He responded by throwing out his line. For a while they fished in silence.

Then he said, "As you saw from the drawings, that whole escarpment under the Assembly is full of caves of various sizes. They're all tidal, none of them are really protected. But, they're easy enough to paddle around in. Except, over to your right. Nobody that I know has ever been in it. It's surrounded by pretty nasty knife-edge shoals, like submerged rows of shark's teeth. Cuts up boats and swimmers pretty good, even if they're very careful. I've seen some of the results."

"Perfect place to hide something," said Teddi.

"Sure, if you're not worried about getting it out in a hurry," said Rajiv.

Teddi twisted her head around. Behind them, a hundred yards or so to the right, some rocks jutted out of the water.

"What's that?" she said, indicating them.

"Part of a small atoll," he said. "In Anuap it's called. *Tukulu Wakaua Ka-enundaka*: Mother Turtle and Her Children. The idea is that atoll's the turtle, and these rocks are its children. Apart from being connected to the Anuap creation story, its main claim to fame is that there's a nice flat mossy slab of a rock, about half the size of a tennis court, right in the middle. It's known as Mother's Heart. Boys and girls sometimes like to…you know." He turned a coy smile on her that she coyly returned. "No value as far as we're concerned," he said, looking away. At which, warmth flooding her, she giddily thought, *Well,*

I guess that takes care of that.

At this moment there was a tug on her line. She reeled in until there was dangling above the water a beautiful multicolored fish the size of a small bass, flipping around in a gasping frenzy. She pulled it aboard, deftly detached the hook from its lip, and slipped it back into the water.

Afterward, Teddi said again that she had learned nothing especially helpful either from the drawings or from their excursions, except to get the lay of the land, and they drove in silence to the airport.

There seemed nothing left to say. They were each left to their own musings. Teddi recycled the events of the last days. Her resistance, strong at first, had been taking a battering. All of the events—the meetings, the not quite coherent but touching bit Shepherd had given her to read from Joe's letter, Horatio's apologetic letter; and finally, most of all, Priya—these had all taken their toll on her clear determination to put all this behind her. Along with the human web that had been weaving itself around and into her, the spice of the intellectual challenge and the adventure, as absurd as good sense said it was, had also gripped her strongly.

By the time they had arrived at the airport parking lot, her revised decision was so clear that she looked at Rajiv in astonishment when he said in a resigned tone, "Well, then, I guess you're off to Tu Vua and parts unknown."

"Oh, no," she said, voicing her surprise. "Going back to Yanu. Get me on the next plane for Guma please."

He gave her a bewildered look, as if he thought she were baiting him.

"You're...really?"

"Yes. It would sure help to have that code Bagram's been working on, whatever it is. *If* it is. Besides, I've got a dive shop to design. I've never stiffed a commitment in my life, no matter how weird the clients. Just how I am," she said, her lips compressed with determination.

"By heaven," he said, smacking his thick hands on the steering wheel. "You are one unusual..." He sat back and shook his head.

Then he cleared his throat and in a matter-of-fact tone said:

"Well, looks like we'll be seeing more of each other, then."

"Looks like," she said.

"We'd better hurry. I booked you on the next flea-hopper for Guma."

"You did what?"

He shrugged, neglecting to tell her that he had also booked a seat for her on a somewhat later flight to Tu Vua.

TAKING OFF FROM South Seas Airport, the small plane banked hard right, sweeping northeast around the Assembly. Teddi watched thoughtfully as it pivoted around the atoll with the small island at its center.

The plane leveled off into a monotonous drone and she dozed off. She dreamed. The image of the atoll came to her, with its so-called 'heart' on which young couples performed rites of consecration and sacrifice to the great Mother Turtle, giving the islands more to sing about. A fissure appeared in the smooth surface of the rock, slick with fluids, and suddenly the surface itself became the large square paving stones of the basement of the Assembly, and she and Rajiv were bending over a stone that was surrounded by loose grout and rocking it until one corner rose up and Simon Glimmer's face peered up at her, then twisted and turned into the beefy shoulder and fangs that had leered at her from the underbrush in the cove. When she looked to Rajiv, she found instead the young tour guide with the wispy goatee, who hoisted her on his back to carry her down into the shaft.

She awoke in a sweat. Her eye fell on the opening in the forward bulkhead through which the windshield of the plane appeared, and into which the shoulder and head of the pilot protruded. The pilot looked around and called back to her, "Enjoying the ride, are you miss?" His voice, straining over the engine hum, had a hint of an Australian accent. A broad smile bent his sharp red nose, and a boyish flounce of golden curls shook over his pale blue shirt as he swung his head around. The several others scattered in the long narrow tube of the passenger compartment seemed to be asleep.

"Very much, thanks," she called back.

"Not too rough?"

"Oh no," she said, and laughed as the plane made a sudden jolt.

The pilot's accent turned her thoughts again to Harley and Simon. She had last seen the *Hespera*, or at least its mast, across the channel from the veranda of the bungalow on Guma where she had awakened from her concussion. They were, probably, still there now. Rajiv's warning, an afterthought as she was about to get on the plane, only whet her curiosity. "Be careful of those guys. We don't know what they're up to. For all we know..." he began, leaving her to complete the thought herself. But, there was in fact only an odd coincidence, nothing concrete, to connect Harley and Simon to her attacker. Their friendliness, Harley's invitation to her to join them on the *Hespera* for the short ride from Yununu to Ini Yanu, might be taken to mean anything. But, the net result for her now was a desire to answer her own curiosity. In addition, there was the undeniable animal attraction of Simon; which, he had made it very clear, was mutual. That definitely spiced things up, and it could be useful. It would not be the first time the flight of pheromones would have aided her in the solution to a problem. She brushed aside cautions offered by recent Los Angeles encounters, which, rather than warning her away, only strengthened the scheming trend of her thoughts. A clear opportunity presented itself here: a puzzle to be solved by use of brains, daring, imagination, intellect—and, ah yes, pheromones. She felt herself in command of them all. Whatever those tantalizing lines of connection between Simon and Harley and her attacker might be, if they were anything at all, she had the means at her disposal of uncovering them. Harley's invitation to go with them on the *Hespera*, though she had declined it at the time—and, again, who knew what that really was about—was a useful entre. As to Harley, as irritating and repellent as he was at the time, she could overlook that. Just another day in the life of a goal-oriented gamer, namely, herself. She had a sense she would find out something interesting by just showing up.

As the plane flew through a break in an island mountain range, preparing for its approach to the Guma Yanu airstrip, Teddi's attention shifted to the contours of Ini Yanu just ahead. A small formation of rock caught her eye. It flattened toward the top, dropped down to water on one side, and was backed by grove of trees on the other. There's my dive shop, she thought happily, as if nothing else was on her mind. The top of a tall mast peeked over the grove, changing the subject back again.

Moments later came a groan of engines and sharp deceleration, then a breathtakingly steep descent.

"'Ang on now, young lady," the rakish pilot called over his shoulder, addressing her as if she were his only passenger. "We're going in now."

Teddi looked past him through the windshield as the plane banked to the right and the world swept dizzyingly by.

XII

On the Beach

APART FROM BAGRAM, who still held down his chair at the head of the table, an entirely new crew greeted Teddi when she arrived for lunch. Not that it mattered much. That other lunch seemed almost a lifetime away, and she barely even remembered the two couples she had arrived with. Besides Teddi, Bagram now had five twenty-somethings on whom to exercise his whimsical charms.

The new guests, a couple and three singles, were fresh from Ogden's official greeting, so they were a bit gaga from their immersion in what they took to be authentically local. And, of course, they were right. What could be more authentically local than Ogden Pelligrew, the old lion of Ini Yanu, protecting his pride? They could not have imagined how complicated 'local' actually was. Even Bagram's effusive welcome, wrapping Teddi with the banner of "hot architect" who would build a "really cool" dive shop—to which the five newcomers compliantly o-o-o-ed—even that could not discourage their sense of the nativeness of the place. And they were, of course, right in that too. What could be more *native* than transforming a ragtag village into a semblance of a ragtag village that others could go blissfully "slumming" in? Such thoughts tartly percolated through Teddi's mind as she surveyed the new talent and Bagram in his new role as arch-deceiver. Not that this was an exceptional performance for him. But it now had the deliberate intention of convincing any ears that might be interested in such information, that Teddi—having recovered on Guma from a bad something-or-other—was now fully restored and ready to commit herself to the dual occupations of play and dive shop design.

For Teddi they were all admirable, Bagram and the twentysomethings. Apart from the young Midwestern couple, there were two guys, software types from Seattle—Brad and Van—and Heidi, a girl from Leipzig. The two guys were both cute in a wet-behind-the-ears kind of way. Just right, she thought, for their tablemate, who fluttered her green eyes from one to the other. Her skin became rose-dappled marble when she said to the table: "*Ich bischen Englische sprache, ach, es tut mir leid,* oh, so sorry, I only speak little *En*-glish."

"So, you're an architect, huh? Pretty cool," said the boy whose name was Brad. He had a long narrow head with hawkish down-slanting eyes and a hawkish nose. His long cheeks were given to puffing out a little on either side when he wasn't talking. Teddi thought he was entirely beautiful. She thought that largely because she was fairly certain that he had no idea of what was going on, and would energetically resist having any idea of what was going on. His only interest in speaking to her was his ardent hope that she would have a reciprocal interest in speaking with him, which would quell his need to puff out his cheeks. He also had the habit of smiling broadly when he finished a statement, revealing a beautiful set of white teeth. They were more beautiful than any she would ever own, despite Horatio Cook's best efforts, and she found herself helplessly admiring those teeth. His smile, apart from revealing them, had the additional function of making his face—which when at rest seemed to carry its hawkish burden sadly—exceptionally handsome in an austere, somewhat homely, Nordic sort of way; something like Max Von Sydow.

"That's right. Architect," she replied chirpily. "I make buildings. You?"

His mouth closed, his tongue slid over his lips. He said, "Software, Seattle," as if the two terms went naturally together.

"Ah," she said. "I live in L.A."

On their conversation went in the gaps between Bagram's pronouncements, creating a sort of intimacy from the small stones thrown into each other's pools. If Teddi were not by now so committed to the goals of her AMNUP friends, and her assigned role in achieving them, she would have felt a little guilty. She would have sympathized more with this really nice timid boy who she was leading on for the single purpose of misdirecting whomever it was that might be surveilling her and them: namely, Harley and Simon and whoever might serve their interests. And, even if not them, someone surely was, if Rajiv was correct in his assessment of the attack made on her on the *Annubis*, which was supported by her recognition of the scoundrel she saw at the railing of the *Southern Explorer*. And why would it not be correct, this assessment, if for no other reason, Teddi argued to herself, than it was Rajiv's? She had by now come to understand the aura of awe that seemed to have attached itself to his name when others spoke of him. His sister's incessant need to tease him only further confirmed this. And, likewise, Priya's, who loved him in the way only a young niece could love an uncle like Rajiv. And she herself...now what *was* she thinking? She tried to assign the warmth that ran through her at the thought to Brad, who made it easy by flashing his beautiful teeth again, laughing at a raunchy joke Bagram had just passed along from one of his bi-polar patients. In fact, if she or anyone were to sternly question her at the moment, she would have had to admit that there was no clear logic to any of her thoughts; only hunches and an eagerness for pursuit. And the stirring hum of equally eager pheromones. She was happier than she had been in days.

AFTER LUNCH, AS SHE had done after her first and only other meal on Ini Yanu, she changed for the beach. If her choice of attire then, in the wake of the assault that had left her on the verge of a coma, was the most modest and enclosing of the three swimsuits she had brought with her, her choice now was something she could dispose of quickly should the impulse arise. She had no clear picture of how that might happen. She had only her mood and energy to go on, and they were both high. The sweet-and-sad-faced boy with whom she had just mingled empty secrets was in part responsible; her vaguely imagined Mata Hari-like venture played a part; the less vaguely imagined object of Simon Glimmer, perhaps a larger one. When she stepped from her enduga, big square shades in place, her pecan-shell skin strategically obscured in electric orange, the thrill of reclaimed physical freedom playing a trill along her nerves, she was ready for whatever might come her way, as well as for those plans still gelling inside her. Halfway along the path to the beach she met up with Heidi. Thin, plain-faced, her lank blond hair dropped between pale shoulder blades over the thin blue string of her halter. She turned at Teddi's approach.

"You look so *cute*," she exclaimed.

"You do too," Teddi exclaimed in return, and they giddily joined hands, suddenly sisters off on the hunt together. They chattered as they went, laughing about the two boys they knew they would find on the beach, having arrived at a conclusion as to who would get whom. Heidi had already shared secrets with Van, a quiet Asian boy. She declared her conviction that Teddi and Brad had already gone into a mind-meld. "But, of course" she added, "we can't let them be too sure of us." So, in the short distance between the manioc patch, where the frail old man dug and planted and smiled goofily up at them, and the sand that spread under a blistering sun, their pact of canny sisterhood was made.

Sure enough, the boys were on the beach, already at work demonstrating the agile planes of muscle and skeleton with a supercharged Frisbee display, the necessary adjunct of their Seattle software geek existence. Minutes later, when the Midwest couple showed up, the Frisbee play broke down in the amateurish hands of all the others. The software boys became disgusted. Soon, all six ended up in the water, pairing off in all possible permutations of boys on girls' shoulders, girls on boys' shoulders, pushing and tugging and banging into each other to the dismay of a school of angel fish, resident manta rays and other natural denizens whose routines they upset with their enthusiastic roughhousing. The couple went off for a swim together, the four singles spread their towels on the beach in a clump. At first, Van's head rested on Teddi's rump, Heidi's on Brad's stomach. A short snooze lead to some brief chatter after which Teddi's head rested on Brad's rump and Van's on Heidi's stomach. And there they lay, cooking in the sun, sharing secrets, growing secretly heated, until the first bell rang for the afternoon dive boat.

"Hey, gotta do this," said Brad enthusiastically, abruptly sliding out from under Teddi's head and leaping to his feet. The couple came from the water on the run to collect their things. Van and Heidi, slowly disengaging from the tangle they had gotten into, pulled themselves compliantly to their feet. But, as Brad reached down to help her up, Teddi said,

"Sorry to disappoint. But I don't think so. Something else I need to do right now. Maybe tomorrow."

As she spoke, they all heard the sound of a motor dopplering by and turned together to see Simon speeding past in the direction of the wharf on a gleaming green and black jet ski. While the others watched, fascinated and impressed, Teddi busied herself shaking out her blanket until he disappeared around the point, heading for where the *Hespera* was docked. Brad made one more stab at cajoling Teddi to come with them.

Declining this too, she gave him a solid slap on the chest. "But I'm counting on you to bring me back a lobster."

AS THE OTHERS TRAILED off toward the village, Teddi's eye shifted in the other direction, further down the beach, to where the line of rocks separated it from the cove. Her feet brought her there with mindless urgency. Climbing over the rocks, she felt soft and liquid, more like a slithering mollusk than a being of bone and muscle, levers and pulleys. Lifting herself to her feet as she reached the top and looking around, she found that things had changed. The decaying sea turtle was no longer there. Then another change struck her. She looked for the opening in the surrounding thicket, the overgrown path in which shifting light brought about the ghostly vision of her attacker. That opening no longer existed; only the faintest suggestion of it remained.

Standing in the sand, having regained her human armature, she realized that she was also looking at her changed surroundings with changed eyes. The place that had so gripped her with dread, aroused only mild interest in her, like an old wound replaced with healthy flesh with no more than a mild discoloration where the lesion had been. The man whose ghost had tangled in these brambles was real enough, and posed his own kind of problem. But, he carried no more weight than that; was no longer a demon that lurked, waiting to attack. The freedom and vigor of her body, which she had tasted during her brief swim in the rock pool on Guma, was finally in full flower.

She waded out into the water, stripped off her bikini and planted it like a flag in a crevice at the end of the rock arm, and swooped in. The water was almost as warm as the air and perfectly clear, like no ocean water she had been in before. When the momentum of her dive faded, she opened her eyes to sea life scurrying away from her intrusion. A large iridescent fish dashed in front of her and then veered suddenly away. She continued swimming underwater, dismaying still more of the locals, and finally came to the surface a good fifty yards into the channel. Her claim to Priya that she had been captain of her high school water polo team wasn't mere bragging. She was a very strong swimmer. She breaststroked for a while until she decided on a direction. At first she thought of crossing the channel, but then decided instead to swim along the shore, out past the rounded shoals that bubbled out from it. She swam a hundred or so yards until she saw, near the shore, a bony cow and a young boy with a stick running toward it. She swam in far enough so that she could cling to one of the outcroppings and watch. The boy saw her and waved, a big grin on his face. She waved back and decided, given her state of attire, that withdrawal was the right course.

As she re-entered the cove she took a deep breath and dove

straight down. Sunlight followed her through the clear, nearly still water. A scattering school of tiny fish sparkled like quicksilver in front of her and disappeared into a shallow reef to which anemones and starfish clung. She swam to it and used it to pull herself up to the surface. She wiped wet hair from her eyes. She was still some distance from shore, but well inside the cove. Turning toward the beach, she scanned the end of the rocky projection for her bathing suit. Alarmed when she didn't see it immediately, she quickly searched the beach for any other presence. No one was there. Swimming closer to the rocks, she saw to her relief that that one had a thin brilliant orange rim. As she slid on her bottoms and then tied the halter behind her, she realized whose presence she had suspected. She also realized that that suspicion was accompanied by a wayward wish.

XIII

The *Hespera*

A LITTLE WHILE LATER, wearing a spaghetti strap mid-thigh black and white checkered sundress and bejeweled flip-flops, Teddi stood at the gangplank of the *Hespera*. She felt top to bottom like a vibrating wire.

"Hello-oh," she chirruped.

She was awed by the size of it. She had seen ocean-going trimarans before. A neighbor of hers in Santa Monica had built one. Over the course of two years, she had sat in the backyard with him and listened to his explanations of the intricacies of building a ferro-cement hull from the inside out; then, the agonies of making the interior and exterior fittings work with the design. Eventually he had sailed off, leaving his life behind. She babysat while the wife he had abandoned spun out of control in Santa Monica nautical-theme bars.

This boat was nothing like that boat. That was humble, plebian, by comparison. This one reeked of money.

"Hey, there. Hello on board," she finally shouted.

The two masts, the tall mainmast stepped amidships, just in front of the cockpit, and the smaller one on the lower afterdeck, near the gangplank she stood at the foot of, had their sails compactly furled. The glistening green and black Kawasaki jet-ski Simon had sped by on, was lashed on a platform flanked by a pair of steps that went from deck to water. She felt a frank hankering for a high-speed ride on it.

"Coming aboard," she shouted out and scuffed her way up the gangplank. Just aft of the cockpit, was a door. As she reached for it, it flew open, sending her falling backwards to the deck. A young man landed on her. He clambered instantly to his feet and with much apologizing helped Teddi to hers. Before he had time to enquire about her business, or she to get herself reorganized enough to state it—a spaghetti strap had pulled down, her hem had pulled up, a flip-flop had bent under almost taking her ankle with it—Simon poked his head out through the doorway.

"Well, surprise, surprise," he said, while she lifted the strap with one thumb and pulled at her hem. "I thought I saw you on the beach as I came roaring by," he gestured to the Kawasaki. "Hear you've been through a rough patch. Glad to see you're okay." He looked her over and smiled. "More of less."

He turned to his crewman. "Have at it, Jeremy." The young man, after further profuse apology to Teddi, turned and ambled down the gangplank.

"So, Teddi," Simon turned fully to her, pulling sun-pickled bronze waves away from his face. "Welcome to me 'umble 'ome."

There then ensued between them a series of formal pleasantries which were followed by a brief tour of the *Hespera*'s topside equipment. During this, in addition to length and beam—twenty by fifteen meters—Simon ticked off such details as horsepower, displacement, navigation equipment and miscellaneous other electronics; informing her as well of the elegance of the lift aft, on which the Kawasaki rested. This brought them below deck to the galley, which gleamed with beautiful mahogany brightwork. He brought out refreshments from a large refrigerator and set them on a handsome teak table. As they were each spooning some very nice passion fruit sorbet into their mouths, he said,

"I must tell you. Your real mission here has been revealed."

"My *real* mission?" she said, almost dropping her spoon in alarm.

"Oh, c'mon. No need to be coy. The *dive* shop. You sure kept mum about that when we were on the ship."

"Well, I just didn't want to get into…" she said, working as hard to conceal her relief as she had, a moment before, her panic.

"Professional envy, eh? Dangerous territory."

"Something like that. Guess I was feeling displaced."

"That's something like what I imagined when I heard. Really no need, though. One project doesn't nix the other. In fact, whatever you're up to might, if the thought isn't too disturbing to you, serve our needs as well."

She smiled and slid her lips slowly over the sorbet-laden spoon. "I don't have a problem with that," she said.

"Great. Maybe later, if you like, I can show you what *we're* up to. But tell me, was that why you shut me down? I mean on the *Annubis* that night. I'd sort of thought…"

She licked the back of the spoon and looked at him, trying to assess the tenor of his remark; if he was just talking or if he had really taken offense. She couldn't tell. So, she responded truthfully: "I know. I guess I did also. I guess you might say that. But, you know, I certainly wasn't banging on all cylinders that night. Oops. No pun intended."

"None taken. Sorry about your trouble. Looks like you've recuperated pretty well. Physically, at least."

"Fit as a fiddle," she said, sucking on her spoon.

After the sorbet, they took a tour of the boat's innards. From the galley, they passed through a lavishly furnished salon with high transoms running along either side. At the far end, there was a short corridor, on either side of which was a door that opened into a cabin. Each cabin had its own small head with full shower, and a queen-sized bed, which one reached with a short ladder. The space below the bed held a dresser and miscellaneous storage. All very shipshape. The bed, Simon explained to her, was set high because it actually spanned the space between the main hull and the outrigger. There were, he told her, four such cabins aboard the *Hespera*. Accommodations for eight, at least.

And hour later, Teddi found herself lying naked on her back on the bed of the port cabin, looking up at a textured styrene ceiling three feet above her. Near the bottom of the short ladder, Simon, also naked, was toweling off.

"Shower's all yours," he said.

"I'm fine. Maybe later," she replied. "Got any more food. I'm hungry again. I always get hungry after, you know…"

"A little work out?" He abandoned the towel to a desk that filled part of the wall opposite the bed. On a shelf above sat his rugby cleats and some tools. He stepped up onto the ladder and, wrapping his hands around Teddi's calves, pulled her, unresisting, toward him.

A HALF-HOUR'S DELAY brought them back to the galley, which again revealed its bounty. From the refrigerator Simon extracted seafood salad and a couple of beers. They sat at the beautiful teak table and ate in silence. Simon seemed as content to be in his own space as Teddi was to be in hers. But, after a while, a nagging curiosity overtook her; a long shot that might risk her Mata Hari objective, which despite all the hijinks of the last couple of hours had retaken center stage. It was a question that might, at the worst, just be stupidly innocent and gamily annoying enough to put him off guard. So, she went for it.

"Is Harley your father?"

Simon stopped in mid-chew and looked at her. He swallowed and took a long drink from his beer.

"Why would you think that? The answer, of *course*, is no." He smiled, but there was a bit of irritation in his tone.

"I don't know. It just occurred to me. He seems to be everywhere in your life. Are you his mascot?"

"Now," he said, answering the clearly intended dig with a wry smile, "*that* could be seen as insulting."

"Oops. Sorry," said Teddi airily. "I'm known for my big mouth."

"How you win clients, no doubt," he said, his smile broadening, displaying the charming crescents beside his wide mouth. He took another pull on his beer, then set the bottle on the table.

"Nope. Pops is a rancher near Alice Springs. I see'm maybe once a year. And Moms, if you want to know, left him and went back to the rez at the end of the seventies. One of those roots kind of things. Hold onto the fragmenting culture. She was a well-educated woman. Big mistake. For her, anyway. Going native just ran'r into the ground. Too much to fight against." He gave her a look that was both question and appraisal, then continued. "No. I hooked up with Harley after college in Armidale. No more rugby scholarship, so I started playing semi-pro, just to keep it up. He became the principle team sponsor a couple of years ago. Then we discovered some mutual interests, and I've worked for him off and on since then. *With* him sometimes, as in this case. As I think I pointed out before."

"Doing what?"

"Well, *this*, for example." He made a sweeping gesture with his hand.

"You're the cook?"

He laughed. "No, I run the place."

"The captain?"

He nodded. "To give it a name."

"Really? I'm very impressed."

"Don't be. Not that much to it, really. As a boat, it's big. But as an enterprise, it's small. I know enough about navigation, the ins and outs of marine charts. The rest is just basic managerial competency. There's a crew that does the real work. I just tell them where we're going and make up the schedules and so forth, and chart the course. They're the ones with the real skill."

"So, there's a crew?"

"Yep. Three of us, all together. Me, the mate who is also the cook, and the steward, who is also the guy who keeps the twin Buicks running and sees to the rigging. Jeremy. You had a brief…ah…encounter with 'em, I believe when you came aboard." They both laughed at this. "I help out with everything as needed. Jeremy, I believe, is off exploiting the local talent at the moment. Or trying to."

"Like you were exploiting me?" she said with a coy smile.

"Rather mutual, no?" he said, lifting his beer to his lips.

"Is that typical here? I mean for the village girls…"

"Well, this *is* a resort, you know. All sorts of birds show up."

"Like *moi*?"

"*Oui. Comme tu.* But, yes, them too. Even especially them."

Her look changed to surprise.

"What? Did you think prudery was the order of the day around here?"

"Everyone seems so formal and respectful."

"Oh, well. I think you're suffering from a little cultural confusion. As the old saw goes, 'things are seldom what they seem.' They may be High Church on the outside. But inside, they're pure southseas."

Teddi flushed, gaping at him, suddenly feeling that she *was* an innocent. He laughed again and took another pull on his beer before going on.

"Sexual repression was just never their thing. You know your modern art, right? It's why Gauguin and all those uptight Victorians came to the islands. These folks really know how to boogie." He swallowed the rest of his beer and belched with satisfaction. She did the same. They lapsed into silence again for some minutes, during which he got them each another beer. He drank deeply from his. Teddi sipped. After a while she asked,

"And where, by the way, *is* your boss?"

"Now, there was a crack to me ribs. *Boss!* I oughta take y' over me knee fer that!"

She mugged back a dare at him.

"Ah, you'd prob'ly love't." They laughed, and he went on. "That's always a good question. The man never seems to sit still for a minute. I wonder why we bothered to bring this barge here if he intended to spend so little time on it. Although it does make a convenient work shack. I don't think Stevenson would be very happy if I had to butt into his little space up there." He gestured toward the village.

"As to where Harley is now, I think the old boy is holed up at the *Augusta* in Indua. He has a meeting there today with some minister or other. We've been keeping a small suite there for such purposes."

The mention of a minister brought to mind Kambula Amatosi, and she asked, "Who might that be?"

He drank and pulled a solid forearm across his lips before answering.

"I couldn't say. Harley handles interfaces with agencies, VIPs and so forth. Not my department, unless it affects me directly. He keeps me posted on what's important. Some big mustached bloke in a skirt, I should think. The usual attire, at least on official rounds. Could be the gent I saw coming out of his room at the Augusta last week. It was late that night," he looked at her coyly, "the night of our little pas de deux at the nightclub in Tu Vua? But, I only caught a glimpse. He took off in the opposite direction." He hesitated for a moment, looking at her pensively before he went on.

"Looked like the gent on the plane we came in on, minister of commerce if I'm not mistaken. Tourist business and such, but also deals with environmental impact."

At this, her voice fallen to its deepest contralto, Teddi said, "I was on that plane."

He looked back at her without expression, keeping his eye on her as he tilted his head back to suck on his beer.

"He was sitting next to me."

He pulled his arm across his lips again, continuing his look.

"You knew that!"

"So…?

"Why didn't you say so?"

"I just did."

"No you didn't. I just pried it out of you?"

"That's true. Would you like to pry out of me what you were wearing on the beach at Waikiki?"

She looked at him and the pecan burnish of her cheeks went maroon.

"It wouldn't'a covered the smallest end of an egg," he said just before she flew at him knocking his beer to the rubberized floor, and him after it with her on top of him.

Later, she sat with her back against the heavily varnished cabinets, twisting on the floor before her the beer he had planted before her along with a small bowl of strawberries. He lay sprawled on his side before her, his head planted on his hand, and reached a strawberry from the bowl and bit through half of it, closing his eyes as he chewed, the picture of contentment.

She twisted the bottle fretfully. *Why would you tell me about this anyway?* Full of grimy insinuation, a furtive midnight meeting with a government official on the take; an admission of underhandedness. She watched his tongue slide over his lips. She dismissed the idea that Amatosi—Stevenson's and Minga's Uncle Jack, a key member of AMNUP—had anything to do with it. But, was the intimation that he might be the scoundrel itself a plant, an artful probe? Likewise, Simon's whole posture of negligence. Was he on to her and just playing her game back? Or had beer and sex made him dumb? She twisted the bottle and stewed.

He opened his eyes.

"Hey mate," he said, "careful what you do with that bottle. You'll dig a hole in me floor. Expensive stuff this." He patted it, then plucked a strawberry and resumed his pose of absorbed delectation.

She sipped the beer for a while. She pondered what she could do to provoke more revelations, without showing her own card. A thought came to her and she said:

"Hey. You told me you'd show me what you and Harley are actually plotting for this place. How about it?"

"How 'bout it?" he replied. Pushing himself up into a cross-legged sitting position, he reached for her robe which lay crumpled on the floor beside him, offered it to her, then reached for his own. A little unsteadily, he led the way out of the galley and across the salon, then through the corridor between the two main cabins. At the end of it was another doorway that opened to an office. A high worktable lined the ten feet of one wall, a portion of it given over to drafting equipment. A computer and printer stood at one end of it. Above the table was a shelf of reference books, some relating to architecture, most to civil engineering. Various pieces of drafting equipment—triangles, templates of various sizes and sorts—hung on walls, littered the table; drafting and sketching pencils stood in cups. Simon had clearly not misrepresented himself as far as all this went.

"Looks a bit like home, no?" he said.

"Yep. You could just put me right to work," she said.

"Careful what you suggest, mate," he replied with a smile.

He stood by quietly while her eye roamed the drawings pinned to the wall and lying on the table; large sheets, primarily renderings of various views of the project. One, which itself contained a cutaway drawing that she immediately recognized as the structure of submerged underpinnings, was a full-blown color rendering of the entire complex. The title read "Royal Reef Inn at Yanu" and a subtitle: "A Golf and Dive Resort by Staple-Birns, Unltd." And then, below that, "Come taste the freedom." Simon moved next to her at the table, draping a familiar arm over her shoulder. She slung hers around his waist and pulled his hip against her own.

"And here young dynamos of both genders from all over the world will come to miscegenate," he said, with an acidity that surprised her.

"Oh, god," she said, laughing. "Let's hope *we* haven't done that."

Her eye scanned the drawing, quickly taking in its details. A blocky structure shot out at an angle from the northern tip of the island, aimed right at the arc made by the protective reefs; a squared off concrete-and-glass lizard that had somehow darted up out of the sand and jungle. The surrounding jungle broke up into a precisely manicured self-parody, with a grand irregular lagoon of a swimming pool in the center, in the middle of which was a group of stone porpoises, spouting water from their blowholes. Shapely bodies, hunky men in Speedos and surfer trunks, pale and bronzed and chocolate-dark, and pale and bronzed and chocolate-dark women, some with halters, some without, frolicked in the pool, on the grass, on chaise longues, on the beach, in the ocean. Beyond the aquatic park, a path through palms led to the golf course—a world-class eighteen-holer, separated from the airstrip by another line of palm trees. Her eye went back to the pool, the beach; the general vision of scantily clad and available youthful beauty. It was, she realized, squeamishly, a rendering of what had been her ideal vacation; a part of which she had just accomplished. Feeling a little woozy, she pulled her hand from Simon's waist and gripped the edge of the table.

"Very lavish," she said, clearing her throat.

" 'Very repulsive,' you meant to say."

" 'Ordinary' is more like what I was thinking," she snorted, a bit ruefully. The drawing before her brought to mind aspects of a revamping of the Marina she had left behind on her desk at Cadmeyer+Fitch+Fitzgibbon. Stale pronouncements from the lips of her boss, Al Fitzgibbon, came to mind: "Who pays the piper…" and "Check your ego at the door"—meaning any indulgence in what he regarded as irrelevant idealism; the second principle being a corollary of the first. The saving grace in the case of that project was that there was no pristine nature left to despoil.

"I don't want to insult your partner…or your work," she said quickly.

"No insult tyken, myte." He slid his hand down and patted her on the bottom. She reciprocated by thrusting her hip against his. Then, noticing some papers lying further down the table beside the computer monitor, she slid toward them. They appeared to be computer generated oceanographic surveys of some sort. Parts of these sheets consisted of tabulations, to which had been added hand-written calculations and notes. There was a logo, which looked like a dunce's hat sitting atop a childish round head. She lifted one of the sheets up and read the title block: INTERIM SURVEY REPORT OF TOTAL ORGANIC CONTENT IN DOWN SHELF REEFAL SEDIMENT FOR YANU GRAND PORTAL REEF AREA.

"Harley knows just what he's up to," he said, tapping his finger against the rendering. "As for me…" he added, nodding at what she was looking at. "Yah, that's part of my work. All figgers. Didn't I say?"

The question brought back their talk on the fantail of the *Annubis* and all that followed, causing a brief shudder, which she turned into a shrug.

"Ah. Well my bit with this, apart from captaining this beauty, is to design the pylons and the support structure. These," he said taking the sheet from her hand, "give me a leg up. As far as the rest of the engineering goes, we may or may not get into the slab. We've got a firm in Sydney on tap for that just in case. Just preliminaries," he waved the sheet he had taken from her and slid it with the others into a black folder with a label she couldn't read. "A final geologist's report will be out next week or so, then I'll get down to the design in earnest. In the mean time…" he moved closer to her, "fun in the sun." His fingers tangled in her hair, and slid over her neck.

She accepted a brief beery kiss, and said,

"I think I'd like that shower now."

"Help yourself," he said in a way that suggested he was also ready to get on to other things. "There's a fresh towel in there for you. If you can find your way, I think I'll just putter about in here while you're at it."

She left him looking over his drawings, reflecting on how decisively he had shuffled them into a folder, wishing she could have another look at the sheet with its grotesquely comic logo. She wished especially she had managed to catch the name that spread in heavy black letters across the top of the page.

XIV

A Conversation

HEIDI SCRAMBLED UP ONTO the wharf from the dive boat, with Van close behind. She picked up the pail she had set there and, seeing Teddi, she lifted it and pointed to the large, gaping greenish-brown pincers that hung from it.

"See what you miss?" she called excitedly. "You come tomorrow. It's very much fun."

From her position halfway down the *Hespera*'s gangplank, Teddi waved and called back, "I can't wait."

Heidi and Van turned to head up the stairs to the village. Brad, just behind them, boosted himself athletically up onto the wharf. Teddi lifted her hand and readied a smile for him, but he turned his sad-eagle eyes briefly on her, puffed out his cheeks and followed the others. Somehow, he had gotten the picture. A pang went through her.

Waving gaily, carrying their own fecund bucket, the couple from the Midwest clambered out of the boat and headed up the stairs. Then came Bagram who turned a brief look on her before following them. She caught up with him at the top of the stairs.

"Did some research aboard the *Hespera*," she said in a near whisper, as they walked into the village.

"Ah. *Re*search," said Bagram with evident sarcasm, his eyebrows raised above his thick lenses.

"I saw some stuff," she went on, ignoring this, "It might be important. Maybe nothing. Anyway, I think someone ought to know about it."

They were approaching a group of guests who had gathered around Heidi and Van to admire the catch. "Why don't you check in with Stevenson," he said quietly. Then, loudly enough for anyone passing to hear, "Well, Teddi. Serves you right for not hitting the reef with us. Maybe Heidi will let you taste her *zuppa di mare*." He turned away to join the others.

Stevenson, already known to be her client, needed no such alibi. She turned and walked back to the maintenance yard. One of the village boys was busy mending a small table and talking to another who sat nearby smoking a cigarette. Both quickly looked her over as she passed them, then dipped their heads and said "G'day miss." Their eyes followed her as she climbed the low porch and knocked on the shed door.

Stevenson ushered her in, then lingered to say something to the boys, which brought a rill of giggles.

"I just told them to put their eyes back in their heads before someone steps on them," he said, looking her over. "They're always busy with everything except what they're supposed to be doing."

"Oh," said Teddi, following his glance, which took in her deliberately alluring attire. Her motives had so shifted since she first presented herself aboard the *Hespera* that she had completely forgotten about it. "Boys," she said, in an effort to shift the subject.

"Yes. Well, here you are," said Stevenson, indicating by his gesture both the room in which they stood, and her presence back among them. He had not seen her since her departure for Indua the previous day when her return was still in doubt. His happiness at her return was evident in the broad grin he gave her.

The room itself was ten-by-ten; efficiently spartan. A high transom above a shuttered window let in steady light. As aboard the *Hespera*, a table occupied most of one wall, equipped with an array of drafting tools including a drafting bar. But here there was no doubt that Teddi *would* go to work. Her fingers itched for the feel of a thick drawing pencil and the receptive grain of tracing paper. Both were often more agreeable companions than humans.

"I hope this is what you need," said Stevenson, his eye lingering dotingly over the table. "I did a lot of drafting in high school, and some in the army as well. But I'm rusty."

Giving the table a quick scan, she said "Perfect." He nodded happily.

Her eye went to the drawing already spread out on the table, which she immediately recognized. She walked over to give it a closer look. It was a modern print of the original working drawings of the National Assembly, identical to the one Rajiv had left for her in her room at the Tukulu, but a thicker pile. She flipped through it all quickly, observing familiar construction practices. Some of the details she recognized from her study of the drawings the night before; which, now that she had been in the actual building, had acquired a somewhat different significance. It was, however, all as one could expect, given the nature of the building and the practices of the time. There was nothing telltale, nothing suggesting a secret anything. When she was done with this quick survey, she folded back the pages of drawings and ran a forearm over the pile, smoothing it out. She turned to Stevenson and shrugged.

"So, you found nothing," he said.

"Nope. Nothing different than what I've already seen. Have you got the other thing?" she asked, referring to the drawing she had unwittingly brought from Los Angeles, although she doubted it would yield anything either.

"Bagram's still working on the code. So none of this tells you anything we need to know?" Stevenson persisted with evident disappointment.

"Not yet, anyway. The tour was great, but it didn't turn up anything, really. Or maybe too many things. Any number of loose stones might conceal a passageway. That sort of thing. We can't just show up with a pry bar, can we? Let's hope whatever Bagram's doing will give us something to go on."

"Let's hope."

"In the meantime," she said brightly, businesslike, "there's the dive shop."

"Indeed there is," he said, his tone shifting with hers. "What say we take a stroll around the property; give it some physical presence?"

"Great," she said, then remembering her mission: "Oh, there's something I need to tell you."

"Let's save it for our walk." He nodded in the direction of hasty footsteps sounding across the porch.

"Hi fellas," he said as they went out to the two boys who stood a short distance away.

"Hi, Steve," said one.

"You were just talking about some kind of building stuff, huh?" said the other, who had been repairing the table.

"Do you suppose it would be possible for a person to have a private conversation around here once in a while?"

"Sorry Steve. Sorry miss," said the first boy.

"That's right. We were," Teddi said answering the other boy's question.

"You gonna design the dive shop, miss?" he said.

"Elias thinks he's got some hot ideas," said the other one pointing to his friend.

"Well," said Teddi, "I'll definitely consult with you, Elias."

"Oh, great," beamed the boy. "Any time."

They went back to their work, jabbering together, as Teddi and Stevenson headed for the beach.

"Little cups have big ears," he said.

"And probably big mouths to go with them," she laughed.

"Yes. But, I think all that will get around now is word that Elias will advise the lady architect about the dive shop. You're a pretty hot item around here, you know. I think he just grew about two feet."

They walked along the rocky shelf she had seen from the plane. Fringed with hibiscus and bougainvillea, it rose a half-dozen feet and followed the beach until it bolted out in a thick rocky outcropping that curved toward the deep inlet protecting the wharf. The view of the wharf was cut off by festoons of close-growing royal palms from which rose a giant ficus with foot high gray roots snaking from it.

The sun was down now. Pink tufts sprouted in a deepening blue sky, shaded into lavenders shot through with iridescent green rifts. The air was wonderfully fragrant, and hugged her skin with gentle warmth. Stevenson was quiet. Despite the serious strains of his face, he seemed so easy in himself that the accumulation of pressures she was feeling dissolved. She settled herself onto a rocky throne and closed her eyes, letting the changing colors, the fragrance, and the softness of the air wash through her.

When she opened them, he was still standing, slouching comfortably with his hands clasped behind his back, looking oceanward, out through the strait toward the reef that stood at its entrance. The emerald hump of Guma Yanu on the other side of the channel glowed at its edges, rimed in gold from the last sunlight. Seeing that look of intimate absorption, she thought that his being had been saturated by many such sunsets.

"It's very, very beautiful," she said quietly, meaning it, intending to convey sympathy with what it seemed to mean for him.

"A possible site for a dive shop, do you think?" He looked aside at her with a smile she couldn't quite read. It surprised her that he would so easily sacrifice what seemed to be such a personal space for business.

"Yes," she said. "That is, if it isn't a sacrilege. Are you really serious about building it?"

He shrugged. "Hard to say at the moment what I mean seriously. Everything is serious. It all depends. But, tell me what you learned." He sat down on the rock beside her. The sky was becoming more violently beautiful, a bloody green-tinged coppery hand laid against a purple sky quickly fading to gray.

"I'm not sure what I learned," she said. "But I know what I saw. For one thing, word's gotten around about the dive shop." She stopped and giggled a bit at the thought of it. "Who knows what Simon actually bought. But, he wanted to know if I was interested in seeing what the competition, as he put it, is doing."

"Not really competition," said Stevenson. "Two different things."

"Yeah. He said something like that too. He even suggested joining forces. But, anyway," she said, waving her hand in the air to dismiss the whole idea, "I did see the tedious mess they've got planned. Déjà vu all over again. Boy, is your life going to change, if they get what they're after." She stopped to watch a parrot fluttering its dusky red wings against the darkened trunk of a nearby palm. She grimly imagined that little vignette becoming the insignia for the resort-to-be, and winced at the thought of what this place would feel like for the two or so years that it would be a massive construction site; and worse, what it would look like after. Her Los Angeles marina job was an insignificant alteration by comparison.

"We know about all that," said Stevenson, his voice tensing with untypical impatience. "What else did you learn?"

"Right. What else? Okay. While I'm standing there at the drafting table with him, looking at this flashy rendering of your disaster, I noticed a stack of papers with letterhead. Calculations and charts of various sorts. But, it's the letterhead, especially the logo, that caught my eye. It didn't seem to have anything to do with designing a resort. Geological studies. When I pointed it out to him, he talked about doing the engineering for the hotel's underpinnings, using those studies of the subsurface for caisson placement, and so forth."

"Right. Makes sense. I always assumed he had some function other than…" He stopped abruptly. *Fucking the local women?* she finished the thought for him in her head, then said:

"Sure. Makes complete sense. But, that doesn't explain the letterhead. Unless, of course, they're making use of studies that have been produced by oil explorers."

"That's what the letterhead was?"

"Right. There was this cute little logo that looked like a round head with a dunce's cap. I didn't pay close enough attention to the company name. Something-something Explorative, Ltd. I remember a bit of the report title, which I did read. Something about 'downshelf reefal sediment...'"

"Yes," said Stevenson. "Makes sense, too. The sort of thing you'd want to have numbers on if you were sinking caissons to support the sort of a building they have in mind. I know at least that much about it. It's been part of the talk."

"Right. Just what he said," said Teddi, impatient herself that that he wasn't making the connections she was. "But, that logo—obviously an oil derrick sitting on top of the world. Yuck."

"Yuck is right. But so what? That information is as useful to a builder as it is to oil speculators. They're probably just trying to reduce their startup costs. I have no interest in defending these guys, but it seems to me…"

"That's basically what Simon claimed. There's something more. I told Rajiv about it, but I guess it hasn't gotten back to you. It happened on the boat ride over to Indua yesterday with Minga. She almost collided with this big ship that was heading out just as we were coming in. It was an oil exploration rig. I got the name: the *Southern Explorer*. And there was a guy leaning against the railing. A big hairy white guy. I'm positive he's the one that broke into my cabin on the *Annubis*."

Stevenson looked at her, struck by the revelation.

"I remember the whole thing now," she added. "Clear as day. I could pick that guy out of a lineup anytime."

"But, still, what can that mean? There's no particular reason why one thing should be connected to the other."

Teddi looked at him, trying to gauge his expression. Was he seriously dismissing this, or was he simply playing devil's advocate, testing her own certitude?

"Sure," she said. "Of course not. But, *Bungshalo!* no? As you guys say. Too many convergences here not to at least make you wonder." She ticked them off: "Simon and Harley on the *Annubis* while this guy breaks into my cabin. He shows up on an oil exploration ship. Simon's using reports that were, for all we know, churned up by that ship. *Bungshalo!*"

Stevenson, smiling at her repetition of the term, nodded.

"Anything's possible. I'll get in touch with Uncle Jack, ask him to get information about the ship's registry. That may tell us something. Too bad you can't go back in there and snag one of those pages, at least get the company name." He thought about it again and said, "Better not, though. No way to know what they're really thinking. If you're on track with this, it could be dangerous. Let's just see what Jack comes up with." She nodded. It was full dark now, the moon was just broaching the horizon, throwing a brilliant wedge of light over the black water in the distance.

"That reminds me. He also had something to say that maybe involved your uncle." She repeated to him Simon's account of what might have been Amatosi's suspicious departure from Harley's hotel room in Indua early in the morning of the day she boarded the *Annubis*. Stevenson guffawed at this.

"This is funny?" she said, startled by his response.

"Well, yes," he said, gathering himself. "It's ridiculous. That's Uncle Jack you're talking about."

"Right. I know that. Your mom's brother. Minister of Commerce. I mean, I don't want to offend you. But..."

From her point of view, it made sense that he was no more immune from being bought off by Harley than was Ogden, or anyone else with influence or something worth owning; which, of course, also meant something worth selling. Why should it be taken for granted that this uncle would be less greedy, more scrupulous than anyone else. Since he also had a stake in what happened to the island it made sense that Harley would look for a way to buy him off, and that Amatosi was himself in a position to shake Harley down. According to this, Simon's allegations couldn't be discounted.

Stevenson looked at her carefully:

"What did you do when Simon started talking about Amatosi?"

"I tried to finesse it, as if it didn't mean much to me except an odd coincidence, and then I changed the subject back to Harley. I didn't want him to see that your uncle's name had any special meaning to me, apart from the fact that we sat together on the plane coming here. He *knew* that, you know? He was on the same plane as me; had his *eye* on me. What does *that* tell you?"

Stevenson shrugged.

"Anyway, you've already said Amatosi's supposed to be one of you guys; I mean, one of us."

"That's right. He is. Definitely."

"But maybe he's betraying us. Even as we speak."

"Definitely not," he said with a placid smile.

"But what about the late night meeting at the hotel?"

"It never happened. Simon was playing with you, to see if you'd react. So it's good that you didn't. Or maybe he was just mistaken. Did he say it definitely was Jack?"

"No. Only that he thought it was, or might be."

"He's wrong. It wasn't."

"You know this for sure?"

"For sure. That night the two of us had dinner together at Government House in Indua. It's the place where foreign dignitaries meet with members of our ministries. There's also a dining room for tribal officials."

"You met in the open like that?"

"Why not? You mean because of my involvement in AMNUP? Everyone knows we're family. After that we went by separate cars to the Tukulu. I was there with my family. And..." He paused and looked at her for a moment, "...and to await the princess from America who didn't show up. Minga was there, and Sanjay. We just needed a little pow-wow to make sure we were clear about things before you got there. Which, of course, didn't happen. Shepherd...it is his club you were dancing at that night, you know...planned to fly in to be here when you arrived by bus, which of course..." He waved his hand dismissively. "The only one who wasn't there was Rotanu, who was stuck in some village matters. So, anyway, the point is, Jack couldn't have been locked in with Harley because, except for the short time we went our separate ways, he was with me. And that wouldn't have been long enough. There's no way he could have met with Harley that night, even if he had wanted to. Which he wouldn't."

"What about his supposed meeting today in Indua with your uncle?"

"Ah, that's what you meant by 'betraying us as we speak.' No reason to think that isn't on the up and up. Harley caught the plane to Indua just before the one you came in on. It's Amatosi's job—Uncle Jack's— anyway, to deal with tourist-related land use issues, check into their legality, make sure they conform to the master plan, and so forth. This won't have been their first meeting either. And it won't be the first time that Harley tries to make Jack see things his way. He's basically retailed the same bill of goods to Jack as he did to my father. But not with the same effect. It doesn't matter. Jack isn't involved personally in this deal. He's just involved in the legal stuff, and he plays it straight. As far as whatever promises Harley's made to Pop that might push him over the edge, Jack's as much in the dark as the rest of us are. Pop knows where Jack stands and has no interest in letting himself in for his persuasion. Those two guys go back together as far as you can go. They each have their own ways of looking at things. As to Harley, don't doubt for a minute that Jack knows what a conniver he is, he and his buddy Simon, and is plenty wary of them. No, no," he said, looking at her earnestly. "The only two-timers here are Simon and Harley. Uncle Jack's with us all the way."

"Then who did Simon see? Or was he just making the whole thing up?"

"You mean at the Augusta that night? Who knows. Maybe he was just probing you to see how you'd react. Maybe there *was* someone slipping out as he was arriving. Any number of these old Anuaps could fit the description of Kambula Amatosi."

The man on the bus came to Teddi's mind. If anyone could be mistaken for Amatosi from certain angles that guy could. But, it was hard to feel suspicious of him. He was so sweet-natured, so gentle, so encouraging. And then she awakened from her momentary idyll to the realization of just what he had convinced her to do.

"I think I know who it was."

"Well?"

"The guy on the bus, he was also a Kambula something or other. Or maybe he didn't give me his name at all. But, it's because of him I took the *Annubis*. He even told me where to book passage."

"No name?"

"None that I can remember."

"Well, of course not, if he's responsible for setting you up. Can you describe him?"

Teddi laughed.

"Sure. He looks like your Uncle Jack."

"Not much help," said Stevenson. Teddi shrugged. "Could, of course, be a coincidence, " he went on. "The guy on the bus could have been completely innocent. Someone else could have been keeping an eye on you."

"Right," she said. "But he's the only one that convinced me to change my plans." She gave him a sheepish smile, "The princess doesn't arrive, remember?"

He smiled tenderly back at her.

"Right on both counts." They both fell silent for a while, then he said, "Well, there's no doubt that all happened according to somebody's plan. What the old guy on the bus had to do with it… who knows? I'll give it some thought. It may not matter much at this point."

The moon had by now launched itself well clear of the horizon, sending a long shaft across the water, spreading onto the beach. Further down the strand, the reflected glow from the lighted dining room barely marked out the little building that housed it from its jungle background.

"We should head back," said Stevenson. "They'll be expecting you for dinner, and I have some business to attend to."

As they were walking back, he stopped and took her by the shoulder. "I wanted to tell you how much your spending time with Pria last night meant. Rajiv told me. He said she seemed like a different girl this morning. It matters so much."

"To me too," she said. "I think she clinched the deal. I mean, I don't know if I'd be here otherwise."

XV

The Code

TEDDI LET HERSELF INTO the office in the maintenance yard early the next morning with the keys Stevenson had given her. She took from her supply bag an array of pencils, a foot wide roll of buff tracing paper, and a roll of drafting tape and laid them out on the table. With a quick practiced jerk, she tore a length of paper off the roll. Then she tore off four short ragged pieces of tape, stuck them to the back of her hand, positioned the paper, and transferred the tape from hand to paper, securing it to the table. Using a thick, soft-leaded pencil she made a quick three dimensional sketch of the space proposed for the dive shop, showing the flat area raised above the beach, and the general contours of the grove behind it. For the next hour or so, tearing sheet after sheet from the roll, she used it to sketch a dozen overlays of possible shapes for the small building and its positioning on the rock shelf, showing also a variety of possible rooflines and arrangements of deck, entry, and window; as well as a boardwalk and stairway that lead back through the vegetation and down to the wharf—to which her pencil also could not help adding improvements. As it made its avid, dreaming way over sheet after sheet, the cold calculations of Simon's and Harley's planned resort lay a close antagonist in her mind, heightening her determination to make something gorgeous, that would seem to have grown right out of the terrain, that would put to shame all their tedious clichés. Her pencil flew over ragged parchment-like sheets. A pile of them had accumulated on the table beside her when she heard a loud knock at the door.

"Teddi! Good morning!" came a familiar baritone. It was Bagram.

"Teddi," he went on with great show as she opened the door. "Stevenson told me I could find you here. Just have some thoughts I wanted to share. Might I come in?"

He entered, carrying a manila envelope. As she closed the door behind him, he peeked through the blinds covering the window beside it.

"Someone after you?" Teddi asked wryly.

"Ach. I saw one of Simon's boys wandering around out there. Probably just heading back to the boat after a night in the hay with one of the locals."

"Spy vs. spy, huh?"

"Just like the good old days," he laughed, snapping his finger against the blind as he let go of it. He set the envelope he was carrying on the work table. From a shelf under the table, he pulled out a board on which was taped the old drawing of the Assembly, covered with a thin sheet of clear acetate. There were cracks where it had been folded, and blotches of decay, and ragged gaps in other places.

"I'm amazed you were able to unfold it without destroying it," she said. The original deep blue of the entire surface was faded, making it harder to read than a new blueprint would have been. But, it was good enough. The suspect leaf-shaped doodle stood out clearly against the background.

"I got lucky," Bagram replied. "If this had been ordinary paper, just unfolding it probably would have broken it up. And, it'd very likely have turned to mush if I'd tried steaming it. But this held up pretty well. It's drafting linen, calendared muslin. Really fine stuff. These boys didn't mess around. A lot of it was still used in the late nineteenth century. Ah, yes. Of course. You know all about this. Part of your kit. Fascinating. Treated just like paper. Same process.

Saturated with ferric ammonia. Ultraviolet light was used to transfer the image from the tracing. Developed in an ammonia bath. Same as that, really, but somewhat less mechanized." He pointed to the small blueprint machine that stood on an adjacent table, a large bottle of ammonia at the ready on the floor beneath it. "The original would have been a crisp Prussian blue. The fact that it's faded out probably makes *this* gizmo a little easier to read." He pointed to the leaf sketch and the scribbling associated with it. "Here," he said, unclasping the envelope and sliding out its contents. "I was able to make some decent copies."

While Bagram talked, Teddi had been looking over the drawing. Even with the rot that broke up its surface, the beauty of the draftsmanship moved her. The quality of the line still showed despite the work of time. Planes and objects were carefully rendered, details differentiated with delicate hatchings and varied line weights, giving anyone with eyes to see a vivid mental picture of what was intended. An elevation of the entire façade was centered on the page. On its right, it showed the shallow steps rising to the enormous, thickly carved entry.

The site plan lay to the left of the elevation, situating the footprint of the building in relation to its environs and approaches. It showed the wide arc of the driveway in front of it, the grove of trees to the east, adjacent to the grand entry. Its slow descent down to the beach, from the plateau where the building stood, was shown with light contour lines. A heavy irregular ruffled line indicated the edge of the palisade just to the north of it. Below the site plan was a small-scale plan view showing the divisions of the main floor, a portion of which she and Rajiv had walked through.

Bagram arranged the sheets he pulled from the envelope in a grid next to the board on which the drawing was taped. Reaching under the table again, he pulled out the sheaf of new prints that Teddi had looked through the day before, and set it beside the old drawing. Teddi turned her attention to the array of photocopies, three neat rows of letter-sized pages. Some zeroed in on details of the crude sketch of the leaf, showing them at different degrees of magnification. Others were devoted to details—from both the relic and the new print—of the tile border that ran around the floor of the Grand Vestibule.

"At first, it seemed pretty hopeless," Bagram began, gesturing towards the photocopies. "I was looking for some indication of an alteration in the tile details on the relic. The presence of this leaf here, of course, suggested that." He pointed to the doodle on the old drawing.

"Apart from that, nothing looked changed. But...ah," he wagged his finger in the air, "...intuition didn't fail me. A close comparison of the relic with the new print did the job. You have to look very closely...see here?...to see that the veins of the some of the leaves themselves have been altered. It's those alterations that make the code. You can clearly see the difference between tiles where the leaves have been altered and where they have not.

"Here," he pulled out a magnifying glass. "Look at this one," he pointed to a tile near the main entrance. "See how perfectly uniform all of the veins are. Same line quality, same thickness, density. That holds up even in the enlargement. Clear, crisp lines. Now, look here," he pointed to another tile, this time one at the right of the entry to the Chamber of Chieftains. He picked up a pencil and pointed with it to several different veins. Teddi could see that they varied in a number of ways. Some were thickened just above the leafstalk that divided them, some below, some close to it, some closer to the tip, and so forth.

"Got it," said Teddi, her eye roaming back and forth between the different sheets to verify the comparison.

"Yes," said Bagram. "Lost in plain sight. But, very clear once you've found it. The enlargements make it clear that these aren't due to random sloppiness, or even the antiquity of the thing. Our draftsman had no trouble drawing a crisp line when he wanted to."

"Right," said Teddi, admiration clear in her voice. "Or any other kind of line."

"Now, look here," said Bagram, pointing to a pair of photocopies. "Both from the same spot. This one is from the new copy, this from the relic. Makes it very clear, no?" It took only a moment's scrutiny to see the difference. The photocopy from the modern drawing had clean regular lines. The lines on the relic were exactly the same, *except* for those lines that had been altered, which had the look of yarn that was unraveling in places.

"So!" exclaimed Bagram, thrusting his pencil conclusively in the air. "Q.E.D. Now it's clear. The code is in the variations."

He lifted another enlarged copy of the leaf doodle itself from the carefully laid out array of pages and set it on top of the two they had been looking at.

"Now, look at the veins on this. Of course, at a glance this definitely appears to be a doodle, done mindlessly by an inexpert hand."

Teddi looked at the offset rows of haltingly rendered lines, some almost smudges, hardly lines at all.

"All by design, deliberate misdirection. See all this variation in the length and thickness of the veins. When I first saw it, it immediately struck me that it was a version of a Gaelic line code. So, I tried it out. See these various locations along the stalk, and the varying thicknesses of each pair of veins. For instance, a short thick vein above the stalk, a long thin one below it. Or, a vein above the stalk that's thick at the top, and a short thin vein below it. Each of those pairs stands for a letter. Twenty odd variations in all. Cumbersome, but simple. And easy to carve into the soft stone of West Wales. You find a lot of 'Gwyneth-loveth-Thomas' sort of thing scratched into old church window sills."

From there, Bagram's explanation flowed on with glacial precision. Fuzzy things here and there, darkenings of lines here and there, such and such references from the doodle to some particular tile in the border, suggesting this and that. At one point Shakespeare made an appearance in the form of a Latin version of Iago's famous epigram—*I am not what I am*—couched in line code. This, it turned out, was merely an index to some other strange distortions in the relic; distortions which became clearly apparent only in the photocopied enlargements. On and on flowed Bagram's analysis.

Teddi's attention drifted to recollections of her tour of the Assembly. The musty odors of the basement came to her, and its heavy timbers and thick painted-over granite pavers. When she returned to the drawing in front of them, again following Bagram's finger as it moved from point to point, object to object, a crude shape caught her eye, like a faint coffee-cup ring or a large letter *C*, close to the leaf drawing. She found it intriguing. But, before she could give it any thought, Bagram wound up his demonstration.

"So, what this all adds up to, if I've got the code right, and I'm quite sure I have," he twirled his hand in the air referring to the lengthy logical chain he had just finished unraveling, "is that certain elements of the atoll—this Mother Turtle, etc.—act as a pointer to the area of the passage, sort of like the pointer stars of the Big Dipper to Polaris. If I've got it right, this is what it says: 'Sight from mother's heart through two lowest children.'"

Bagram's reached a long index finger across the page of the new copy to tap a few inches above the footprint of the building, close to the edge of the drawing, to a point that would have been several hundred yards offshore.

Letting his finger rest there, he said, "The Mother."

He pulled his finger away revealing the little circular group, the name in small letters beneath it: "Mother Turtle and Her Children." Below that, the name in Anuapúan: *Tukulu Wakaua Ka-enundaka*.

"Right," said Teddi. "Rajiv pointed it out to me when we went out in his boat. I had a bird's eye view of it on the flight back."

"Well, you have the picture, then. The idea is that from some point here, you could sight through two other aligned islands and your bull's eye would be the point at which the secret passage came out to the ocean." He paused reflectively for a moment. "Odd, no?"

"Odd?" she said.

He smiled and raised his eyebrows. "Well, if this was supposed to show you your means of escape *to* the sea, would you expect it to show you how to find it *from* the sea?"

"Oh, right," she said, getting his drift. "If you were already safely at sea....So this isn't much good for helping you find the way out."

"Yes. I was expecting something on the order of 'press the third stone to the right' to make the door to the escape route spring open. Makes one wonder what this Brightman fellow was up to."

"Right, like maybe he was only interested in getting *into* something. Must've been worth it to him, to go to this trouble," she said.

"More than a tin of soda crackers," Bagram chuckled.

"So you think Horatio's ancestor was a crook? That the famous legend's all wrong and this has nothing to do with an escape route? Just a ruse to cover some other grand scheme, like stealing the crown jewels or whatever? You think that's it?"

"It's been occuring to me. But, who knows. There's some value in knowing what the terrain is like you're going to escape into, where your route meets the ocean. Maybe there's some other clues yet to be found. But, anyway, this gives us plenty to go on. From our point of view, it doesn't matter which end of the passage it points to."

"Unless," Teddi said tartly, squinting teasingly at him, "it doesn't point to anything and this is all nonsense and it *is* just a doodle."

Bagram snorted. It was not a possibility he was willing to consider, not even in jest.

They focused again on the drawing. The atoll was only faintly shown even in the new copy. "Can't tell much from this," she said, pointing to it. There was no way of determining from it an alignment of three islands of any sort.

Bagram pulled a crisp folded sheet from the envelope. It was a marine chart of the waters surrounding Indua. He opened it up and spread it on the table. The scale was large enough so that the promontory on which the National Assembly stood was clearly depicted, as well as the area around it for several hundred yards. The atoll itself was well delineated, as were the islands associated with it: the so-called *Heart*, that moss covered flattop rock that Rajiv claimed did service as a rendezvous of young lovers; the surrounding jagged rocks that made up the ring of the atoll itself; finally, a diffuse scattering of smaller islands, not much bigger, most of them, than large rocks. The chart was cluttered with markings, symbols, numbers, abbreviations, most of which meant nothing to her. She picked up a large plastic triangle and used it as a straight edge to plot an alignment of two such rocks with the Heart. There were a few that sort of qualified, but only two really likely suspects. Bagram pointed out the markings that showed height at low tide.

"The *lowest* two children," he said, recalling what the code, as he had translated it, specified. That narrowed the possibilities down to that single pair, which went off in a southeasterly direction. The line intersecting them made landfall at a point below where the grove of trees climbed the escarpment to border the Assembly on the east. She had scrutinized the whole area carefully during her 'fishing trip' with Rajiv and had a clear picture of it in her mind.

"It's all pretty much out in the open," she said. "Don't see what you could conceal there. I might have missed something, though. Maybe Minga could take the *Xanadu* around and…"

"Done!" exclaimed Bagram. "I called her this morning and suggested she take her latest batch of oglers for an excursion in the area. It's really pretty, anyway. Not bad fishing as I recall."

"Not bad," she replied, warmly recalling Rajiv's admiration of her skills. "I rescued a parrotfish from my hook out there."

"Kind girl," said Bagram, patting her on the shoulder. Then he pushed himself away from the table. "I'll leave you to your reflections. You may see something in the drawings that gives more information. We should be hearing from Minga by tomorrow morning anyway."

He went to the door, opened it a crack, peeked out, then opened it wide and bounded from the porch to the ground. Brandishing his hand in the air with a flourish as he strode off, he called back, "See you later, I'm sure, Teddi."

Glancing around, she saw the eye of the boy on her.

"Good morning Elias," she waved to him. "You're at work early."

"Yes miss. Just thought I'd get this done before breakfast. That way Joseph won't show up to bother me."

"Think I'll try to get some work done too, while it's still not too hot."

"A'right miss," said Elias, smiling broadly and waving back at her as she disappeared into the office.

She continued to study the drawings, going back and forth between the new print, the marine chart, and the relic. There was nothing exceptional, nothing revealing, nothing suggesting a secret exit. There was no detail at all in the architectural drawings of that area of the escarpment that the line she had projected aimed at. The only details were of the other end of the building, at the west tower. It was into the sub-basement there that the young tour guide had led them—the dank and moldy *catacombs* as he called them—where he gave his theatrical little campfire rendition about the secret escape route. She studied this area on both the new print of the original and the relic. Again, there was nothing revealing.

After a while, she slid both onto the shelf below the table and turned back to the piece of buff tracing paper she had taped down on the desk, with the stack of sketches beside it. She picked up the fat sketching pencil and for the next hour she gave herself over to the more fruitful uncertainties of creation.

By the time the breakfast bell rang, there lay scattered around her on the table—and on the floor behind her where a few had fluttered down in her haste to get on to the next budding idea—a dozen or so raggedly torn pieces, adding notes and sketches of possible floor plans and details of elevations to the already sketched out ideas for the massing of the dive shop. That it might never be built hardly mattered. Her imagination had its own purposes and pleasures. But, as a tactical matter, when she went out, she made a point of leaving her efforts spread out in plain site of the window, counting on the sweetly eager Elias to make sure that word of her efforts got around.

XVI

The Reef

HER PLAYFUL WORK ON the dive shop, purging the frustrations of her quest for the secret passage, had put her in a rambunctious mood. In the dining room, she gave her tablemates a boisterous greeting, particularly Brad who looked glumly away as she entered. She rested her hand on his shoulder and planted herself in the chair next to him. When shortly after breakfast, the dive boat with Casper at the helm pulled away from the wharf, they were seated thigh to thigh on one of the long benches, their arms lying stretched along the railing behind each others' shoulders.

As the boat rounded the headland into the channel, Teddi looked back to see the Kawasaki, tied off near the *Hespera*'s swim steps, bobbing in their wake, dappled sunlight glinting off its shell. She still felt a pang of regret that she hadn't gotten Simon to take her for a spin on it.

Her last chance had come when they were saying goodbye on the fantail of the *Hespera*, after she had showered and primped herself back into the condition in which she had arrived on board. The sumptuous machine rested on its lift like a gorgeous cat after a regal meal. It turned its beautiful glinting eyes on her and hummed its seduction, harmonizing with the remnant of physical vibration between her and Simon. When the words *How about a ride?* arose in her mind, she bit the lips that were about to utter them.

Instead, she carried on a detailed, instantaneous, internal dialogue which argued the relative value for espionage purposes of riding or not riding. Would it, on the one hand, convince him of the possibility of an alliance? That would be useful...*and* dangerous. Or would it convince him that she was really just another a thrill-seeking babe; a score he could revisit any time, using the jet-ski as bait? That could be annoying. The dialogue closed with their farewell kiss. The seductively humming beast had drifted off to sleep. She walked down the gangplank.

Now, as it disappeared behind the headland, she slid a bit closer to Brad, and her hand that lay behind his back decisively clasped his shoulder. She recalled her conversation with Stevenson about Simon, which made it clear to her, if not yet to Stevenson, that she had slept with the probable enemy; and that she could not count on his stupidity. The willing Brad, to whom she would probably be some degree of a disappointment but never an enemy, was for her like underbrush to hunted prey.

As they pulled further into the channel, one more thing came to her: the previously unconsidered fact that the Kawasaki was not at rest on its lift—humming in placid self-satisfaction—but moored in the water, ready for its next assignment. *Where are you going?* she wondered. *What will you do?* She nestled still closer to Brad, their long lean thighs, his pale, hers dark, each giving the other the comfort they needed.

The boat head north through the channel, toward the reef. They spoke little. Opposite them, their elbows resting on the gunnel, Van and Heidi were turned to each other, apparently unaware of anyone else until they were persuaded, reluctantly, to shift their attention by the change in engine pitch and speed that signaled that they were close to the reef. The water now was a very clear medium turquoise. Below it, some thirty yards away, the rough shape of the reef worked its way up from below until it surfaced as a multicolored metropolis of fantastic shapes. Twenty odd feet from it, Casper threw out a sea anchor and cut the engine. He then gave a shy, sweetly smiling rendition of the rules of diving decorum and safety, with special emphasis on the buddy system.

"Okay, buddy," said Teddi, buoyantly, sticking out her hand for Brad to shake.

"Buddy," he replied, taking hold of it. They slipped on their equipment and paddled off together toward the reef. Ahead of them swam Van and Heidi. The couple from the Midwest, hardcore reef hounds as she had learned, had been in the lead, but almost immediately disappeared from sight. Teddi looked just in time to see the woman's plaid-covered bottom slip beneath the water, followed by tan legs and green flippers. Their snorkels reappeared in tandem for a moment some fifty feet ahead, off the far side reef, just as Teddi and Brad arrived there. Heidi and Van were already clambering up on it, warning each other to be careful not to crush the delicate residents. They seemed, for the moment at least, to be content so sit on the reef's edge, hold hands, and remark to each other on the local beauties. A rippling series of *O-o-o-o*-s could be heard coming from Heidi. On the dive boat, Casper—Walkman clipped to his belt, headset in place—had thrown out a line and was settling himself in a beach chair.

Looking quickly over to Heidi and Van, his face twisted with mild disdain, Brad threw a thumb in the direction of where the Midwest couple had been a moment before. "*Those* guys have the right idea," he said. "C'mon. Let's go for the main event."

Without waiting for a response, he pulled his mask into place, adjusted the snorkel's mouthpiece, and pushed off backward into the water. Teddi followed suit, though with less exuberance, unaccustomed to the equipment despite being a strong swimmer. She lowered her face into the water and watched as Brad followed the steep and brilliantly colored scarp of the reef down into darkness. A swarm of tiny silver fish, incandescent in the sunlight, fluttered away from him. Then he too disappeared into the gloom. She pushed herself down along the face a little, no further than she could go and still breathe through the snorkel. Suddenly, less than a yard in front of her, there hung an iridescent blue ellipse, speckled with bright yellow spots. Its mouth frozen in a long regretful sweep, the fish looked at her with a pensive eye for a long few seconds and then, as if exasperated, turned ninety degrees away and disappeared.

Brad had been gone for what seemed a long time when she felt a tap on her shoulder. He indicated that he wanted to talk and they came up out of the water.

"You should see what it's like down there. It's stupendous."

"Sorry. I'm not a very good buddy, am I," Teddi laughed sheepishly.

"No, no. I'm the screw up. I shouldn't have taken off alone like that. But really. It's amazing. C'mon. It bottoms out a little ways down. If you think it's cool up here, you should see what's happening down below."

A dozen feet down, the reef leveled off into a miracle of color-splashed forms that spread out in all directions. Some splotches of color swam right up to her, matching her curiosity with their own. An angelfish, as big as a large frying pan, pushed its thick, smirking, cadmium yellow lips toward her. It hung like a glowing lampshade for a long second before it made a slow turn, and whiplashed off between two schools of palm-sized turquoise fish floating like leaves amid the gnarled limbs of a huge branch coral that grew like a mountain oak out of the vertical face of the reef.

Riveted by vision after vision, unaware almost of the need to breathe, she again felt a tap on her shoulder, and turned to find Brad pointing upward. They pushed up to the surface, grabbed a breath and went back down; this time all the way to the flat mantel. They swam over it together for a while, propelled by their fins, following its contours.

They drifted out over an abyss. The brilliant plane had given way to complete blackness. The power of the void was startling, like the sudden drop of an elevator. Then euphoria set in. For long seconds Teddi drifted, unpropelled, maintaining her face-down position with little adjustments of hands and fins. When Brad's hand touched hers, she felt a moment's irritation, and then twined her fingers with his. For some seconds they floated like that. Then the fingers pulled away from hers and she turned to see him pointing urgently surfaceward. The sight of the bright surface glistening above them shook her out of her reverie.

She reluctantly swam up with him. Once she got started, she had adapted quickly to the equipment and was now feeling that this buddy system imposed unreasonable restraints. It was clear that Brad's lung power wasn't equal to hers, or maybe his sense of adventure, or pleasure in the intense silent peace of drifting over the abyss.

They broke the surface and clung to the edge of the reef. Heidi and Van had disappeared. Fifty feet away, on the other side of the reef, Casper sat with his eyes closed, headset in place, an unattended fishing line hanging over the side. Beyond him, coming from the village, she could just make out a small glistening object heading toward them, barely distinct from the jungle background or the water it moved over. She knew it was Simon on the jet ski.

"Listen," she said. "I know how important this buddy stuff is, but I really need a little more time by myself down there. Couldn't you sort of keep an eye on me for a little while from up here?"

She could see him flinch a little.

"You don't want me to go down with you?"

"No. Not that. I just happen to have these super lungs, and it's so beautiful down there I hate to come up before I have to."

"Lucky you," he said, a little morosely.

"Oh, come on," she said, smacking him on a well-developed deltoid. "It's just a freak. Some people have big muscles. I have big lungs." She took a deep breath as if to demonstrate. He looked at her skimpily covered torso.

"Not so big," he said impishly, reclaiming his deflated manhood.

"I said *lungs*!" she barked at him, punching him again, relieved that his spirits had revived. She needed to count on him. She looked over the water at the steady approach of Simon. In the brief minute or two since she had first noticed it, the Kawasaki, coming on at full tilt, had gotten close enough so that she could see clearly see Simon standing up and leaning out over the handlebars.

"C'mon," she said, pulling Brad by the wrist with one hand and pushing her mouthpiece into position with the other. Fingers intertwined, they dove backwards into the water and swam down until they were close to the horizontal mantle. They passed close over a large bed of brilliantly colored polyps, as thick as she had ever seen on the shoals of northern California beaches. Unlike them—muted shadings of dusky greens and blues—these were brilliantly colored. Closed, they had carmine lips, surrounded by brilliant orange and lavender. Open, as many were, they looked like bright orange daisies. Just beyond this bed, a giant lacy fan was being nuzzled by a magenta fish with yellow fins, whose black eye glistened through a yellow mask. As they watched it watching them, Brad tapped Teddi on the shoulder and pointed upward, and then swam for the surface, leaving Teddi to continue below on her own. She swam out past the mantle over a precipice, and allowed herself to just float there, enjoying the vertiginous euphoria, trying to hold at bay the image of Simon racing toward them.

Her lungs had just begun to ache when out of the gloom and just above her came a shape that was darker still, looming large, its wide black wings fluttering in the radiance from above—a giant stingray, harmless but ominous. Teddi backpedaled away from it, using her fins to grab onto the mantle and turn herself. Then, feeling more of a pinch in her lungs, she swam the short distance toward the cliff with the idea of pulling herself to the surface more quickly than she could swim. The ache in her lungs was growing quickly. As she grabbed on to the rock and started pulling up her foot slipped on a hard slick ridge and landed in a gelatinous mound. Before she could pull away, something clamped her leg above the ankle. As she pulled, it clamped tighter Panicked, she looked down and saw her foot disappear into the scalloped indigo lips of a giant clam that was half-buried in the angle between the mantle and the face of the reef. She tugged again and felt another painful tightening against her leg.

Panic left her. Her mind completely clear and purposeful, she let go of the rocks and bent to put her fingers between the hard brilliant lips, struggling to pry them apart. The will of the animal fought with hers, and she felt the bruising hurt of its responsive efforts as it clamped harder against her ankle. Then there was someone beside her, another pair of hands prying along with hers.

The hands pulled away from the clam's mouth and slid down under it. She could see Brad's face as he kneeled, trying to tug the clam from the grip the rocks had on it. Suddenly he stopped. He pulled his mouthpiece away, pulled Teddi's out of her mouth, put his lips against hers and blew breath into her. She instinctively inhaled. Then he climbed up the rock wall to the surface. She reached below the clam and tried herself to pull it free. She could wiggle it a little, even slide it, but it was solidly locked in place. She heard clamorous voices above her, and then silence. In her oxygen starved giddiness, she was struck with sympathy for this stolid thing with which she was locked in a death dance. Everything became hazy, distant, and it came to her as an unremarkable fact that she was about to die. In a moment her mouth would involuntarily open, the sea would enter, her lungs would fill.

Something pressed between her lips, forcing her mouth open. A strong breath pushed into her, reviving her instantly. Fully alert, she opened her eyes wide and saw on the other side of the cumbersome mask the face of Simon looking thoughtfully at hers. He turned and then it was Brad who was holding the mouthpiece to her mouth, his face a mixture of relief and worry. He took it away from her long enough to take a breath, and then returned it to her. For some minutes, they hung there together trading the mouth piece back and forth, anchored together by Teddi's foot still trapped in the clam which held on with ferocious primal force despite the fact that life was being literally stomped out of it.

Then Simon was there again, a tank strapped to his back and a knife in his hand. He went to work on the clam, sawing away at the muscle that held the two shells together. A moment later, she was free and swimming up. As she broke the surface, she pulled off her mask and snorkel. Casper was in the water and swimming toward her. He reached out as if to take her in tow, but she waved him off and swam with strong strokes toward the boat alongside of which the jet ski bobbed. When she reached the boat, she let Casper support her and help her to clamber in, painfully grating her bruised shin against the railing as she did. He pulled himself aboard after her and, taking a first aid kit from under the bench, sat next to her to examine her wound.

"I think he probably got the worst of it," he said. An angry looking bruise swelled above her ankle. "You'll be as colorful as this ocean in no time, I'm guessing." He smiled ruefully at her. "I'll get the others on board and we'll get you back to the village. I think we've had enough undersea adventures for this day."

Brad and Simon swam toward them, each holding half of the clam shell.

"Your victim," said Simon, smiling brightly and holding out the shell toward her. She took it, and the half that Brad held, and put them in a pail that Casper handed to her. She wondered how many years had gone into making its shell, saw the gash where the sharp edge of her fin had sliced into its body, and felt again an odd sense of grief that she had been responsible for bringing its long life to an end. She felt at the moment more sympathy and commonality with it then she did with her rescuer, who was now remounting his jet-ski. Brad had gotten himself on the boat and had settled himself next to her. Simon's eye went from one to the other.

"All's well then, I guess," he said.

"All's well," she said, seeing something in his expression that she was unable to read. "Thanks to you."

The smile she gave him didn't linger, making it clear that her feelings for him stopped at gratitude. By now, the others had pulled themselves aboard. Heidi sat beside her and put a sisterly arm around her.

"See you back at the village," Simon said, as he cranked up the Kawasaki. This was clearly intended for Teddi, who did not respond, occupied by her wound and the attention it was getting from the others.

"See you there," Brad called back to him in comradely tones, flush with the bond of fellow-rescuer, feeling in addition some gratitude that Teddi had not invited special attention from him, and that Simon did not seem to claim any. Simon threw off the rope securing the jet-ski to the boat. Casper started the engine and urged it around in an arc back in the direction of the village. As it swung slowly around, Teddi looked up long enough to see that the expression on Simon's face had changed from one of friendly concern to brooding reflection. She also saw beyond him, near the horizon, a barely visible blue hull with a derrick rising above it. It held her for a moment, and as she looked quickly away from it, she saw something flicker in Simon's expression, some recognition, an *aha!* A moment later, she looked at him again, and the sympathetic smile had returned. But the mask that had slipped momentarily had been only awkwardly replaced. The look in his eyes was piercing and calculating, and meant for her alone. Brad was wrong. It clearly did make some claim on her, though not what he might imagine. Seeing this, a shadow of foreboding came over her relief at being rescued. As Casper pulled out the throttle and the boat picked up speed, hitting against the peaks of the waves kicked up by a sudden breeze, she looked back to see Simon still sitting on the jet-ski, looking thoughtfully after her. When she looked again, he had turned away and put the machine in motion, heading out beyond the reef, in the direction of the blue hulk that hovered on the horizon.

XVII

Departure of the *Hespera*

SIMON'S BROODING LOOK had more staying power than the beauty of the reef, more than the terror of near-drowning. It trumped the throbbing of her bruised ankle—medicated and bandaged by Mona—as it now lay propped on a pillow on its own chair beside the dining room table; trumped Bagram's mock-heroic celebration of her "epic victory over the barbarous clam"; even broke through the distancing glaze of whatever it was he had popped in her mouth some time earlier. The eyes—with their fringe of creamy blond curls and their frame of quiet ocean, jet ski, ocean-going petroleum exploratory—the eyes dark, snake-eyed, bored into her, probed, questioned, sorted, surmised. *What did you see, what did you think, when you looked from me to the derrick-laden ship? And what did I see when your eyes slipped back to mine and slipped away as fast as they could, holding no hint of friendliness or gratitude; what rapid rolling of your mind to what conclusion?*

She lurched to her feet, upending chair and pillow, abruptly halting Bagram's elaborate description of her victory over the bivalve. Both he and Brad—from whom he had had the story—rose and called to her at the same moment. She landed badly on the bruised foot and almost fell. Brad, reached to help her. But, she brushed him off, took another step, regained herself and went the short distance to the door where she paused, said "Sorry. Need some air," and lurched out into the thick twittering night leaving behind their objections and offers of aid.

Once outside, she was uncertain where to go. She wanted mainly to flee her thoughts. Her first impulse was to go to the beach, to the shelf where she had sited the dive shop. But, that felt too exposed, so she headed toward her enduga. She could keep company with the pigs in the nearby pen for a while.

She had just come into the open, beyond the protection of the dining room and the jungle that shadowed it, when she saw a form with a familiar gait approaching from the direction of the *Hespera*, and she immediately regretted not taking Brad up on his offer to come with her. She quelled an impulse to turn back to the dining room and, instead, kept walking as if she didn't notice his approach, hoping that she was not his goal. But, his path clearly aimed to converge with hers.

When Simon was within a dozen feet of her, he said, quietly, "Teddi."

Without looking at him or changing her pace, she said,

"If you don't mind, I'd like to be alone now."

"But I do mind," he said. A long stride brought him beside her. He wrapped his fingers around her upper arm, forcing her to stop. She stiffened and turned to face him.

"I beg your pardon," she said, pulling her arm from his grasp. His eyes scanned her face, noting her alarm.

"I'm sorry. I just want to talk to you," he said, taking on the look of wounded entreaty she had seen before. It did nothing to reassure her. This was not a social call, however much he might be giving out the appearance at the moment of a spurned lover, a charade for which she had provided him adequate pretext. This was clearly all business.

She looked away, breathing heavily, the pain and her confusion getting to her. She had been a bad Mata Hari. She should have been content to play at making him jealous. Better, she should have clasped her two rescuers together to her sleek bruised body, had Casper pull out his camera, take a picture of them holding up the trophy clam-halves and her mangled leg; joined them together in celebration. What had she been thinking of? Not thinking. She saw what she saw; he saw her seeing. She took a deep breath, exhaled, turned to him. She tried to see the mask of the wounded, vulnerable man; she saw the calculating viper stare behind it, coldly violent, repulsive. Her eye skittered past him.

"Really, I just need to spend some time by myself right now," she said quickly. Then, as if to encourage and falsely placate the false face, "I mean I'm grateful and all for your pulling me out. But..." she shrugged, plastering a wry distancing smile on her face, spurner to the spurned, hoping her camouflage would do the job better than his; leaving him with just this impression of a sex hungry ditz, in her checkerboard spaghetti strapped easy-off who flopped in his lap for an afternoon, then flopped out. When she turned and took a step away, his hand was on her arm again. She stopped.

"Nothing? After we spent three hours..." His voice was low and imploring, his own mask held in place by a perfect response to her bitch-cool retreat.

She turned the screws in her mask, tightening her smile to outright sarcasm. "Is that why you came out to the reef? To stake your manly claim on me?"

They both knew it wasn't so. They played on. His viper eyes twisted up ironically.

"All that..." he gestured in the direction of the *Hespera*, "...nothing more than a handshake, eh?"

"Oh, c'mon. Sure it was fun. But, what'd you expect? I'm not the only *bird* on the island, right?"

He looked at her carefully for a moment, her question hanging on her face, then said,

"Well...okay...if that's the way you want it."

"It's the way it is," she said. "Friends?" she stuck out her hand.

His eyes scanned her face for a moment.

"Sure," he said, slidding his hand, thick and warm, over hers. "Friends. Sure you wouldn't like some company."

"I'm fine," she said, wiping her hand against her hip, as if to clean off whatever residue of pleasure might remain on it. "G'night."

"'Night, mate," he said softly.

She gave him a slight nod and turned to walk away, seeing as she did the same brooding silence in his eyes she had seen on the reef after he had rescued her.

He stood watching her for a while as she limped off in the direction of her enduga. Then he continued his own progress toward a light that peered weakly from another enduga through the heavy growth from whose shadow she had emerged.

WHAT HAD SHE DONE? she wondered as she limped toward her hut. Effectively convinced him that she actually bought his wounded lover pretense; that she was merely an unfeeling bitch, hopping from one joy ride to another? Or had she convinced him, as she suspected and feared, that she was gaming him as calculatingly as he was her? She needed to talk to someone. She looked back toward where she had left him standing, and found no one there. Instead, another figure came across the moonlit green from the general direction from which he had come. For an anxious moment she thought it was Simon himself returning. But, the figure was too tall, its gait too loose, and she realized with relief that it was Stevenson, heading toward the dining room. She hurried as best as she could to intercept him. As he saw her hobble toward him, he stopped and waited.

"I've *got* to talk to you," she said. "I'm worried."

They walked together past the dining room, toward the manioc patch where they could be out of range of prying eyes or ears. Stevenson listened patiently while Teddi told him of her encounter with Simon.

"But what could he be suspicious of?" he asked, when she had finished.

"Listen," she said. "Something happened out there I didn't get to tell you about. I hadn't really processed it—I guess I was still sort of in shock and whatever. But, seeing him just now brought it back.

That ship was out there, the *Southern Explorer*. Maybe a mile or so off toward the horizon. I could hardly see it. It almost blends right in. Anyway, I saw it just as we were heading off, and then I saw Simon give me a kind of funny look, as if he wondered what I knew about it. I think that guy that was on that ship that I saw when I was heading into Indua with Minga, the guy who broke into my cabin on the Annubis—I think he recognized me too and realized that I knew who he was. That's why he took off so fast and disappeared. I think Simon's heard about it all. That he knows what I suspect."

"You really think they're in close communication?"

"Maybe. If they're all hooked up the way it seems they might be. What we talked about yesterday. But, the important thing is I don't think Simon was coming out to the reef because of me. I think he was heading out to do business with that ship. My run in with the clam sort of waylaid him. He headed out toward it afterward."

"Really?" he said. "That's interesting. Or not. He might have completely legitimate business with them. He might have been off on a diving jaunt. That reef's a big place. Anyway, even if he is up to something, it's hard to see how he would have put all that together. I mean that your glancing in the direction of the ship would have clued him into anything."

It was a reasonable comment which did nothing to deter Teddi's concern. She decided to let it go for the moment.

"Well, maybe not. But, I'm convinced he's got something to protect. And he has reason to be worried that he spilled the beans to me. I mean, I don't think he meant to leave all that stuff on his table for me to see; you know, those geology workups with the strange letterhead. He took it out of my hands as soon as he could. Anyway, he fed me some spurned lover bull just now, and I fed it right back. I doubt he was convinced any more than I was. He thinks I know *something*. That's enough to make him dangerous."

"You're certain you're not reading too much into things? After all, this has been a very emotional day for you. You have plenty of reason to be upset."

"That may be true," she responded. "But it's not that. I think I *can* read him. And, I'm afraid he can read me too."

Stevenson stood quietly for a while, deep in thought. Then he said,

"I don't see a problem here, at least not for us. If anyone has a problem, it's Simon and Harley. I think it may be about time to bring all of this to a head."

"What do you mean?"

"I think Pop can be made to see the real nature of Stable-Birns Ltd. Your drawings might help, if I can use them."

"Oh, they're just some crude preliminary sketches. I wouldn't want…"

Stevenson chuckled.

"This is no time for artistic pride. I saw them. They're *beautiful* crude preliminary sketches. I think they might just be the smidgen of additional lubrication we'll need to get Pop over the hump. He's a man ruled by his heart, even though it's confused about some things. He likes you. He doesn't really care much for Harley."

As they headed back, he said softly,

"You know, there is also the other possibility."

"Meaning?"

"Oh, you know. That it really was you he was coming out for. After all, he had to know there was a dive in progress." He turned on her a sly smile. "He is a man, too, you know. Who knows how much of *him* is ruled by his heart?"

She shrugged off the suggestion impatiently.

THE NEXT MORNING after breakfast, Teddi resumed her work in the office. Craftsmanly self-respect made her convince Stevenson that his case would benefit from a nicely presented sketch or two, and she hurried to produce a couple of overlays that gave a clear and artistic representation of her ideas. To these she added a quick small rendering which showed a handsome view of the building as she had come to imagine it hugging the rock on which it would sit, fringed in front with bougainvillea, the giant ficus and tall palms shooting up behind it. A few figures headed down rock steps toward a dive boat alongside a newly conceived wharf. All very prettily sketchy.

She had just enough time to review her work and stamp it with qualified approval when Stevenson arrived to collect the result. On his way he had passed Ogden giving his pitch to the newest arrivals, his lament and warning of the dangers of change to the Anuap way. The timing would be perfect, he said. Ogden would be unprepared for the revelations that were coming. If the combination of Teddi's drawings and the charges he would level against Simon and Harley didn't work a revolution in him, nothing would.

Stevenson looked her work over with clear admiration. Patting her on the shoulder he said,

"You have a way with a drawing."

Teddi scrunched up her face dismissively. "Do you like it?"

"Oh, yes. Very much. But don't you think you should give yourself some credit for this?" He indicated the lack of any information regarding its origins or purpose. "Besides, for Pop, the formal touch is useful."

So she taped the drawing down again and quickly added a title block:

PROPOSED DIVE SHOP	
THE VILLAGE RESORT AT INI YANU	INI YANU ISLAND, ANUAPÚA
KAMBULA SHANGANO OGDEN PELLIGREW AND FAMILY	
PRELIMINARY DRAWING	9-23-2000
T. L. P. SHEPHERD, AIA	LOS ANGELES, CA, USA
Theodosia Shepherd	

While she did that, Stevenson cranked up the ammonia printer. Sharp odors filled the poorly ventilated room, making Teddi's eyes water as she worked. He went off with the rolled copy still reeking of ammonia.

AFTER STEVENSON LEFT, she put away her materials and made a neat roll of her sketches. She thought about going to the beach to bide the time until she heard back from him. She was also anxious to hear what Minga had discovered, if anything, about the marine terrain around the Assembly. She doubted seriously that anything new would come of it. Her own observation of the area, her study of the drawings, her own intuition all stacked up against that possibility and seemed to make nonsense out of the whole project. Unless, there was another way of looking at things.

Unable to resist, she pulled the old drawing and the fresh prints out and arranged the two beside each other on the table.

There was, she noted again, no difference between them apart from the decay and various sketchy additions that had been made on the relic. She studied the new print. A detail in the lower left section of the sheet showed the structure of the western tower and its underground supports. To the west of it, the palisade dropped down and, over the distance of a hundred yards or so, finally broke up in a jumble of boulders that ran down to the ocean. But, the terrain that the building was let down into, that contained its substructure, appeared to be the solid limestone that formed the bulk of the underpinnings of the island. It must, she thought as she studied it, have been arduous pick and shovel work; in all likelihood done by imported labor. Probably the first wave of Rajiv's ancestors and whomever else the British contractors press-ganged into service.

She turned her attention to the same section of the relic, and spent some time comparing it with the recent copy. She still saw no difference between them. Anxiously, she peeled back page after page of the copy, looking for more detail. She finally came upon an enlarged floor plan of the sub-basement, where the guide had put on his freak show about natives on the warpath. It showed the pattern of the stone floor, the slabs of rock laid on heavy wooden beams and sleepers, just as she had seen them from beneath. Above the detail drawing on the top page was a plan view of the same area, just as it appeared on the faded relic. The grid of paving stones on which they had stood showed plainly in each. She pulled a magnifying glass from her bag and compared the two drawings carefully. Among the lines defining the grid of floor stones on the relic, the lines demarcating one particular stone were somewhat darker than those of the others, thickened compared to them, as if the hand of the draftsman had idly run around them a few extra times.

Idly? Like a falcon pinning its prey with its sight, she planted her index finger on that stone. She carefully scanned the immediate surroundings. To the left, in the area where the palisade would drop down to the sea, in the hatching that indicated the surrounding rock, there was that barely noticeable open ring, like a large carelessly drawn letter *C* or the faint stain from a coffee cup. Neither would grab the attention of the uninterested and uninformed. But, together—"Bungshalo!" she exclaimed to herself triumphantly under her breath—it was a convergence that absolutely demanded attention. This intuition was fortified by her recollection of the dream she had had on the plane from Indua, of a lifted paving stone and descent into a shaft. There was also the comment by Bagram, suggesting that there should have been an indication of the escape route, if that was really what was intended. And here they were, the sketchy indication of the cave, its mouth opening seaward, and the outline of the trapdoor leading down to it. If Horatio Cook's ancestor were responsible for these as well as the leaf code, he very likely didn't have theivery in mind, after all.

She pulled from under the desk the pages which held Bagram's scribblings about the code, and the final telling phrase he had translated from it: "Sight from mother's heart through two lowest *children.*" Then she pulled out the marine chart and considered it carefully once more. There was no doubt the code, as Bagram understood it, suggested that the escape route would be located near the east end, of the building. But the telltale markings she had just been studying were found on the drawing of the *west* end,

She taped the chart to the table to keep it from curling up on her while she worked. Laying the edge of a triangle against a pin she stuck dead-center into the Heart of the Mother, she again went through the exercise of seeking alignments, with the same result as before: a line through two small islands pointed to a location on the east side of the Assembly. She was sure this was wrong.

Exasperated, she yanked the pin from the Heart and stuck it into the open water in the middle of the circle of rocks. And then it struck her. She pulled it out, quickly plotted two diameters of the atoll, and stuck the pin back at the point of intersection. Laying an edge of the triangle against it, she swept the chart to the west, the location of the suspect markings, and quickly found an alignment of two tiny low-lying islands just seaward of the buoy marking the hazardous shoal.

The line through them went right to an area near the west tower, close to where the palisade tumbled down to the ocean. She recalled from the tour several paving stones whose grout seemed to be breaking up, suggesting multiple possible causes. One in particular had creaked a little when she stepped on it. It had crossed her mind when she first noticed the thickened grout line in the drawing, but she had dismissed it because of Bagram's certainty about the meaning of the code, the meaning of "heart."

Now that all changed. Her imagination leaped into a detailed holographic vision. The shifting paving stone lifted away to reveal a narrow shaft down through the rock. A ladder leaned against its wall; better yet, steel rungs were embedded in the rock. A horizontal passage below lead to where a small vessel was concealed, kept in constant readiness—a hidden vestibule sealed off from a larger cave through which the boat and its frightened occupants would be delivered to the safety of the ocean whenever the crisis came. The hazardous shoal made it an unlikely hiding place. Those fleeing could wait there until the tide was right. Their pursuers would be looking elsewhere.

The important thing now was that Bagram had swallowed the misdirection intended by the code-maker—presumably old Brightman himself—and that, consequently, Minga was on a wild-goose chase.

Teddi quickly left the work shack and went looking for Stevenson. Instead, she found Bagram coming down the path from his hut, accompanied by two women who both seemed overcome with laughter. His voice swirled in the air, his hands fluttered at the trees, the sky, the earth, seeming to lead everyone and everything in some baroque orchestration. When he spied Teddi, she also became a member of his orchestra.

"And here's Teddi," he said with delighted emphasis. The threesome all came to a halt and waited for her to reach them.

"Teddi, these two young ladies just dropped in from the sky. Theodosia Shepherd, may I introduce you to Marlena Chumac and Isdora Dumkac." As the three shook hands, Teddi realized she had seen the women before. They were part of the group that had arrived at the Tukulu when she was there having dinner with the Guptas. She said as much.

"Right you are," said Bagram.

But her curiosity about them was quickly eclipsed by her discovery, and she said, "Would you mind if I borrow him for a few minutes?" She was pulling him away by the arm before she had fully gotten the words out, and called back, by way of apology, "We've got to talk."

"No problem, I'm sure," laughed the one called Marlena, a tall blond with a tan somewhat weathered face. "You run along now, Bagram," she called after their receding figures.

They followed a path that led in a circuit, past Teddi's enduga and through a little group of fan palms and azaleas behind which was the village's pig sty. Gola was standing in a pen with several shoats, tossing out kitchen scraps to them. She made a point of dropping some close to herself, so that the little piglets would nuzzle her before rooting in the ground. When she saw Bagram and Teddi approach, she turned her wide toothy smile toward them.

"Hi Uncle Baggy."

"Hi Gola, honey," he replied.

They stood close to the pen, their hands on the bamboo railing, and watched the girl feed the pigs for a while.

"Uncle Baggy?" said Teddi.

"As you know, I'm here a lot." Bagram smiled, then he turned to her. "You look a little breathless."

"I am, I guess. I think I've figured out something important," she said. Before she could continue, he broke in.

"Let me tell you something first. I was actually about to go looking for you. We got a call from Minga. She said that she took the *Xanadu* around that side of the Assembly we talked about, on the east. There's even a little beach that she could pull up to, just below the tower. She saw nothing there, nothing useful. She wandered around at the base of the palisade. It's just more or less a sheer sandstone cliff. She wandered up and down the beach for a hundred yards. Nothing."

"That's right," said Teddi. "That's what I think too. And…"

Bagram held up his hand, interrupting her.

"*And*, she said that she looked at her own marine chart and figured out that a line projecting from the *center* of the atoll—also, in a sense, the *heart*—goes through two of the smaller islands to a point near the other tower, on the west side."

Teddi's eye widened, she said breathlessly, "What else?"

"Nothing yet. She said she'd try to take her boat around there today, early enough to get a good look. You know about the shoals. It'll take some careful maneuvering, but she'll get close as she can. Waiting for low tide will make it easier. She'll get close enough to get a good look with binoculars anyway."

"I know what she's going to see," Teddi burst out. "At least I'm pretty sure. I've looked over the drawings some more…a lot more, actually, and I think I understand how it all works." In a rush, she told him about the results of her researches and speculations about the layout of the escape route.

She had just finished when the little girl, busy with her pigs while they talked, called out,

"Hi, Joseph."

Teddi turned and found the boy who had been keeping Elias company in the maintenance yard standing behind them. His usual wry, gamy expression had been replaced a by solemn mask, and he delivered the message in a way that left no doubt about Ogden's expectations.

"Our father has called a meeting. He wishes you both to be there."

Teddi looked questioningly at Bagram, who shrugged.

"Of course," she said.

"After you, Joseph," said Bagram. "See you later, Gola honey."

"See you later, Uncle Baggy honey," the little girl called back, pushing a nosey shoat away from her skirt.

As they followed Joseph back along the path toward the dining hall, Teddi, gesturing toward the two women who now sat in front of it, said to Bagram,

"Where are the others?"

"What others?"

"The rest of their crew. The ones I saw at the Tukulu. Who are they anyway?"

"Those two are underwater experts. Trained very well by Tito. But they went underground after things came apart and Milosevic took over. Righteous girls they are. They'll sell their services to anyone but assholes. They're our security."

"Security? What do you mean security?"

"Didn't anyone tell you?"

"About what?"

"About how we're going to hold the place once you get us inside."

She recalled a bit of an earlier conversation.

"Somebody, maybe Shepherd, said something about having 'cover.' I thought maybe he was talking about those tough brothers of his."

"Too dangerous. For them. These are nice reliable mercenaries. Security professionals. They know how to get a job done."

She looked at the two women, extravagantly female in their bikinis, stretched on chaise longues with tall drinks in their hands.

"They're working right now," he said. "Sentinel detail. Protecting a high-level meeting. Right ladies?"

The two women smiled and nodded, holding up their drinks.

"And the others?"

"They're all multi-talented, but *their* special expertise is lockdown. They'll join us when the moment is right."

Teddi suddenly had a new sense of respect for her cohorts. The plan might be comic-opera insane, but it was being prepared with tactical astuteness.

"Hard to believe," she nodded again at the two women.

"No more than you," he said, smiling.

Looking out at the channel, Teddi saw a familiar blue shape sliding through it. The Hespera was moving out under power toward the breakwater. The sight of that alarmed her. While she knew that Stevenson was going to lay out everything he knew about the dynamic duo to Ogden, hoping by that to bring about his conversion, she hadn't reckoned on the idea that Simon would also be made aware of her suspicions about him and his partner. She now imagined that Ogden had simply gone ballistic and ordered them off the property, citing their suspected role in the attack on her as cause.

"What's going on?" she said, frightened by this prospect, grabbing Bagram's arm and pointing to the boat as it slipped through the channel.

Bagram followed the course of the trimaran for a while. He shrugged.

"I have no idea. They're heading out. Why?"

Just then, Stevenson hailed them as he came along the path from the maintenance yard on his way to the dining hall.

"What's going on, Stevenson?" said Teddi, when he had caught up to them.

"What's the problem?" he said, noting the anxiety in her voice.

She pointed to the *Hespera*, now disappearing behind the dining hall.

He grunted.

"Guess Simon's decided to pull out. At least for the time being."

"Why," she said, a panicky catch in her voice, "What did Ogden say to him?"

He looked at her intently, then understanding her concern said,

"Not to worry. He didn't spill the beans. I told him what I had to tell him. I was right. Pop's with us now. And he's no fool, our father. He didn't need me to tell him that he had to keep things close to his chest for now."

"So what…?"

"Seems that Harley was caught in the act of trying to bribe a state minister."

"Oh?"

"Right. And he picked the wrong one. He thought he was on safe ground. He thought that because there was a family connection and, of course, he was hooked up with Ogden, that a little palm greasing was in order."

"Uncle Jack?"

"Right you are. Kambula Amatosi Jack Sprague, Minister of Commerce and Tourism. Jack has no compunction. He just called in the gendarmes and off Harley went to the pokey. He'll be indicted in a couple of days. Then he'll be out. And, of course, he'll find the right official to pay off and that will be that."

"So, why's the *Hespera* leaving?"

Stevenson thought for a while.

"That you would have to ask Simon. My guess, though, is it's probably a sort of twofold move. If there's any real nastiness, the Hespera's a sitting duck parked right here. Better to get it out of Anuap waters. And then there's the oil ship you saw yesterday. Maybe, if you're right about this, and now I think you probably are, he's going to hook up with his buddies—or his bosses—on it to get their help with Harley. I suspect that those guys, whoever's in control, know all the right buttons to push, even if Harley himself doesn't."

"Sounds about right," said Bagram.

"How long will they hold him?" Teddi asked.

"A couple of days or so, maybe less. Not long," said Stevenson.

"Oh," said Teddi. her sense of relief from the initial anxiety aroused by the *Hespera*'s departure immediately dashed. The thought of Harley out of jail and the two of them dwelling resentfully on their loss, plotting their revenge, two cold-hearted mercantile pirates on the loose, sent a chill through her.

"I'll see you inside," Stevenson said, and headed for the dining hall.

Teddi and Bagram followed the path toward it, passing the two bikini-clad, pina colada sipping sentinels.

"Greetings ladies," said Bagram, cheerily.

One responded with a casual, "Ola, Bagram."

The other, the one Bagram had earlier introduced as Marlena, raised her sunglasses in a more ardent salute.

"Soon my love," she said, breathily.

Teddi looked at Bagram.

"Security, huh?" Teddi said with a smirk as they passed out of earshot, doubting this was mere tactical theatrics.

"Also my girlfriend," he smiled and shrugged impishly.

XVIII

Leaving Ini Yanu

Whatever Stevenson had said to Ogden after he had left her that morning, whatever the current circumstances— and even her drawing—meant to him, the change in him was clear. The meeting that took place in the dining hall was attended by the entire adult extended family of Ini Yanu. Casper headed the younger contingent. Alyosius and Elias sat near him, seeming to have been quickly initiated into a new station in life, as had Joseph who also sat with them. The manioc-planting elder gave ceremonious import to the event as the last remnant of the former generation, despite his vacant smile.

Ogden gave an account of the immediate circumstances that had brought him to the decision to sever his connection to Stable-Birns Unltd. and free himself from the seductions of the grand resort. He joined to that his other, even more radical, conversion: his abandonment of the dream of maintaining the racial purity of the indigenous Anuaps and the priorities that came with it. It was all pretty much according to Stevenson's calculations. Teddi didn't try fathom it.

"And anyway, what racial purity?" Ogden said with a chuckle, displaying his rather *un*indigenous profile. He seemed a man suddenly liberated from an old useless burden, in whom there arose a new youthfulness. That did not keep him from acknowledging and making clear to the others the somber business that they faced, and the need for caution. For the present, word of his change of heart was to go no further than that room.

These warnings, however, did not interfere with his mood of celebration. Mona broke out a stock of an elixir made from the root of a plant known locally as *mafulu*, the intoxicating pepper, boiled down to a dense syrupy substance that tasted like clay, made palatable by mixing it with coconut milk. She did that now in a bowl reserved for the purpose. The bowl then went from hand to hand around the room. A sense of gaiety took over. The children were brought in. The long dining tables and chairs were pushed to the edges of the room. A boom box appeared from which came Anuap style reggae-zydeco, and everyone, including the old uncle, was up and dancing.

At a break in the music, Ogden raised his hand and called for their attention. Finding Stevenson across the room he walked over to him and took his hand in his own, then turned to the others.

"It should be said...I should not simply slide over what you all know," he said, his voice low and full of feeling. "I have, in my stubbornness caused much pain to those I love." He waved off objecting voices. "But, that's over. Now..." he said, his voice breaking, wrapping his arm tightly around Stevenson's shoulder, "...now, all of my children will have a home in Ini Yanu." Stevenson's face clenched and he lifted a hand over his eyes. At the thought of Priya finally reconciled with her grandfather, Teddi's own eyes filled with tears.

AFTER THE SUDDEN AND decisive conversion of Ogden Pelligrew, Teddi wondered if all of the elaborate plotting that she and they had been caught up in was still necessary. Certainly if someone with as much influence as Stevenson's father—not to mention Amatosi, and Shepherd's adoptive father Rotanu—aligned themselves with the sentiment for change, then others, or enough of them, could be brought along without the risks the AMNUP steering committee's subversive scheming entailed. But *No!* said Stevenson, and *Very much no!* said Mona.

Ogden spoke an earnest warning. "These old buzzards are

tough old birds and they control much power and know how to use it. They are not," he said—and he knew this because, as he said, he was one of them, "afraid to throw the military against any opposition. There will be no effective demonstration, no mass appeal to conscience, no media presence in the world, *without* the theater you've proposed."

He bent his head and looked away, overcome for the moment with the perplexities of his own situation. "I cannot now imagine," he went on, "how I would have done what only yesterday I thought I must do. We are in a more dangerous situation than you know. We have no real options *except* to make theater of it." He paused, took a deep breath, and looked at them with a soft smile before going on. "And, of course, we'll likely, very likely, fail anyway. We might all just end up in the pokey," he said.

To which Mona responded,

"Don't you worry. If you do I will bring you some good fish soup to keep your old bones strong." He turned a warm smile on her and pressed her fingers to his lips.

It was decided that the next morning Marlena Chumac and Isdora Dumkac would fly back to Indua where Minga would be ready to employ their diving skills to investigate the sea cave she had found. As Teddi looked over the drawings again later that day, she had not an iota of doubt that they would find things more or less as she thought them to be. There was too much pointing in that direction. Unless, of course, Bagram was utterly wrong and the code he himself was so sure of *was* merely meaningless doodling. But her faith in Bagram was as strong as her faith in herself. It all added up to the exciting expectation that by the following day, or the next at the latest, the details of the cave and the entire escape route would be revealed; that they would then be able to lay their plans for taking the Karoja, the august Assembly of Chieftains, hostage. She said as much to Stevenson.

"We can only hope," he said, with a cheerless smile. "Time isn't exactly on our side."

THEN A DAY PASSED of empty waiting during which Teddi did everything she could to put her brain on hold. She took a swim before breakfast, and then lolled on the beach with Brad and Van and Heidi. In the afternoon, she went to the airstrip on Guma to see them off. She and Brad exchanged e-mail addresses, promising to hook up some time or other, some place or other; hugged, kissed, and said goodbye. Likewise, she and Heidi assured each other that each would always have a place to stay in L.A. or Leipzig. Dinner brought some new tablemates. That night, she lay in her steamy enduga rescued from time to time by the plop of a coconut in the soft sod from obsessing about caves and secret passages.

The next morning brought a set back. Awakened early by a knock at the door, Teddi found a glum faced Stevenson announcing that he had news from Minga. They walked in silence to the rock above the beach. The early sun glistened prettily on the water. High above, a macaw screeched. A flight of pelicans scumming for breakfast made a few speculative dives, then flapped off around the headland. Teddi struggled to be patient while Stevenson collected his thoughts.

"Lovely, isn't it?" he said, after a while. He lifted his arms as if to embrace the scene, took a deep breath, and sighed.

"You're making me crazy, Steve," said Teddi, her anxiousness to hear Minga's report clouding over any interest in the setting.

"Well, maybe I'm taking this too hard," he said, turning to her with a tolerant smile.

"What?" she said sharply.

"I mean, even if there's no secret passage, we've gained something. Pop's with us now. That means, whatever big chief Iratago might want or think, at least three kambulas are on our side. One of them, Uncle Jack, being a pretty big fish himself. Pop's got plenty of clout. And with them, maybe more will come out." He breathed deeply again.

Hearing this, Teddi sank in disappointment.

"At least for us, personally," he went on, "even if that fails, we have a success. My darling father and darling daughter, and my darling wife will no longer be estranged. I'll be able to bring my family here. That is great. And," he said, turning to her, raising a prophetic finger, "you can't account for time. Maybe we're the moment that announces the change of tide. So. We can be patient, if we have to be."

He sat Buddha-like, hands folded in lap, a beatific smile spread on his face. Teddi wanted to throttle him.

"Are you going to tell me what happened?" she growled.

His smile fell.

"What happened. Okay. Minga took Bagram's two diver ladies in. They made a good show of it, spear guns and everything. They got into the cave. They saw a cave, nothing else. No boat, no sign of entry to a passage. Nothing. Minga being Minga didn't buy that. Sometime around midnight she and Sanjay putted around the other way in a dinghy from the Tukulu's wharf so she could check it out at low tide. Sanjay tied off just out of reach of the perilous shoals. There was enough moonlight for Minga to work her way through them to the cave. It was the high low tide, so the water hadn't dropped out completely. But there was plenty to see. She had a good torch with her."

"So?" said Teddi, overcome with impatience.

"So? So nothing. Same, same. The ladies saw nothing. Minga saw nothing. They went back to the Tukulu and bandaged up her cuts. Sounds like she made a nice mess of herself on those rocks. She called me just a little while ago, just before I came to you."

"So, that's it?" said Teddi.

"Seems like it might be," said Stevenson. "Minga sounded pretty discouraged."

Teddi's mind raced. If Stevenson managed to find something of a silver lining in this, she could not. Perhaps he was right, that there were other kambulas, secret AMNUP supporters, who, seeing Ogden's conversion, would come out; that even if the Karoja voted the way it was expected to, nothing is finally carved in stone, including carvings in stone; that the turning of the tide might be slow, but that it would eventually turn. And anyway, he was right about one thing. He had his own personal reason to be happy in the promised reconciliation of his family. But for Teddi, the discovery of the passage had become a purpose of its own. She worked at not being distracted by doubts, at holding in her mind her picture of the cave and its relationship to the Assembly building, going back to the holographic image of the escape route her imagination had cooked up the previous day, refining it.

"I'll find it," she said abruptly

"Yes?" said Stevenson, doubt evident in his voice.

"Being in the cave at high tide wouldn't help. You wouldn't see much unless the passage opens right into it. Unlikely. Going in at low tide and just looking around might or might not be useful. I know what I need to do. I'll go myself."

"With that?" Stevenson said, pointing at her shin, still livid where the clam's shell had closed on it.

"I'll manage," she said. "When's the next plane?"

XIX

A Sea Cave

THE MID-DAY SUN lit up the reddish rock of the Assembly on the palisade above them with golden highlights. The tide had turned and started running swiftly out. Minga struggled to hold the *Xanadu* in position without surging disastrously forward into the barely visible arc of jagged shoals or careening backward into the two islands that stood close together like a pair of ragged canine molars less that fifty feet to her stern.

Marlena Chumac, in a yellow and blue short-legged wet suit, tank attached, mask on forehead, reviewed the plan with Teddi. She would go in first and survey the interior of the cave for a place where they could set up until the tide receded; from which they could study the changes in the interior for anything that might suggest a hidden vestibule. They would have a long time to make these observations. The lowest tide, when the entire surface of the interior would be open to their inspection, was still several hours away.

"Go!" said Minga, putting the engine in neutral during a lull of the tide. Marlena quickly pulled down her mask, gave Teddi the thumbs up and went backward over the side. Teddi watched her blue and yellow clad form with its silver canister as she made her way toward the cave, pause, adjust direction, move forward, then disappear below the surface.

Five minutes later she re-emerged, breast stroking through the choppy water. Teddi and Minga helped her aboard.

"We should do fine," she said. "There's a little shelf a little to the right of the opening. The tide's dropped enough by now so that we can rest there."

They readied themselves while Minga pulled the boat into position, holding it as close as she could to the cave mouth. Marlena quickly went backward over the side and headed for the cave. Teddi, wearing only goggles, slid into the water and swam close behind. When Marlena slipped below the surface, Teddi did the same and followed the glow of her torch and the glint of sunlight off her tank, as she guided them around the jagged minefield of submerged rocks, then under the arch of the cave mouth into its interior gloom. They broke the surface together, and Marlena led the few strokes to the shelf she had found.

Still under a foot of water, it was large enough and with enough headroom so that they could sit side by side, legs dangling over its edge. The little sunlight that made its way through the opening glowed eerily in the mass of water that filled the cave, as if it had its own deep source. Marlena turned her torch to the dome, lighting up starfish and algae and iridescent clusters of mussels. Shoals of little fish swimming nearby glittered in the reflected light.

Marlena swept the torch slowly around the exposed cave, particularly the area closest to the Assembly building, opposite the mouth. They speculated on what it might conceal, what its drippings, its sea life and encrustations might or might not disclose about what lay behind it.

When conversation fell off, Teddi asked the question that had been on her mind ever since Bagram had introduced them, about her and the whole crew of mercenaries that he had enlisted.

"Why are you doing this?" she said.

Marlena smiled. "I wonder about you too. You mean besides for money?"

She shifted her position so she could sit up further on the shelf and rest against its back wall.

"Okay. I go first. For one thing, Bagram is very persuasive man."

"Have you two been together long?" said Teddi.

"Ha. Not much together. Just every once in a while. But, yes, for a while now. Long enough for me to know he's big troublemaker."

"You mean like his troubles with Ceauşescu?" Teddi asked, recalling what he had said about his sudden departure from Romania.

"Oh yes. And all the other brutal bastards like him," replied Marlena. "Some here too, no? For me, after Tito died and the whole country fall apart it got to be just too horrible. Much too horrible."

She slipped into the water, pushed off and floated face down for a while. then paddled back and clung to the ledge.

"Listen," she said. "I saw one best friend have another arrested and tortured because suddenly he became enemy. Just like that. No reason except one is Serb, one Croat. Can you believe this?" The elegant feline curves of her face inverted into a deep scowl. "How can one live in this way? I could not. I left."

With other friends who could not live that way—Serbs, Croats, Montenegrins, Bosnians among them—she made her way first to Kuala Lumpur. All trained divers, they took on salvage contracts, and did deep-sea geological surveys.

Hearing this, Teddi immediately thought of the engineering report that Simon had been quick to take out of her hand and bury in a folder.

"Do you know Harley?" she asked.

Marlena at first didn't make any connection.

"The guy who was going to build the resort at Yanu," Teddi explained. "The guy that just got arrested for trying to bribe a Minister. Harley Stable-Birns."

No, Marlena said, she knew no one by that name. But she and her friends did some deep-sea work—setting core bits in sediment—for an exploration company near Papua that had initials like that.

"S-B Deep Sea Exploration Unlimited, I think it was. Something like that. Oil."

"Omigod! It's gotta be Harley!" cried Teddi.

Marlena went on to say that it was her recollection that this company contracted with exploration rigs, ships that hired out to do the actual exploration. They were middlemen, not themselves ship operators.

"And you know what else is funny?" Marlena continued, following her own thought, seemingly immune to Teddi's excitement. "That cute pilot, the Aussie that jockies the plane to and from Yanu? He didn't recognize us. We know he didn't because he tried to hit on us. But we recognize him. Guess what? He's very versatile. He flew the chopper that brought us out to the *Southern Explorer* to do our dives. Small world, ya?"

"*Southern Explorer?*" said Teddi, barely able to contain herself.

"Ya, that's right. It's their ship, S-B, the one they use. You know something…?"

Bungshalo! Dots not just connecting but colliding by the second.

"It's even a smaller world than you think. I'll tell you later. C'mon," said Teddi, pushing off into the water which had now fallen well below the ledge. "Let's find this damned passage and get out of here."

Without waiting for her or her torch, Teddi began feeling her way around the perimeter of the cave, pulling herself along on its outcroppings.

Marlena quickly threw the beam of the torch ahead of her, showing her the way. The water was by now well below the shelf, far enough down so that Teddi could touch bottom and keep her shoulders above water. She made it all the way around, going slowly, feeling everything within her reach, hoping for a telltale crack or crevice. Her fingers slipped over crusty knobs, over slimy bulges, into crevices. But nothing announced itself as worthy of special attention, either visually or by touch. It took her nearly an hour to make the circuit.

"Nothing," she said, deflated for the moment with frustration.

"Neither could Isdora and me. Maybe there is no…" she began.

"No. Don't even go there!" said Teddi sharply. Her voice echoed eerily against the dome, grown larger with the drop in the tide.

She started a second circuit, and then she heard it. It sounded at first like steam beginning to whistle from a kettle, then it became a hiss, then a steady hum. They both turned their heads in the direction it seemed to be coming from. By this time, the water had dropped to mid-shin and the hum had become a hollow, agonized moaning that changed in pitch as the tide changed direction. Marlena turned her torch toward the sound. In the area that had already caught their attention, just opposite the cave mouth, the beam found a large shallow egg-shaped bulge. It was about three feet across at its widest and five feet high, encrusted like the rest of the cave with colorful splotches. The bottom bellied out, and a ragged ridge formed a margin at the top which seemed to separate it from the surrounding rock. Despite that, except for the sound that clearly came from that direction, it was not strikingly different from other features of the cave. The eerie repetitions of hissing and groaning continued as the receding tide sloshed slowly up and down its base.

They moved toward it carefully, so that the sloughing of their shins through the water wouldn't muffle the sound. When they were a few feet from it, they heard another sound, a quiet intermittent knocking, as if from a soft collision of objects rocking in the tide.

"The boat!" Teddi said in a tense excited whisper, as if the cave itself had treacherous ears. They moved closer, stepping carefully through the now ankle high water. The moaning stopped, leaving only the rhythmic repetition of the dull knocking sound and the soft sizzle of the tidal flow draining down the crevices of the rock face. A pile of rocks, rolled in by immemorial tides and dropped in depressions along the cave wall, emerged at the base of the bulge. They worked together to pull them out of the way and fully expose it.

In the few minutes it took to clear them away, the tide had reached its lowest ebb. They stood on the slick exposed floor of the cave. Water drained from under the bulge in a thin sheet that rushed against their feet. Crabs came out from crevices to peer at them. The only sound was the murmur of the tide behind them, beyond the cave mouth, their own breathing, the sizzle of water streaming down the rock, and the rhythmic knocking that seemed to come from behind it. Then came a final soft thunk, and the sound ceased. Water continued to drain out over the rock for a little while, then it too stopped.

Teddi picked up a grapefruit sized stone and, stepping back a few paces, threw it with both hands at the wall further to the right. She picked up another of about that size, and threw it at the section of the cave wall from which the sound seemed to come. The difference was obvious: the first clearly was higher pitched than the second. She repeated the experiment with the same result.

"You're right!" exclaimed Marlena. "It's hollow back there."

They slid their fingers behind the crevice that crawled up one edge of the rock. They pulled and tugged together. It didn't budge.

"It's too heavy for us," said Teddi.

"Not just that," said Marlena. "It's sort of glued in place with all this stuff." She pointed to the buildup of coral on the edges of the stone. She grabbed a rock and began pounding it against the accumulation. Chunks flew away with the impact. They tried pulling it back again. Still no luck.

"We need something," said Teddi.

"Like a crowbar, maybe. I'll swim back to boat and see what Minga has." Teddi went with her to the opening of the cave. The tide had now fallen well below the threshold, exposing a slick slope that went down to the hazardous shoal. Minga sat in the *Xanadu* fifty yards away, mostly hidden from view behind the two large rocks. They waved at her and she waved back.

"Back in ten minutes," said Marlena. Leaving her tank and mask with Teddi, she eased her way down the slope and then pulled and picked her way through the jagged rocks to open water, where she swam toward Minga with long strokes.

Teddi turned back into the cave and stood for a moment facing the object of her assault. With its clinging fringe of sea life and dark gleams, it stood like a primitive sculpture, challenging her to reveal its meaning. She picked up another stone and again attacked its crusty edges, working feverishly to breaking down its mute resistance.

XX

A Discovery

STRETCHING HER ARMS OVERHEAD with the stone between both hands, she pounded away at the top edge. After some minutes of this, breathing hard, hands and arms aching, she dropped the stone which, now that the tide was coming in again, splashed and thudded dully. Wondering what was taking Marlena and the crowbar so long, she lifted the torch and inspected her work. What had been an accumulation of choral and sea flora was now reduced to a jagged edge. A pair of small eye stalks suddenly appeared in her beam, bending in slow speculative motion; pincers reached out, opened and closed beside them, and tiny claws grasped the broken ridge. The miniscule being, the size of a penny, pulled itself up, acknowledged her in a slow turn to the right, then, as if escaping from a long imprisonment, dashed in a quick line down the flat face of the rock, paused where the bulge began, scampered halfway over its curve and dove, disappearing in a little splash between her feet. Taking the appearance of this tiny creature as a positive sign, she reached up, hooked her fingers over the edge and felt them slide into empty space. Her heart leaped and, damning into silence the yelps of her tender shin, she planted a foot on the belly, grabbed onto a nearby knob of rock, and struggled to pull herself up to peer into the crack. *C'mon, Marlena. I need you*, she thought as, trembling with the effort, she pressed her cheek to the jagged edge and lifted the torch so its light shone into the crevice.

Through a three-inch long ellipse, a half-inch wide at the widest, she could see to a varied surface that seemed to be several feet away. At first, all she could make out was a grayish rocky texture. But just at the edge of her field of vision she clearly saw a rusty spike poking from the rock, with the curve of a heavy rust-corroded chain link encircling it. In a frenzy, she dug two fingers into the crevice and pulled back with all her might. Tugging and jerking violently at the unwilling rock, she thought she heard a grinding, as though it was beginning to move and part. Then a voice said,

"Would this help?"

Her blood froze.

She turned to find Simon standing just inside the cave mouth, dressed in a wet suit, a crow bar dangling from his hand. Next to him, also in a wet suit, was the crewman from the *Hespera*, Jeremy, the one who had tumbled onto her when she first came aboard.

"Is it treasure you're looking for, Teddi?" said Simon, smirking. To his companion he added: "An adventurous bird, this one." The face of the young man, that had seemed so sweet the last time she saw it, was now unnervingly hard and hollow.

"Where's Marlena?" said Teddi, her own voice steady despite the dread that his had instantly aroused.

"Marlena?" he said after what seemed like minutes. "Oh, the tall blond bird? No need to be concerned about her, Teddi. She's quite comfortable, I should imagine. Before long, she'll be all cozied up in her own luxurious stateroom on the *Hespera*. But you? You, my girl, are not quite so comfortable, now are you?" Simon motioned his henchman forward.

"Just hold out your wrists, now Teddi, and let Jeremy make a nice little bracelet for them. We need to make sure that you stick around while we do a little research here." Jeremy advanced, plucking from his belt a plastic tie. Teddi backed away along the wall of the cave.

"There's no use, you know, sweetheart. We're two big tough men and you're one little woman." Both of them moved toward her. Her feet went out from under her on the slick surface, and she went down, banging her head hard enough to daze her. They were both on her and when they were done, her hands were strapped and a nylon rope held her feet tightly together, its other end jammed into a crevice behind a knob of rock to which it was tightly knotted. They set her so that her back rested against the rough wall, across the cave from the rock she had been pounding on. Then the two men turned back to it. Simon handed the crow bar to Jeremy.

"Just jam it in there and see if you can get it to budge," he said. "Right about here, sweetheart?" he smirked at Teddi, pointing to the area of the gap through which she had seen the chain.

The shock of the blow had given Teddi a sudden dreamy sense of clarity.

"I know what you've been up to, Simon," she said in a sort of sing-song, smiling strangely at him.

"Oh, do you? Just what might that be?" he said. Jeremy forced the crowbar into the gap and they both threw their weight against it. There was a grinding sound as the rock broke free of its attachments.

"That resort was just an excuse. If you have your way you'll destroy that reef with oil rigging."

"Could be right about that. We all have our alibis, now, don't we? What's yours?" he said, pausing briefly to turn an expression that was half-smile, half-snarl on her, before urging Jeremy on to more effort.

Another pry, another tug, another groan. The rock pulled away a bit from the surface it rested on, then thudded softly back.

"Think we've got it," said Jeremy, with a wink in Teddi's direction.

"I always thought…you were a clever girl…Teddi," Simon said, breathing heavily from the effort. "But…progress…y'know. The world needs it." He paused, catching his breath, and looked at her directly. "And that, my girl, is what this place has always been about. I suppose you've heard about the sugar plantations.

Your mistake," he said, returning to his labors, "is that you're trying to defy progress. That's the problem with me bloody Abo ancestors, including m' poor Moms, rest her soul. Just couldn't get with the program."

The two men pulled at the now liberated stone. It came away slowly at first as they threw their weight back, exposing only a thin crescent of an opening along one edge. Then gravity started to work in the other direction and the stone threatened to fall on top of them. Shifting position quickly to support its weight, they eased it down on the cave floor. Simon shined the torch into the now fully exposed opening. Resting on the bottom of the thick encrustations of the coral choked passage lay the decayed remains of a coracle, a rusty chain still leading from its prow to the spike Teddi had seen through the crack. Exhilaration at the fulfillment of her calculations overwhelmed her dread. Everything, so far, was as she had imagined it. It was evident, as Simon moved the light around it, that the passage continued back for some distance and then stopped at a vertical wall that rose up beyond the limit of the tunnel's roof. She could just make out the iron rungs fixed in it. Ignoring her restraints, she struggled to her feet.

"I want to see!" she shouted with childlike pleading. She managed a few short hops before her feet went out from under her. She landed badly, crashing her shoulder and cheek against the stone. She lay still, overcome with pain and frustration, bitterly brought back to the reality of her situation.

"Well, well," said Simon, ignoring her completely. "How very interesting." He headed into the opening with the torch. Reaching the back wall, he pointed the torch upward above his head, and was quickly swallowed up in darkness. A shifting and grinding noise came from inside, followed shortly afterward by a thunk. Then he reappeared.

"It seems," he said, smiling, "that what we have here is a secret passage leading right up into the belly of the house of the National Assembly. D'you know that, Teddi? 'Sthat what you expected to find? Or were you and goldilocks out there just doing some casual cave hounding?"

He was quiet for a moment, then he came over and sat beside her, tight against her. She squirmed away.

"You see," he said, slipping a muscular arm around her shoulder, grasping her thigh with an iron grip so that she couldn't move. "I also know a bit about what *your* alibi is. Always 'ave." A sound escaped him she had never heard before, between a bark and a wild cry. He grasped her chin with his other hand and forced her to look at him. "Always 'ave, you see?" He slid his hand slowly over her cheek and down along her throat, let the other slide up along her thigh, throwing her body into frenzied revolted jerking, which brought from him more of that ghoulish laughter.

"Ah, there was a moment..." he said. He released her and she fell into a heap on the cave floor, which pulsed with the now foot deep slush of the rising tide. He studied her with amusement, a few more barks bursting from him, before he continued.

"Of course Harley—not always so clever, he is—got 'imself into a bit of a slam, you see; sort of got his conk rubbed in it; looked for a moment like the knobs were really going to give the job to'm. Couldn't let that happen. That called for my quick departure from Yanu day before. I know how sad that made you. Anyway, he got out of his depth a bit. Seems he tried to suborn your chummy seatmate on the plane from L.A.—old Amatosi. You remember him, don't you? Anyway, he sort of got his signals crossed, did old Harley. Should've been speaking to someone else. But I got there, got it all straightened out. Turns out Harley's *proper* connections exert quite a bit more power. They saw to it that all of the charges against him were deferred, which around here is as good as dropped. And then our primary connection, who happens to be quite high up—oh, yes, quite—in this beastly little government, pointed out that since the bloke Harley wrongheadedly tried to deal with is unwilling to play by the rules, unlike that other bloke from your crew who was quite happy to do his fair share...Ah! Don't know about that, do you? Well you will. In any event, since he had the goods on us and could really bolex up our affairs, it stood to reason that we should get the goods on him, or at least his ruddy playmates. Give us a little leverage that might come in handy. So, here we are, playmate. We already know a lot. We know all about what you were carrying, even if you didn't. And I think you didn't. Had our man been a little quicker, or if you'd made yourself more receptive to our arrangements, you'd have been saved a heap of trouble. We could've had some fun together, girlie. Even more than we had."

At this repellent reference, Teddi tried to crawl away, but he twisted the rope that bound her feet around his hand and held her tight.

"Who spilled the beans? you'd like to know. Oh, I bet you would. Well, you're resourceful. And you'll have a little time to think about things now. Why don't you try that one on?"

He let go the rope, turned away from her and sloshed a few steps toward the passage opening. The water had risen again to calf-height, causing the coracle to resume its rocking.

"Well, here," he said, gesturing toward it, "we have evidence that you have become a full participant. Conspiracy against the state is not highly thought of, not even in a backwater like this. You've taken a big risk, girlie, you and your friends."

He turned back to Teddi, and stood over her. She tucked her head to her knees and tried to go as far away, as far into herself, as possible.

"So, now that that's settled," said Simon, "let me tell you what's going to be, so as to allay your anxiety a bit. We're going to go back to the *Hespera* and call in the authorities. We'll take your girlfriend in too—she needs a bit of first aid, I'm afraid. In the meantime, you'll just stay here and ponder things. I know you 'ave a lot to think over. And I trust that you'll figure out how to keep you head above water while we're gone."

He again fingered the rope that held her feet together.

"I think you have enough slack here to ride out the tide, just in case it takes us a while to get back. I suggest you rest, conserve your energy. You might have some hard work ahead. I may not make it as timely as I did the last time you got yourself into such scurvy underwater trouble."

The height and surge of the tide had grown in strength so that Teddi could not keep her head-tucked position. She struggled to get to the cave wall against which she could at least rest for a while. She scooted on her bottom, pushing against the slimy floor with her heels, aiming herself in the direction of the ledge where she and Marlena had first sat. With each push, the surge of the returning tide knocked her to her side. She ended up crawling on her knees, pulling herself along with the heels of her bound hands. So involved was she in this struggle to reposition herself that it was not until she heard again Simon's strange animal guffaw, that she realized they were still there, entertaining themselves with her misery.

"Here, here," she heard Simon's voice behind her, between those barks of dismal hilarity. "Physical comedy just isn't your thing. C'mon Jeremy. Show some manners. Give this poor girl a hand." A hand slid between her bound hands and wrenched them out from under her. She was dragged along, half-floating in the tide, the plastic straps biting sharply into her wrists, and dropped face down in the water beneath the stone ledge. She struggled to push herself out of the water and get herself turned around with her back against the wall. Looping her arm around a nearby bulge of rock, she managed to steady herself against the shifting surge.

SHE WAS ALONE. There was a long timeless stretch, measured only by the continually rising tide. As she worked at adjusting to its changing motions, agonizing questions came to her—immediately about Marlena, what had happened to her; what had happened to Minga; what would happen to them all. The water rose. She clutched jagged handholds between the bleeding palms of her bound hands. When she floated up to the level of the shelf, she pulled herself onto it with her elbows. She rested for a while, until the water filled the little space, forcing her out, pushing her higher toward the dome of the cave. The air space shrank and she thought, dully, that this is how it is going to end. Was that what they intended, Simon and Harley: to leave her to drown in this cave? Maybe they *were* that vicious, but what would that gain them? No. They meant to frighten her, not to kill her. They needed her. Dead, she accused them. Alive, she was a witness for the prosecution. No. They hadn't abandoned her. Her dull acceptance of an unreasonable fate was now overcome by an unreasonable hope. They'd been intercepted. Rescue was on the way. As the water rose, she clung to this logic.

Something bumped her from behind. Her body twisted with involuntary panic and she found Marlena's tank bobbing coyly in the wake made by her sudden movment, its mouthpiece bobbing close to it, both just out of reach. She fought down her panic and paddled carefully to keep them from moving further away. When she reached them, she slid her arms around the tank in a bear hug, letting it carry her weight with its buoyancy, resting for a minute with her cheek against it. Then she held it far enough away so she could read the gauge. It still held a half hour's worth of air. Gripping it with her legs, she reeled in the mouthpiece and slid it between her teeth. Then she clamped the knob of the valve between her sore palms, turned it just enough to test the air flow, then closed it again. The water had risen to the point that there were barely three feet between its surface and the dome. Letting the mouth piece go, she resumed her embrace of the tank, buoyant with its half hour of life.

A TUG AT HER FEET startled her. As she recoiled from it, she realized that they were now free. She felt another tug at her hands, and then they were also free. As the air tank, no longer caught between her bound hands, started to drift away, she wrapped it tightly with her arms. Fearfully, she opened her eyes to a sharp light through which she could just make out the shape of a face mask and, above it, a headlamp and a blue-hooded head. A hand grasped one of hers, pulling it from the cannister. She frantically jerked it back. The masked figure swam off a few feet, across the tiny pond that was all that remained of the water surface inside the cave. A hand reached across it toward her. The light shone on long feminine fingers, on the small pool that rippled between them, on the small glistening rutted dome, what was left of the cave interior, to which a starfish clung like a piece of rusty corroded iron. Suddenly abandoning the tank, Teddi reached toward the hand. It grasped hers, and she let it pull her down into the water where it released her. Then she swam, following the figure and the beam of light. A minute later she rose gasping into blinding sunlight. She felt a touch at her elbow, and turned to find herself looking at a confused image that quickly resolved into her own reflection in the glass of a diving mask. A voice ahead of her called,

"Teddi!"

She turned abruptly and saw Minga, leaning from the stern of the Xanadu Reefer, a dozen or so feet from her. She turned back and looked into the smiling face of Isdora Dumkac, Marlena's cohort whom she had last seen stretched out on a chaise longue on Yanu. Her mask now perched on her forehead, Isdora swam close by, lightly supporting her.

"I'm okay," said Teddi, and the two of them swam the short distance to the boat where Minga helped them both aboard.

Minga pulled up the sea anchor and got the boat under way. Teddi settled herself in the chair beside her. Once the *Xanadu* had come around and pulled clear of the threatening rocks, Teddi gripped Minga's arm.

"Where's Marlena," she said, sudden panic in her voice. "Something happened to her. Did you see?"

"I saw everything. That's how come Isdora showed up. Not to mention everyone else. Don't worry. She's safe. We got her. And, by the way, your little boy toy too. You'll see."

With that, she pushed the boat up to full throttle, tore around the pair of islands behind which she had anchored earlier, and then out to sea in a wide arc around The Mother. Once they were clear of it, Teddi could clearly see the outlines of the *Hespera* a few hundred yards in front of them.

"Hey, what's going on," she shouted in Minga's ear. Minga half turned and gave her a wicked smile. Teddi looked again and saw floating off the stern of the big trimaran a frumpy little wreck of an ancient runabout that she knew could only be the *Rama*.

XXI

Aboard the *Hespera* Again

LOOKING OVER THE LOW GUNNEL of the *Hespera*'s afterdeck, Teddi could see two blond young men in surfer trunks reclining on chaise longues. Rajiv, emerging from below deck, hurried over to help her up the ladder. Leaving Isadora on deck with her two cohorts, Minga and Rajiv took Teddi below where they found Bagram with Marlena and two of Bagram's other hired guns. They lounged in easy chairs, their Kalashnikovs on the floor beside them. Marlena sat in another easy chair, hands planted regally on its wide leather arms. Bagram sat behind her. A lamp had been brought close and was trained on the back of her head. They both looked up as Teddi appeared.

"Teddi," shrieked Marlena, leaping up, despite Bagram's sharp "Don't move!"

She walked unsteadily over to Teddi, and the two women embraced. The back of Marina's head sported a pale tonsure in the middle of which was a raised purple circle with a red gash running through it. From the gash hung a black thread with a needle at the end.

"I was in the middle of surgery," said Bagram, plaintively, as he also hugged Teddi. He turned Marlena around so she could see his handy work.

"Ouch!" she said.

"But, I don't feel a thing," said Marlena, smiling and hugging Teddi again.

"That is because, my darling, your skull is about as loaded as it can be with lidocaine, not to mention what the rest of you is loaded with. Wodka I think."

Rajiv, who was quick to reconnoiter the possibilities of the *Hespera*'s galley, produced drinks and snacks, and the three of them sat in elegant chairs while Bagram completed his surgery, planting kisses on Marlena's skull as he worked.

"What happened?" said Teddi.

"Voila," said Marlena, pointing to the area that held Bagram's attention. "What happened to you?"

"You first," said Teddi. "You're in worse shape than I am. I just got a little scared, is all."

"I got clobbered with that damn crowbar, then they tape me up with duct tape and throw me into their smelly rubber raft while, I guess, they went to mess you up. I had no idea. I just lay there in the bottom of the boat and thought about geese."

"Geese?" said Bagram.

"Yes, geese, mister psychiatrist. Geese fly. Good thing to think about when you're taped up in the bottom of dinghy with blood gushing out of skull. You have problem?"

"Not I," said Bagram, tightening a suture. "I like practicality in my women."

"So, that's it. I lie there. They come back. They shove me around a little but don't throw me in drink. Maybe I'm hostage. How should I know? Anyway, next thing I know, we're bump up against this tub, then there's a lot of noise and bouncing around, then I'm falling through water and thinking I'm going to be dead soon. Then Baggy's pulling me up by the neck of my wet suit. Then he's sticking his needle in my head. So," she held up her hands and nodded conclusively.

"They probably thought of you more like evidence than a hostage," said Teddi. She recounted for Marlena Simon's stated intention to supply Iratago with his information about the secret passage and AMNUP's goals, to be used to discredit them; and, very likely, to bring legal action against them for plotting against the state.

"A little payback for Jack's having Harley thrown into the slammer. But, it serves their purposes anyway," said Rajiv. "I think maybe we've caught a lucky break here. If you're done messing with this poor lady's skull, maybe we should conduct a little investigation."

Leaving Marlena in the company of her compatriots, he led the others into the workroom where Simon had first introduced Teddi to the proposed resort, and inadvertently let slip clues regarding their true purpose. Everything was as she had last seen it, except for the stacks of paper neatly arranged on the table, geological reports evident among them.

From the other side of a door that opened off the room to the left came a muffled bellow.

Teddi looked at Bagram who said, "Here, let me show you. Time for a little well-deserved *schadenfreude*."

He opened the door, revealing a small storeroom. A narrow beam of late afternoon sun shot through a transom, choosing for its target a shining pinkish mass surrounded in pale brown that Teddi quickly saw was Harley's forehead. Adjacent to it, in half-light, was Simon's forehead. The two men were cheek to cheek, as if they had been tangoing together. But their embrace was involuntary. A thick band of duct tape swathed their lower faces and mouths. An arm and hand of each was also taped together, and more tape went around their waists and their legs, binding one of each together, completing the tango effect. More grunts came from the men, and they struggled together against their restraints, their eyes flashing wildly in the direction of their three observers. Minga broke into unrestrained laughter. Teddi looked at them blankly: Simon no longer desirable, Harley no longer threatening. The only feeling she had for them was exactly what she would have had for defused bombs.

"That's awful!" exclaimed Minga between guffaws. "You're torturing them,"

"Our friends have their own way of doing things," Bagram said merrily, gesturing over his shoulder toward the two men who lounged in the salon. "They're well practiced. I wouldn't argue with them."

More frantic grunts came from the two men. Teddi looked around the room and saw that they were not alone. Against the opposite side of the hull, sitting down more or less comfortably on a large coil of rope, but well gagged and tied, were the two crewmen of the *Hespera*, one of whom was Jeremy, Simon's henchman in the cave. He turned his face away when she looked at him. Seeing him did for her what the sight of Simon and Harley had not done. A sudden volcanic rage, fueled by the magma of all the indecencies she had suffered, rose up in her. She flew at the man, grabbed him by the hair and drove his head against the steel plate of the hull.

"You dick!" she screamed. "You don't treat people like that!'

Blood poured from the wound the impact had opened and she smashed his head against the hull again with all her force before Bagram reached her and pulled her away. She gasped for breath through her tears. The man cowered, and pulled as far away from her as he could.

"Let's kill the bastards," said Minga throatily, leering at the two tangoers. "Or maybe we should get that fat friend of theirs to just sit on them." She took a long step toward them and made as if she were about to launch a boney knee at them. They cringed back as far as their restraints permitted.

"Easy, easy," called Bagram to the two excited women, caught himself between rage and laughter. He gently herded them out the door and closed it behind him.

"Don't worry. They'll get what they deserve."

"Hope so," said Minga, breathing hard.

"Whew! Where'd *that* came from?" said Teddi, astonished at her own violence.

"Oh, I can imagine," said Bagram.

"I don't do things like that."

"Really? Looks like you just did. And they do deserve it, that and worse. But, all in good time."

They turned their attention to the papers arrayed on the table. There was that obnoxious logo, the dunce's cap that doubled as an oil derrick dominating the world, and the possibly damning letterhead. She could read it now. It did not make the clear link she had hoped for, a direct nefarious connection between Harley and Simon and the *Southern Explorer*. But it kept the door to it open.

"Let's get to the bottom of this," she said.

"Right," said Bagram. "A treasure hunt."

"Oh, wonderful. Treasure hunt," said Minga, grimacing at the piles of papers. "What might we be looking for?"

"Okay. Here's the deal," said Rajiv. "We've long known that our Minister of Mineral Resources, also Kambula Iratago—one of his other hats—has argued against many safeguards of the natural environment. He's been especially irritated about the activities of the various reef protection organizations. It turns out that there's strong evidence that reefal slopes harbor substantial oil fields. I've done some research. Big strikes have been made in these kinds of formations along the Indonesian plate limit, to mention one."

"I know something about this," said Teddi. "There was some stuff about it on the sheet I was looking at before Simon jerked it out of my hand."

"Then we should find that here," said Rajiv, and went on. "A few months ago, Amatosi happened to be sailing off The Mother when he saw the *Hespera*, which he knew was Harley's boat, sailing before a fast wind toward the marina. And who should be sitting on the deck, cooler in hand, laughing with Harley, but Iratago."

So, that was what Simon meant when he said they had other friends in high places, thought Teddi, her mind running in tandem with Rajiv's account.

"Of course, that ministry's only a secondary portfolio for our Chief of Chiefs. But, it provides a hook into Harley's and Simon's scheming, which their little joy ride together on the Hespera certainly seems to confirm. But, you know, it only suggests connivance, in addition to all the other circumstantial stuff…their trip on the *An-*

nubis—owned by Iratago, in case you didn't know—the attack on Teddi on same. Etcetera, etcetera. All good reasons to suppose, but we need more than that to nail him down.

"So. Okay," he said, gesturing to the piles on the table, which Minga had already started digging into. "Here's our opportunity. Evidently these guys were careful record keepers. Let's see what we can dig up."

Minga flipped open a manila folder neatly labeled ENVIRONMENTAL GROUPS, and studied something in it. After a minute, she said:

"Those guys," she said, gesturing toward their captives in the store room, "must have figured they really had something when they got the two of us together. My guess is that flyboy snitched that you," she nodded to Teddi, "came back here, to Indua, this morning, and they put a tail on you. And they already had an eye on me. Look." She handed Rajiv the sheet she had been studying. It was a list, and she pointed to the first item on it.

"See?" she said. "Right on top. Prime suspect."

Teddi looked quizzically at Rajiv.

"NaSoRP," he said. "National Society for Reef Protection."

"Environmental group, huh?" said Teddi. "So?"

"So?" repeated Minga. "So, you are looking at it."

"You are it?"

"And," said Rajiv, "so is Stevenson, so is Shepherd."

"And a whole lot more. We're officers. But as far as today's events go, I am it. They had a tail on you, they saw us hook up. Oh boy. A two-fer. They could nail NaSoRP and AMNUP at the same time. Plenty of evidence to go around. What a gift to present to Iratago."

"Yah. Served us right up. Not surprising he wasn't worried about a little collateral damage," said Bagram, giving Teddi a rueful smile. "You're right. You were only supposed to suffer for your sins, not die. They needed you as evidence."

"Now we're pirates and kidnappers to boot," said Rajiv. "We'd better make the most of it."

"Very good," said Bagram, rubbing his hands industriously together. "What's the plan?"

"Well," said Rajiv, gesturing to the neatly arrayed table, "there's *our* trove. Just fortunate these boys weren't expecting guests. They've sort of prepared the way for us. If there's one thing that's better than a crook, it's an orderly crook. My guess is that we'll find in this heap enough to accuse our would-be accusers. Let's divide it up and see what we come up with."

Whereupon they fell to work, methodically excavating the piles of folders and paper in front of them.

"Aha, some treasure I think," said Bagram, shortly, and spread out the folder he was studying for the others to see.

Titled GENCOMM it contained a neatly organized stack of memos in front to back date order, containing summaries of conversations and other communications with someone most often referred to as "the General," but occasionally as KI. There could be no doubt that these pertained to a single person, nor who that person was. KI obviously stood for Kambula Iratago. The memos told of the means and methods of circumventing the environmental laws of Anuapúa, the very laws that the General, a.k.a. KI, was charged with protecting. There were also notes about an AMNUP conspiracy in the works, and mention of various of its principles.

"Oh, lookee!" exclaimed Minga, "a paragraph just for me—'particularly meddlesome turncoat.' That's me all over." She cackled gleefully.

Teddi, in the meantime, had come upon a folder with the label YANU REEF—SCHEMATICS. In it were charts that, even with her slight knowledge of geology from Civil Engineering 101, she understood to detail the geological composition of the undersurface of Yanu Island and its incorporation in the reefal slope.

"And, look at this," said Rajiv, holding up another folder. It was labeled PET RES PROJ and contained statistical analyses and summaries of petroleum yield projections in billions of barrels, correlated with the difficulty of recovery, and projected dollar returns under varying market conditions over the next twenty years.

The four of them stood in a tight group at the table, surveying the contents of the three folders thus far discovered. Standing between Minga and Teddi, Rajiv flipped through the pages of one folder after another.

"Looks like more than a little finger in the petroleum pie," said Bagram.

"Right. But, we need something more to really stick it to them. Let's keep at it. Time's awasting," said Rajiv.

They returned to their independent researches. Finally, all the folders and stacks of loose paper had been handled and studied, and nothing more of significance turned up.

Minga nudged Teddi,

"Hey, why don't you go beat those guys up some more? Maybe they'll spill all the beans." Teddi rolled her eyes at her.

Bagram had begun pulling open the drawers of the bank of filing cabinets beneath the desk. Three of the four drawers opened easily. All were empty, their yield was evidently what they had already poured over. The fourth did not open.

"Could be that's the baby," he said.

"We need something to break it open," said Minga. "I'll go look."

She had taken a step toward the door when she heard a voice beyond it saying,

"Hey, Marlena. Look what you left in your boyfriends' boat. Maybe you can find a good use for it."

"Sanjiji!" exclaimed Minga at the sight of Sanjay, a ghoulish smirk on his face, offering a crowbar to Marlena.

"We've got one," she said, turning a quick smile on Marlena as she dragged Sanjay and the crowbar back to the office with her. In a minute, the face of the drawer was torn away, and its contents quickly stacked on the table. In a folder labeled DISPURSALS, they found what they were looking for.

"Here," said Rajiv, sliding his finger over a dated list with names and numbers. The eyes of the others followed.

"The noble Jason Featherstone," said Sanjay. "It seems he's been well provided for."

Interrupted by an occasional variant, the name filled most of a single ledger sheet as the recipient of some twenty payments, all for 10,000 USD.

"And who might that be?" asked Teddi.

"That would be our beloved leader, Kambula Iratago," said Rajiv, his finger continuing to travel smoothly down the list. Then another name appeared above his finger. His hand stopped suddenly. He gasped. A grunt came from Sanjay. They looked at each other sharply, and, before Teddi could make out the name, Rajiv abruptly closed the folder.

Too abruptly. Both Teddi and Bagram looked at him, then at Sanjay, whose attention seemed to be occupied elsewhere. Another quick disturbed glance then passed between Rajiv and Sanjay. Teddi was about to ask what they had seen when Rajiv pre-empted her.

"Well, that's all we need," he said clearing his throat, the triumphant tone he aimed for struggling with something else. "Let's pack this all up and make sure it stays safe."

"Problem?" said Bagram.

"Ha," said Rajiv, recovering quickly, "Many problems. The main one now is how we're going to turn this to our advantage."

"That seems simple enough," said Bagram. "We've caught him with his finger in the honey pot."

"That may not be enough," said Sanjay. "He still controls the army. There's nothing to say that he won't simply stage a coup, when it comes down to it. He'll have plenty of backing among the old guard."

Teddi again saw a look go between him and Rajiv.

"What is it?" she said, feeling a sense of alarm, definitely not liking what was in that look.

"Well," Rajiv said, ignoring her, responding to Sanjay's cautions, which precisely mirrored his own. "We'll just have to let that be whatever it is for now. We have three days until the Karoja meets in full assembly. That's how much time we have to work it out as best we can. For now, let's get this tub secured and get ourselves back ashore."

"What about those guys?" said Minga, pointing to the storeroom.

"One of them's got a pretty nasty gash," she smiled at Teddi, who flinched a little, but only a little.

"Oh, god, yes. I really went crazy." The tremulous undercurrent in her voice taking on the character of a suppressed giggle.

"Never fear," said Bagram. "The doctor is in. Just a little stitchery." He added, grinning maliciously: "The question is, do I operate with or without lidocaine?"

XXII

A Different Place

BY THE TIME RAJIV guided the *Rama* with Teddi and Bagram aboard into its slip in the Indua marina, the last long rays of the sun had retreated and a humid dusk had settled. The others had remained on the *Hespera* to continue sorting through the revealing documents. Afterward, Minga and Sanjay would come in on the *Xanadu*, bringing Marlena with them. Isdora, with Bagram's two other mercenaries who remained on board, would take the *Hespera* and their prisoners into international waters, well out of immediate range of Indua and easy pursuit.

Footlights dramatically ignited the palms surrounding the Princess Augusta, lending the old hotel an ethereal glamour. A blue micro-taxi was parked near the end of the jetty. A woman stood leaning against it, smoking a cigarette. She wore a slinky silver dress with spiked pumps to match. She appeared to be waiting for her partner for the evening to emerge from one of the upscale yachts that surrounded the frumpy *Rama*. As they approached, Teddi saw that it was Joyeeta Gupta, who flashed a quick look at Rajiv, who rolled his eyes in response. Throwing away the cigarette, she got into the front seat beside the driver, and the three others crammed into the back.

"You look lovely tonight, sister," said Rajiv as they drove off.

"Special events call for special attire," she said over her

shoulder. "Got word that a gang of Iratago's finest was hanging out on the Indua road. Better to look a bit touristy, I thought."

"If that's what you call it," said Rajiv with a chuckle. Then, seriously, "A change of venue?"

Joyeeta nodded. "Everyone else is on their way up to the house."

Teddi looked from one to the other for a clue to the meaning of this "house." Both ignored her. Joyeeta continued: "Steve's coming in by plane about now. He'll meet us up there. He may even be there. I just got a call from Shepherd. He's already there with his brothers." They were, in fact, not headed in the direction of the Tukulu. The entire atmosphere, including Joyeeta's extraordinary attire, breathed crisis.

"Shepherd's been in touch with Jack," she said. "It seems his contacts have given him nothing useful. There's no way of knowing what Iratago cooked up with that Harley guy. But, for sure, he pulled levers to get Harley out quickly, even though he still faces indictment. Apart from that…" she shrugged.

"Well, he's not going to be doing anything for a while," said Rajiv, a sense of pride at the success of his operation sounding in his voice.

"So I'm told," said Joyeeta, reaching back to take his hand. There was no sisterly carping now. They were clearly a team. The quick glance and sympathetic smile she offered Teddi, made it clear that, for the moment at least, she was not included.

Just then, a column of jeeps filled with Anuap soldiers roared past them and out of town in the direction of the Tukulu. Joyeeta watched them race by.

Turning back to Rajiv, she said, "I got the word. Poor Shep." Another quick sad smile fell on Teddi as she turned once more to face the front.

Poor Shep? Teddi thought.

"What the devil is going on, you two?" said Bagram, twisting suddenly in his seat to look at Rajiv, asking the question that had been hovering in Teddi's mind ever since that silent communication had gone between Rajiv and Sanjay in the office on the Hespera.

"Do you expect us to rely on our interpretive gifts here?" he said grumpily, squinting at Rajiv through his thick lenses.

Teddi's own agitation was heightened by the fact that Bagram—Uncle Baggy—also was being excluded. She was not comforted when Rajiv, looked back at him with pursed unsmiling lips and said in a flat, alien voice, "We'll get to that. Patience. Please."

Bagram harrumphed, and slammed himself against the seat back, jarring her and further raising her sense of apprehension. The world had turned upside down. She realized how much she had come to depend on them, on their close connections with each other, and with her. It was bad enough that they were in flight from enemies. But being excluded was unbearable. Worst of all, being held at a distance by Rajiv. The feelings that she had first had an inkling of when they met in Indua, and which had begun to speak in a clearer voice after she definitively cut things off with Simon, muttered their own sense of betrayal.

The little car turned into the center of town, climbed through streets that became narrower and narrower, populated with fewer and fewer buildings, until they found themselves on a road that wound through a hilly woodland. After a few minutes, they turned off into a gap in the trees, and followed an overgrown road to a gate at the end of it. As the car stopped before it, one of Bagram's people, a rifle slung over his shoulder, stepped from behind some bushes, unlocked the chain on the gate and pulled it open. Bagram nodded to him as they drove through, making it clear to Teddi that their being there did not in itself mystify him.

After going a short distance along a dirt road, they arrived at a clearing. Two cars were already parked there. One was a Mercedes with government plates, which startled Teddi for a moment. Then she realized who it must be.

"Uncle Jack?" she said. Rajiv and Joyeeta replied with a nod.

A man approached from a house that stood a short distance from the clearing. It was a large old Victorian, capped with a widow's walk. No doubt elegant in its time, it was now almost disastrously run down, a fallen porch at its rear and a partially collapsed section of a lower roof revealing the lack of attention it had been receiving. A light coming from a pair of basement transoms backlit the man so that it was not until he was quite close that Teddi saw that it was Stevenson. Joyeeta threw open the door and ran to him, stumbling in her spiked heels. They stood together with their arms around each other while the others climbed out of the little car. Rajiv in the meantime had hurried off toward the house.

"I hear you had a terrible time today, Teddi," Stevenson said ruefully, as she and Bagram approached them. "A nice adventure we've cooked up for you."

At that moment, footsteps came from behind him, and Shepherd emerged from the gloom and hurried by with an elder who Teddi quickly recognized as Uncle Jack. He paused as he came close to her, but Shepherd pulled him along, giving her a short nod as they rushed past. The two got quickly into the Mercedes, which immediately pulled away and headed for the gate.

"That's okay," she said to Stevenson, watching in perplexity as the car drove off. "I survived. My problem right now is nobody's telling me what's going on."

The look on Shepherd's face as he had hurried past her hung in the air, ghostly and despairing. She looked from Stevenson to Joyeeta. She realized she had never seen them together before, and could see now how closely they were joined; at the moment, most strongly through a common sense of devastation. Clearly, whatever it was, something very bad had happened which, however much she might be involved in its consequences, still drew a tight circle that kept her out. She turned to watch the car as it pulled through the gate. Bagram also looked after it and nodded, seeming to come to some conclusion of his own.

"I think, perhaps, you need to take some time for yourselves," said Bagram. "I'll be in my little hovel when you need me." He turned to walk off, then paused. "If you've got a cabin ready for Teddi, I'd be happy to show her the way." He added, with forced joviality, "Not that much to choose from if memory serves."

"That would be great," Teddi said quickly, taking Bagram's readiness to withdraw as a cue for her to back off also. "I'm falling on my face anyway."

"No wonder, after all you've been through," said Joyeeta, taking her hand and kicking off her glamorous heels. "But, I'll take you. I told Madhu to set one up for you. Come on." And laughing, the clinging dress swishing against her as she walked nimbly barefoot over the rough ground, she led Teddi off toward a group of low blocky buildings that could just be made out in the trees.

In the short time it took them to walk to the little building the stresses of the day finally had their way with her and she was overtaken by the exhaustion that she had thought she had used only as a pretext for excusing herself. When Joyeeta flicked on the harsh light in the little room, the only thing that mattered was the bed, its sheet already turned back. She barely took note of the distinctive animal odors bleeding through a recent swabbing of bleach, or the bowl of fruit on a small dresser. Her daypack stood beside it, and she thought briefly about digging out something to change into. But, as soon as she sat on the bed she keeled over. A moment after her shoulder hit the mattress, she was asleep. Joyeeta slipped the light blanket over her, turned out the light and left.

A KNOCK AT THE DOOR awakened her. It was followed by Rajiv's voice. She was up in a second, feeling for the switch on the lamp beside the bed. The funky odor that she had at first ignored stung her nostrils. As she rose to go to the door, her eye went to her daypack and the bowl of fruit.

"Give me a minute," she said. She stripped and ran for the shower. Finding the tap dry, she turned back for her bag, and discovered beside it a bowl of water, a washcloth and a small towel. She dipped her hands into the tepid water, splashed herself strategically with it, quickly toweled off, then dug in her bag for fresh underwear, a blouse and a pair of shorts, thanking Joyeeta under her breath for thinking to bring it for her. She could hear the impatient pacing of the man outside the door. She grabbed a mango from the fruit bowl and bit into it, dousing herself with juice, as she went to open it. Rajiv stopped and turned to face her.

"Teddi," he said, a broad smile replacing the coldly somber mask she had last seen him wearing.

"Rajiv," she said, returning his smile, her relief enormous, and taking another bite of the mango, sending a trickle down her chin and arm.

"Hungry," she said, holding it out to him. He took a bite.

"Good mango," he said, wiping juice from his chin with the heel of his palm, holding her eyes with his own.

"So, are you going to fill me in now?"

"I want to show you something," he said. "Take a little walk with me."

The half moon was high. There was a slight chill in the air, a slight cooling breeze. Everything was still, except for the occasional chirrup of a cricket. They walked back to the parking area and then turned toward the path leading to the main house. Rajiv stopped before what seemed to be a shoulder high clump of weeds just beside the path.

"It's amazing how things grow here," he said. "We try to keep this cleared. I send a man up here every week just to do that. As you can see, there's not much else we're able to do." He gestured to the house and its obviously broken-down state.

"Do you own this place?" she said.

In answer, he pulled out a pocketknife and cut away at the foliage. The moonlight showed what seemed to be a thick block of concrete with some lettering on it. It was, Teddi saw, a ground sign of some sort. It was not until he shined his flashlight on it that she was able to clearly see the letters that stood out from its face. When she saw what it said, it took her breath away:

R. J. SHEPHERD CENTER FOR INTERCOMMUNAL STUDIES

She looked down at it for a while, unable to speak, feeling as if she were looking at a gravestone, like the one that had been installed at her father's grave only a few weeks earlier. The name on that was the same, except the initial letters were spelled out: Rupert Joseph

Shepherd. He had hated the name "Rupert" and never used it with his friends, some of whom expressed astonishment at the unveiling ceremony that she had orchestrated. But, she knew he also felt a peculiar sense of loyalty to it, which she took into account when she designed the stone. Here, below the three inch high oxidized brass letters, was an equally discolored brass plaque. It read:

> DEDICATED TO COMMUNICATION AND UNDERSTANDING
> BETWEEN OUR COMMUNITIES.
> JULY 31, 1973

And below the plaque, in smaller cut letters:

> FOUNDING COMMITTEE
> GOPAL S. GUPTA, ESQ. ~ MME. SAMHITA GUPTA ~ R. JOSEPH SHEPHERD
> MME. RUTH PINKERTON (DECEASED) ~ KAMBULA AMATOSI JACK SPRAGUE
> KAMBULA ROTANU REGINALD PINKERTON, ESQ.

Teddi's eyes filled with tears as she scanned the names.

"Your dad?" she said, pointing to the first name.

"Yes. And Steve's and Minga's uncle, and my mom, and Shep's mom," he went through the list. "And, of course, your dad. He never really left, you see. He put up a lot of his own money, found more when we needed it. The whole thing fell apart, of course. They did what they could," he said, pointing to the names.

Teddi's eye fell on the bottom row, the one name Rajiv had not included. She pointed to it. "Shepherd's step-dad?"

"Yep. A barrister, like my dad. They had an office together. Seems Rotanu was the one who convinced Joe to go for the bar."

There was something in his voice that suggested special import. And then it struck her, shocking her with a sense of the obvious, the inevitable, that had been murkily, lazily swirling around, ever since the attack on her aboard the *Annubis*, in the guise of the kind old man on the bus who had directed her fate. It was not a coincidence after all. It had been carefully plotted by someone who had foreknowledge of her movements. She now clearly understood why Sanjay and Rajiv had suddenly become so secretive aboard the *Hespera*; why Joyeeta had uttered that tragically Delphic *poor Shep*, and why Shepherd had thrown her a blank, haunted look as he went off with Amatosi. She understood that this discovery had been for them an excruciating shock. It was Rotanu, Shepherd's mother's brother, his adoptive father, the absent man. It was *his* name they had found on the payoff list below Iratago's. That was why Rajiv wanted her to see this—to see both the depth of the betrayal, and something more she could not yet fathom.

"Is he the mole?" she asked, knowing already the answer.

"You see why we needed to not talk at first," he said, turning to her. Then, with a short laugh, his face contorting into a Janus smile, "There's more to come."

She nodded, sensing a somber pleading in his voice, the something more. She impulsively lifted her fingers to his lips, which he held and pressed against them.

He turned off the flashlight and pocketed the knife. They stood close together for a while, the moonlight throwing their tandem shadow onto the sign and the growth that clung to it.

XXIII

A Confession and a Plan

THE SCENE THAT GREETED TEDDI when Rajiv pushed open the door to the basement room stirred an uncanny memory of Tintoretto's "Last Supper," with its flights of dark angels, as if hewed out of the mother rock of a cave. But, the radiance was completely missing: no eternal flame, only one bare bulb glowed dimly from a tarnished chandelier. And, instead of the man whose halo poured munificence onto adoring apostles, the shadows at the far end of the long table admitted just enough light so that Teddi could make out the defeated face of the man who had once buoyantly enticed her aboard the *Annubis*. He looked up as she entered and trained his eyes on her for a moment, before looking down again at his hands lying listless on the table before him. Strangely, she felt no anger, not a bit. There was no longer any doubt that this man, the curiously missing character in the drama of the last weeks, this Rotanu Reginald Pinkerton, had played a conscientious and foul role in a plot in which she, among others, was a deliberate victim. He was a mole, a betrayer, a turncoat; he was the Judas in this painting. Thanks to Rajiv, she knew all this—what she had been guessing at for days—before she entered. And, thanks to him also, whatever rancor she might have had stored up in her—and she might have had plenty given her specific suffering due to his deceptions—had wonderfully dissipated. But for him, her presence itself was enough to make him bend his head in deep embarrassment, though there was little if anything in her that asked for it. She had caught in his look toward her a sense of hopelessness. She couldn't do anything about that. She stood quietly, her eyes sliding over the rest, who also sat solemnly at the long dimly lit table. A strange calm seemed to absorb them also, like a wallowing of tide between ebb and flow. Joyeeta sat beside Stevenson, their arms intertwined on the table. Shepherd sat at the far end, at right angles to Rotanu. She recognized the three larger men beside him as her rescuers from the randy rugby players who accosted her in the club the night of her arrival; and whom she now understood to be Shepherd's cousins and step-brothers, Rotanu's children. Bagram, Minga and Sanjay sat beside each other with their backs to her. Out of the corner of her eye she saw Amatosi, Uncle Jack, leaning against a heavy stone fireplace, arms crossed over his chest. When she turned toward him, he raised his head and nodded, then fell back into his half-lit, reflective pose.

The stillness and silence were eerie, and if it had not been for Rajiv behind her, who moved closer to her, grounding her in the moment, she would have felt herself to be an alien onlooker. As she felt the comforting radiance of his body behind her, she became aware of an absence. Ogden surely should have been there. She looked quickly around again to make sure she had not missed him, vaguely wondering if his absence was due to his having, suddenly, reverted.

A minute later the void was filled, the question answered, by the sound of a car, its engine cut, crepitating over the nearby gravel drive and grinding to a halt. The others heard it also. A car door closed, quick steps grew louder as they came over the gravel, then up the stairs onto the porch, through the front door, pounded across the floor overhead, then down the stairs to the basement. Then there was Ogden, just behind her, moving around the table, exchanging greetings. He went to where Amatosi stood at the fireplace, said something quietly to him, then turned toward the table and came closer.

If one could have looked into his mind at the moment, one would have seen, along with other emotions and thoughts that raced in competition with each other as he struggled to compose himself, one tableau superimposed on another. Over the current scene, there was the picture he had looked at least once a day for twenty years, the one that hung in his office, of his army pals, his life-long friends, and the strange diversions that brought them to this moment: three present—himself, Amatosi, Rotanu; one dead, Bokanjo Claudius Cook, father of Teddi's dentist, Horatio, and so, in a strange way, instrumentally present; one—Iratago Jason Featherstone—the enemy, the hound that now hunted them, and so, also strangely present. Through that screen he and Rotanu now peered at each other. It was Rotanu who spoke first, addressing Ogden in a voice as warmly melodious and beguiling as Teddi remembered it from her trip with him on the bus to Indua.

"Greetings, my brother, Shangano. The turtle has made many turns in its wanderings since we spoke last."

"The turtle's shell has coarsened and deepened," replied Ogden, with wry intonation, "and its cries to the dolphin and its young have softened."

They smiled at each other, both aware of the out-of-placeness, the ironic misuse of these ancient formulations of salutation after a long lapse; the real and deepening divisions that had frayed their bonds over the years; the battering of cross-tides in just the last few days that had landed them on the same shore. It was the best language available.

"*Bungshalo!*" they both gutturally exclaimed at the same moment, and laughed. The others held their silence.

"You're a crazy old man, Reggie," said Ogden, his lean face pulling together, caught between tears and laughter.

Rotanu looked at him, his own face undergoing a similar change, then said,

"The ocean is deep, Oggy...as you know." The other nodded and pulled the palms of his hands over his eyes. Rotanu went on, his voice shaking: "I had no idea how deep my ignorance of myself was. But, a man cannot be absolved for not knowing himself."

During this exchange, Amatosi had left his retreat at the

fireplace and approached the table. Now, standing just beside Ogden, he spoke up.

"There will be opportunity for more of you self-recriminations later Redge. But, time is not our friend at the moment."

Addressing particularly both Ogden and Teddi, he said: "Kambula Rotanu Reginald Pinkerton is our brother, our friend, our cohort. He has gone away, and now he is back. He is contrite. Much more importantly, he has a plan we can put to use to reverse his mistake, and maybe even turn it to our advantage. Miss Shepherd, Teddi, I so much enjoyed your companionship on the long flight from Honolulu. Despite that, you know now, I'm sure, that I was a fraud. You were, as I'm sure you also know, subject to two plots: one, our brother's aforementioned mistake; the other, our connivance with our brother Horatio Cook, that brought you here. I wish circumstances now were happier, so that you could more easily forgive me. It has been your misfortune to be caught up in our woes, against your will. I must own my part in that and ask your forgiveness. I will leave Rotanu and the others to make their own amends."

Rotanu turned to her and nodded, a bleak grimace on his face. From the others came muttered assent. Amatosi went on: "I'm sure there won't be any disagreement when I say you would be perfectly right if you now chose to simply walk away and say good riddance to us all."

Teddi took it for the ploy it was and without skipping a beat responded, "Not a chance."

Having gotten through this necessary demurer, a smile spread on Amatosi's face. He took the hand she reached out to him between his own and patted it, expressing his real gratitude.

At the other end of the table, Rotanu stood up. "Peace, brother," he said, lifting one hand toward Amatosi and bracing himself against the table with the other. "This should be mine to say. That is, if, after what I've done, I even have the right to speak. Who knows where we would be now if I had not stuck my foolish hand in the middle of things?"

He looked around to the others, his eye finally resting on Teddi.

"As Jack says, now is not the time for me to maunder about my sins, let alone try to explain them. But, Miss Shepherd, daughter of my..." He stopped, overcome. There was a breathless quiet while he recovered. "I take all blame on myself, if things do not work out well. There is a plan. I wish I could undertake it by myself, but...not possible. You are the daughter of the man who was my greatest friend. As things turned out, I have made myself his enemy, and because of that, yours. I have put you in the greatest danger."

He paused again, his face now showing neither pleading nor regret as he looked at her, perhaps seeking in her the fragmented remains of the friendship he had betrayed. The room was thick with the breath of the past. The pause seemed to go on and on, belying the need for urgency. When Rotanu spoke again, it was as if he were addressing a ghost, speaking directly to Joe Shepherd, with Teddi serving as a medium.

"So. One more great risk to run. The sun will be up in two hours. We have till then to lay the ground."

"Let's go through it again," said Rajiv. "Teddi needs to hear the details."

"If I may," said Rotanu to Teddi, "I will fill you in on our way. That is if you can tolerate sharing the ride, and the risk, with one such as myself...if you will be generous enough to trust me."

He turned to the others. "I think we should quit this place immediately. It is quite likely that the fruitlessness of Iratago's stakeout of the Tukulu will have stimulated his imagination, or that of his surrogates. We are only lucky that we have not had a visitation here yet. In fact, it is a little unbelievable that word of Jack's arrival there with Shepherd and my resulting...ah... *extraction* hasn't come up on their radar. We may be surrounded as we speak."

Turning to Bagram, he said,

"If that's so, can your folks draw them off, do you think?"

"They would be positively thrilled, I'm sure," said Bagram. "Madcap wild goose chase is part of their stock in trade. Who else don't you need with you? Maybe a couple of you guys," he said, pointing to Shepherd's brothers. "I'll go along for the ride. Then the rest of you take your chances. Scatter to the winds. And I agree. We should move right now."

"Let me take the lead," said Ogden, avid for any opportunity to make amends for his own misguided dealings. "If they're out there, they must have seen me come in. I expect they'd have a special interest in me."

Within fifteen minutes, the mercenaries, accompanied by Bagram and Shepherd's three brothers, had piled into micro taxis and were heading away from the R. J. Shepherd Center by various routes. No sooner did they drive off than engines could be heard starting up beyond the road. The others waited until the sounds of cars scattering over the hill, pursuers and pursued, faded. Then they, also, quit the Center. Teddi rode in the Mercedes with Amatosi and Rotanu.

"You are sure about this?" said Rotanu, after he had filled her in on the details of the plan. "I have already made one bad plan for you."

"Wouldn't miss it for the world," she said, her voice tremulous now with the excitement of adventure.

"Your father's daughter," he replied, his voice catching as he took her hand in his.

THE FLAG OF THE NATION of Anuapúa consisted of a coppery depiction of the Great Mother Turtle against a teal background, with a broad emerald green stripe below and a broad ochre one above. It was a pretty flag; one which by its color scheme and bland references to its aboriginal background, sought to soften any tensions that might arise on account of that. One of these fluttered from the stern of the government launch that Teddi—flanking Harley on one side with Rotanu on the other—watched tie up now to the Hespera. The sound of the motor quit, and first a mass of grey curls appeared over the gunnel followed by heavy shoulders and torso covered in a traditional orange and black print. Large hands pulled at the top of the ladder. It was only when the full-skirted figure had planted massive sandaled feet firmly on the wooden deck that the head rose and the eyes confronted them. They glared with cold, determined fire.

"And where, Mr. Stable-Birns, have you been?" Kambula Iratago half-bellowed. He turned curtly toward Rotanu, and said, in a voice full of righteous disgust, "Good afternoon my brother. Where did you dig this fellow up? Was he off guppy fishing?"

He then turned his gaze on Teddi. The face was large, heavy, imposing, the most bullish qualities of indigenous and English strains pressed into its flesh.

"So, my girl, daughter of the infamous Joe Shepherd. You see what trouble you get yourself into meddling with other people's business. But…ah…the mango doesn't fall far from the tree, hah? It is a mistake your father delighted in making. I am sorry to speak ill of the recently deceased. Despite all, you have my condolences."

He looked briefly and conspiratorially at Rotanu again. Then, turning to the Australian, he said,

"Well Harley, old fellow, are you going to explain yourself. You've never been one before to be enigmatic and tight-lipped." He grinned and winked at Teddi.

Harley's face was red. His eyes blank. His mouth moved, but nothing came from it.

"What? You act as if you're drugged," said Kambula Iratago. "Too much into the sauce, eh?"

At that moment, a sound of a commotion came from the launch. Garbled exclamations were followed by a loud splash, then another. Iratago turned slowly, to see what the matter was. As he did, Teddi dropped the pose of surly defiance she had been struggling to maintain. At the same time, she let go of Harley, whom she and Rotanu had been holding up by his belt. Harley collapsed in a heap on the deck in front of them. Looking past him she saw what Iratago saw. She had also seen what he had not: the immediately preceding action. As the two kilted army guards who had come out in the launch with Iratago had just settled against the railing to relax while the Kambula attended to his business aboard the *Hespera*, yellow wet-suited arms wrapped them and pulled them overboard. While they spluttered in the water, the two figures climbed aboard the launch, dismounted submachine guns from around their necks and aimed them down at the two men who now paddled submissively beside them, ordering them to the *Hespera's* ladder.

"All secure down here," Teddi heard Marlena call out.

All was also secure on board the *Hespera*. Harley—drugged, in fact, thanks to Bagram's pharmacopoeia—lay moaning, stuporous on the deck. Two more figures with Kalashnikovs at the ready had emerged from below deck, along with Bagram, Rajiv, and Shepherd.

Kambula Iratago, his wits not dulled by shock and outrage, quickly understood the situation, and turned with a vengeful glare on Rotanu.

"So, the turncoat is a turncoat," he spat out and addressed him with full formality. "Kambula Rotanu Reginald Pinkerton, you have made a bad decision. You at last had chosen the right side in this, and now you are a defeated man. You will never get away with this."

"It is you, my brother Kambula Iratago Jason Featherstone, who will not get away with your bad business." It was Amatosi who spoke, now emerging from the main cabin. "Please, come below. There are some things we need to show you. We have some matters to discuss that should be done in more comfort."

"You, Jack? Well, you do not surprise me. We have always known of your loyalties. The cat will have his day, as they say. But I say, you cannot get away with this. Give me back my men and get off this boat and we'll ignore all of it."

It was the ploy of a desperate man, and all knew it, except perhaps for Iratago himself.

"You are not in a good position to bargain, my friend," said Amatosi. "There are some things which you need to see. Please come below." The two mercenaries had by now stationed themselves, rifles in hand, beside the truculent old man, who allowed himself to be led down into the main cabin.

XXIV

Return

"TWO HANDS!" SHOUTED OGDEN from the sidelines. Priya, slouching, hand on hip, glowered at her grandfather, then bent to pick up her racket. Her next serve, a rifle shot just nicking the outside corner of the service court, was barely returned by her opponent's weak forehand flick. The ball looped in the air, falling just behind the service line. Priya had plenty of time to position herself and, while the other girl raced to recover from the momentum that had carried her in the wrong direction, unloaded with a two-handed rocket shot into the opposite corner.

"Game. Set. Match," said the umpire as Priya flew into the air with both arms over her head and Ogden Pelligrew flew into the air with her. So did Teddi who leaped up from her seat beside Rotanu, who also rose—a bit more sedately—and added his applause. Teddi threw her arms around him, planted a kiss on his cheek, then hurried down to the court where Pria attacked her with hugs and kisses before she remembered sportsmanly decorum and went to the sideline to offer her hand to the girl she had just defeated. Then she gathered her gear and returned to sit with her family. Over the public address came the announcement:

"Kambula Iratago Jason Featherstone, President of the Karoja and Honorary Chairman of the National Junior Tennis Federation to make the awards." Iratago seemed larger and more powerful than ever as he took center court. Pria rose. Bouncing from foot to foot, she awaited his call.

Afterward, as they sat at an umbrella covered table on the patio of the new café, an exchange occurred between Amatosi and Iratago that, because of its easy insulting banter, might have caused the casual eavesdropper astonishment that any vexed history had ever run between these two.

Amatosi leaned over and said to Iratago, "Well, you desperate old goat. I hope you are pleased at the honor bestowed on you. I don't know how you came to deserve it."

Iratago gave a short gruff laugh. "In the usual way, you foolish old rooster." He parenthetically rubbed his thumb against his index and middle fingers.

Except for Priya and the girl she had just beaten—who in any case were too busy giggling with each other—everyone at the table knew exactly what he meant; and furthermore, that it was offered without the cynicism or bitterness that an outsider, informed of that vexed history, might have supposed. Although the agreement that finally settled matters was worked out between the four kambulas, all the other adults present had been duly informed. So, when Iratago indicated that money was the basis of the honor of announcing the winner, Teddi, Minga, Stevenson, Samhita, Joyeeta, Sanjay and Bagram all knew that he was referring to the two-hundred thousand dollars—an amount equal to his payoff from the oil company—that he had coughed up for the refurbishment of the R. J. Shepherd Center. It had been used, in particular, for the fine clay court on which his awardee and her opponent had just done their work, and the café in which they now sat.

More significantly, as part of the recompense they demanded of him, in his opening address to the Karoja at the Constitutional Convention he called for a complete reconciliation between all communities. In particular, as the centerpiece of that reconciliation, he called for the revocation of Statutes 14.6 and 15.3 which were together responsible for sustaining the second-class citizen status of ethnic Indians. The Bukharat were nowhere in evidence on that occasion, verifying both the seriousness of Iratago's commitment and the widely held belief that they were under his control. Whatever bitterness he might have still harbored at the change of circumstances appeared to be as well. Or they had both—the Bukharat and his own displeasure at the new arrangements—been washed away as easily and completely as cane syrup by rain. It was, no doubt, a transformation worthy of some speculation. But Teddi did not bother with that. She accepted it—as she accepted all of what had happened to her since she first touched down in Anuapúa—in the light of the miraculous. Nothing else could provide adequate explanation.

It was now June, nine months after the Convention; a time in the world, or at least some parts of it, when such wished for fairy tale endings were still possible. The further announcement—this time by Priya herself—that both she and her recent victim had won scholarships to a tennis institute for promising young players to be held at UCLA in July (thanks in large part to Teddi's and Horatio Cook's interventions) was, for the moment at least, additional evidence that complete happiness was a human possibility. Several bottles of wine made the rounds, which left the two girls strangling on giggles and the others roaring with laughter, Iratago most profoundly. In the course of this, someone noticed the absence of Shepherd and Rajiv.

"Where the hell did those two get themselves off to?" said Stevenson. In the sudden silence—they had flushed everyone else out of the café with their boisterousness—loud sounds were heard from the direction of the nearby tennis courts.

"Fault!" shouted one voice.

"Fair!" cried another.

"That was bloody out, you giant fraud!" bellowed the first.

"Call me a fraud, you world class liar!"

The two girls got up and ran off laughing like a pair of demented ostriches in the direction of the courts.

"I didn't know they played," said Rotanu in dismay.

"Neither did I," said Samhita.

"They don't," affirmed Joyeeta, sneering, her capacity for sisterly sniping again in full flower.

A few minutes later, the girls returned dragging the two men by their tennis rackets. They stood before the group, each with an arm around the other.

"He won," said Rajiv, poking Shepherd in the stomach with his racket.

"No, he definitely won," said Shepherd.

"You're right, I won," said Rajiv, as Teddi reached over and took his hand.

"As did I," said Shepherd, as Teddi reached out her other hand to him.

There could not have been three happier people, except perhaps for the two girls who had thrown themselves in a giggling clutch at Priya's handsome grandfather, who might have been happiest of all. Mona, in the most flagrantly colorful muumuu she owned, stranded with beads and braceleted in silver, sat by with a knowing smile which may have expressed relief more than the cut-loose exuberance of the others; fitting for a woman whose recently fragmented family, nuclear and extended, was busy wrapping itself into a seamless embrace. When Samhita Gupta's hand found hers, she lifted it to her lips. The look that they shared spoke of their relief, but also of the loses they had each, and jointly, suffered.

"Isn't it fitting that Horatio was such a culprit in all this?" said Samhita.

"Yes," Mona agreed. "It has all come full circle."

When the revelers broke up, Teddi and Rajiv took a stroll together over the grounds. It was now a construction site, wherever the work was not already completed. The courts were finished, as was the lower room of the house, which had been transformed from the grim clandestined meeting room that Teddi had first seen into a pleasant dining room adjoining the lovely patio where they had just been sitting.

They teetered a little as they walked hand in hand, from an excess of wine and an excess of happiness. The broken-up earth—deposited in heaps by a yellow skip loader, looming nearby like a giant crustacean—was no help to them, except for allowing them to fall into each other's arms at the slightest misstep. The necessary embraces and kisses that followed put in jeopardy their intention to survey the work. But, Teddi's eagerness to see what had been accomplished finally claimed equal place with her eagerness to replenish her stock of cuddling, and together they looked at the repairs to the porch and the roof of the house, the new plumbing lines for the cottages that were already laid in the trenches dug by the skip loader, the cottages themselves that had been stripped to their framing and, in a few cases where the jungle and rot had claimed them, down to their slabs. When all was done, the main house and cottages together would house and feed fifty people comfortably. A cricket pitch was in the works in a field just beyond. It would double as a baseball diamond, or a soccer field.

To say that this survey made Rajiv at all anxious would be an exaggeration. But, this was Teddi's first day back after an absence of several months, and the work which she meticulously specified before her departure—including the new clay tennis court and its small grandstand, and the newly rolled out crushed rock parking lot where the big roller still stood—had been his responsibility to carry out. So he was both relieved and hugely pleased that his work got the same stamp of approval that his own person was getting.

They stood before the concrete ground sign where Rajiv had first, that early morning nine months before, introduced Teddi to what was then the neglected remnant of her father's work there. As had been the case with the Great Seal in the vestibule of the National Assembly, history had overtaken the sign, requiring a new name and new brass lettering to be mounted on its freshly scrubbed and sealed surface. It now read:

CENTER FOR THE IMPROVEMENT
OF UNDERSTANDING BETWEEN PEOPLES
DEDICATED TO THE MEMORY OF RUPERT JOSEPH SHEPHERD
1944–1999

A new bronze plaque below added the following to the names of the original *Founding Committee*:

ADJUNCT FOUNDERS 2001
RAJIV GUPTA~ SANJAY GUPTA~ DOMINGA PELLIGREW-GUPTA~ STEVENSON PELLIGREW

A construction sign stood nearby, identifying the work underway:

REFURBISHMENTS AND EXPANSION OF
The Center for the Improvement of Understanding Between Peoples
Sponsors:
The Grand Karoja of the People of Anuapúa
The Agarbathy-Mango National Unity Party (AMNUP)

Supervising Architect:
T. L. Patel-Shepherd, AIA
Offices: Los Angeles, California, USA   Indua, Anuapúa

Project Management:
Gupta & Pelligrew Associates, Unltd.   Indua, Anuapúa

Teddi's supervisory function was carried out mostly at long distance. Apart from the two short trips she had made in the course of the last several months, she had been on the phone daily with Rajiv, trading e-mails several times a day, whenever a critical decision arose; or for any reason at all.

"We're almost on schedule," said Rajiv. "And the response we're getting…unbelievable." He spoke as if she weren't already minutely aware of everything. "We have to hurry. Next month, Bangladeshi and Bengali kids. Then some Israeli and Palestinian businessmen. Then a gang of Nigerian Catholic and Muslim clerics. Some kids from parochial schools in Kansas and Yemen. It goes on and on. Come to this beautiful place, play some tennis, kick the old bean around, take a swim, hang out in the café. While you're at it, solve the world's problems. What more could we wish for?"

Teddi close beside him, said, "Just beautiful."

"Yes, yes. I think our outreach has been very…"

"I was thinking of something else," she cut him short, slipping her arm around his waist and pressing herself to him. He wrapped her in his arms and held her.

Over his shoulder she saw a view like the one she had wished for the Tukulu when she had first arrived there the previous September. It was a simple and beautiful twilight scene. Some of it was her doing, faithfully executed by Rajiv and his crew: a sandstone terrace with a few benches looking out over a low stone parapet. Beyond that, a sparse group of palms stood like sentinels, and beyond them the ocean, its horizon incandescent with the setting sun. The scene was perfected by two figures moving close together, slowly across it, both roundly protruding about the middle. They were Minga and Joyeeta who had managed, more or less simultaneously, to become pregnant in celebration of Minga's and Sanjay's wedding the previous October.

"Look," said Teddi, pulling Rajiv closer to her and turning him so he could see them also. The two women made their slow traverse, disappearing into a grove of mango trees just as the last light died on the rim of the ocean, as if they had pulled a scrim across a stage, leaving behind a twilight glow. Watching them, Teddi mused on the strange ironies that had brought them all to the present moment.

"*Bungshalo!*" she said under her breath. Rajiv smiled his most radiant smile at her, as Rama must have after Sita had overcome all obstacles to return to his embrace.

OF COURSE, THE SECRET PASSAGE never found the use they originally intended for it. The intervention of Harley and Simon had been responsible for this course correction. If those two had not followed their brutal stratagem, it was unlikely Iratago's misbehavior would have been uncovered, or Rotanu's betrayal either. Their original fantastic plan to take the Karoja hostage might very well have gone through, with who could know what disastrous results.

As it turned out, Iratago made the speech they required him to make. Ogden, as a member of the Karoja's executive, made one in the same vein, likewise insisting on dismantling the regulations suppressing Indian rights and privileges—the infamous *point six* and *point three*. The two speeches each gave support to the other—although most agreed Ogden's was the more provoking, the more impassioned. But, the two old guardians of Anuap prerogatives were the guidons that turned the head of the herd.

Amatosi added his own powerful voice; as did Rotanu, who had recovered his, and who may have spoken most passionately of all. He was, according those few who knew of the troubling circumstances, his old self.

Others who found in these exhortations the expression of their own deepest desires soon followed, first in a trickle, then in a flood. Still others—whose cautious habit it was to go along to get along—seeing the new trend, swelled the numbers. In the end, the statutes were revoked virtually by acclamation. In the release of the tension that had gone into maintaining a past that was no longer viable, an atmosphere of celebration swept Indua and spread throughout the islands. Only a few bitter holdouts muttered to themselves.

At some point in the happy tumult that followed, Harley and Simon were allowed to slip out to sea aboard the *Hespera*. They had been held temporarily in prison, with numerous charges lodged against them, none of which, for obvious reasons, could be pursued. However, they were admonished not to even think of returning, they or their sea-going oil rig.

Of the contents of the secret passage itself, nothing much survived. In the three days it took for the happy conspirators to come back to the Assembly, descend to the catacombs, lift away the paving stone Teddi had correctly suspected—and Simon had tested—and climb down the iron rungs imbedded in the native stone, in less time than that, the tide had torn the rotting coracle loose from the iron ring that had held it in place for more than a century, had swept it out of the cave and splintered it beyond recovery on the jagged shoal that guarded the entrance. If there had ever been any treasure to supply a motive for a greedy assault on the cave, that too had been swept away. What remained was the passage itself, a corroded iron ring embedded in the rock wall, and a few links of corroded chain hanging from it, attached to nothing.

ABOUT THE AUTHOR: M. A. Hassan grew up in Los Angeles, studied at UCLA, lived for many years in the San Francisco Bay Area, and now lives, writes and teaches in New York City.

Made in the USA
Charleston, SC
08 December 2009